The Familiar

Allison Snell

Front cover design by Vince Wathen
Design, typesetting and publishing by
UK Book Publishing
www.ukbookpublishing.com
ISBN: 978-1-914195-40-2

In the beginning

The late afternoon sunlight flickered on the nametag that hung from the cat's collar. 'Barnaby' sat on the windowsill, looking out, and surveying the commotion in the street below. His ears twitched as the footsteps grew louder. He turned his head, following the direction of the sound, and focussed his attention on the slowly-turning door handle. As the door began to open, he crouched guardedly. He watched with suspicious, large eyes as the man entered the room.

Without relinquishing his gaze, Barnaby watched as the stranger walked towards the bed. The man glanced briefly at the animal, before returning his attention to the sight ahead of him. That fleeting glimpse was the cue that Barnaby had been waiting for: an indication that the visitor posed no threat. Barnaby relaxed his stance, and with a chirrup-like mew, arched his back in a long, feline stretch. He carefully eyed up his route, via the bed to the floor, before finally making his jump.

The inspector noticed the body flinch as the cat rebounded from it, using it, seemingly rather callously, as an intermediate step in its launch to the floor. The sudden spasm had brought, for a second, a glimmer of life into the young woman's body. Now, it was still again.

The inspector was feeling a little cynical today. Why should he waste his time with a simple suicide? There was, after all, much more pressing business to attend to back at the station. Ridiculously, he couldn't even say that the poor girl was actually dead; you had to be a qualified medical practitioner to know that, didn't you? So why was he there? Just to nose around the ugly scene and write a report? Now, were he a detective in one of those clichéd, murder-mystery paperbacks that his wife loved reading, there would be clues left around for him to find, wouldn't there? Perhaps there would even be a few red herrings to really test his investigative skills? But this wasn't a paperback novel, was it? This was real life. This was 1984, and this was Willsby. You had suicides, not murders, in Willsby.

The inspector took a deep, resolute breath as he rolled the woman onto her back. Hardly flinching at the sight, he scanned the body with a cool, analytical gaze. The knife was firmly embedded in her chest. It was a typical self-inflicted stab wound with little to see from the outside, the fatal injuries having occurred deep beneath the pale mantle of the woman's skin. There was no doubt in the inspector's mind; it had been the single stab wound that had killed her. Her hands were wrapped around the handle, and her chest had taken the full brunt of the knife's thrust. There was no sign of a struggle. The inspector was initially puzzled by the cuts across the woman's right forearm; but then a theoretical vision began to form in his mind, to quench his suspicion. She had probably first considered slashing her wrists, maybe as an initial suicide attempt, or maybe as a prelude, mustering up the courage, for the frenzied, final penetration?

The concocted vision stayed in his mind as the inspector stared at the woman's gaunt, colourless face. Her wide eyes stared through him, and her grey lips hung open.

"Don't take my word for it," he muttered under his breath. "Remember, you're not qualified to say if she's dead or not. She could always be putting it on."

His facetious humour caused a smile to creep over his lips, which he ashamedly tried to hide as he remembered his young colleague who stood at the door. He glanced across to the man who, no doubt disturbed by what was his first experience of such a violent death, showed a distinct disapproval of his senior officer's disrespect. The inspector coughed quietly, almost apologetically, as he regained his professional composure and looked around the room.

He noticed a diary on the bedside table, picked it up, opened it to the first page, and read a couple of lines. Now, had he been that paperback detective, the handwritten ramblings might well hold some vital clues. For this suicide, however, it would simply make an interesting psychological study for anybody with the time, or inclination, to read it. He had neither, so instead, he continued his visual examination of the room.

On a small table next to the door was a typewriter. The inspector hunched his shoulders as he craned at the paper message.

"That's the suicide note," said the young officer at the door.

He seemed proud of his deduction.

As the inspector read the typed note, his eyebrows crept together beneath the deepening lines of his forehead.

"What is it?" asked the young police officer, noticing his colleague's puzzled expression.

The inspector remained silent with his thoughts. The young officer

3

was growing impatient.

"Sir?" he prompted.

"How odd," murmured the inspector, waving the diary that he held and pursing his lips in contemplation. He was looking at the misspelt and poorly typed message in front of him. It didn't make sense. The diary was written with perfect spelling and grammar; the two pieces surely couldn't have been written by the same person?

"Sir?" quizzed the young officer again.

The inspector said nothing, ignoring his colleague and continuing to scan the room. His eyes followed the painted walls to the fireplace, above which on the mantel, were two further items that caught his attention. The first was a vase of neatly arranged flowers. He lifted the vase to his nose. The water smelt fresh. He had also noticed, on his way into the flat, their discarded cellophane wrapper in the kitchen pedal bin. It seemed odd to the inspector that a woman, about to commit suicide, should go to the trouble of arranging flowers. Perhaps they had been a present to cheer her up? A sarcastic smile crept across his face as he pondered the thought; the gesture had hardly been successful, had it?

Next to the vase was a photograph; two men, one dressed in racing leathers, smiled out from the picture. The inspector wondered if this pair may be able to shed some light on the woman's motives for taking her own life. He studied the photograph for a while before turning his attention to the window, from where a loud purr was now emanating.

The cat had returned to the sill and was peering into the room from behind the blue curtains. Perhaps it was just a case of his mind imposing human attributes on the animal, but the cat seemed to be watching him, with the same inquisitive expression that he himself had earlier been surveying the scene. The inspector could almost imagine the inevitable worry lines etched on the cat's forehead, beneath the dense covering of black fur.

The inspector approached the animal, holding out a reassuring hand.

"We'll have to sort someone out to come and get you, little chap," he said as he stroked the cat's head.

It was at this moment that the inspector caught a glimpse of a silver BMW pull into the cul-de-sac outside. The car slowly passed the house. Briefly, the driver's face stared up at the window before the vehicle accelerated hastily out of sight. The inspector looked again at the photograph. Perhaps it was only a coincidence, but that face did look familiar. He radioed down to the police car parked outside and watched as it sped off in pursuit of the silver car. Let's face it, that would have been what any self-respecting paperback detective would have done in the circumstances, wouldn't it?

Chapter One

It was April 1984 and the first meeting of the new speedway season. Standing just inside of the stadium entrance, Charlotte took a deep breath. That distinctive smell of speedway, and the sounds of the bikes warming up in the pits, engulfed her senses. It had been two years since she'd last been to the Willsby stadium, but as she pushed her body through the wormhole of the entrance turnstile, the memories of her previous visits flooded back.

Speedway can have that effect on you. Once one of the most supported sports in the country, spectator numbers have gradually declined. Its demise, most probably, due to the absence of big sponsors rather than to anything lacking in its entertainment value. After all, it has all the ingredients to appeal: excitement, danger, team camaraderie, and a hefty sprinkling of heroes and villains. However, as a result of the dwindling numbers of spectators, the lack of cash injections, and the desire of owners to cash in on the lucrative house-building potential of their land, many of the racetracks around the country have been forced to close. Those that have remained open have missed out on refurbishment. Consequently, revisiting them, after a period of abstention, can make one feel as if time has stood

6

still inside those ramshackle, timeworn spaces.

This was exactly how Charlotte was feeling as she stood looking around the stadium. The commanding clubhouse stood ahead of her. The building housed the changing rooms on the ground floor, and the hospitality bar on the first. The bar area led out onto a roofed balcony where the entertainment could be watched in comfort, sheltered from the unpredictable British weather. It was, without doubt, the best viewing spot for spectators, but out of bounds to all but selective guests and sponsors until after the racing when, for a small fee, it became the venue where the fans could brush shoulders with their racing stars.

A couple of doors to the balcony were ajar, and glimpses of the privileged occupants could be seen through the narrow gaps. Charlotte remembered how, as a child, she had looked up at those same doors, envious of the people behind them, and longing to sample the clubhouse's delights for herself. Her father, however, had always put paid to any such doing. He was an extremely strict man and had wanted to protect his little girl from unsavoury influences: apparently, bars and speedway riders, he felt, featured quite prominently in this category.

As the building stared down teasingly at Charlotte, she realised that there was no longer anything to stop her from fulfilling her childhood dream. She was sixteen now, and it had been almost two years since her father's death. Perhaps she could visit the clubhouse later that evening?

Temporarily slipping thoughts of the temptation from her mind, Charlotte headed off to the more familiar spectator areas encircling the racetrack. She stopped on the grass bank overlooking the first bend; it had always been her viewing position of choice in the past.

Charlotte looked around. The stadium was filling up. The flow of fans through the turnstiles had increased, each clutching their clipboards with their crisp, new score card attached. They dispersed into the stadium to assume their territorial viewing positions. To her right, figures milled in the pits. They were different faces to those she remembered, but their actions were predictable and reassuring. Mechanics tinkered with the bikes and shouted to one another above the sound of the engines, whilst groups of absorbed fans looked on.

It was hard to believe that it had been so long since her last visit. She'd heard very little of the club during that time, apart, of course, from that unfortunate episode last year that had made the national papers. Sam Orpin, the manager of a local garage and one of the club's sponsors, had been convicted of murder. Murder, no less: an unfortunate accident by all accounts, during a burglary at a local property. It had been the evidence given by one of the Willsby riders that had secured his conviction and had seen him imprisoned. It had been in all the newspapers; it was hardly the sort of publicity that the club wanted really.

As thoughts of the story skimmed through Charlotte's mind, the riders appeared from the changing rooms and began their walk across the centre green to the pits. They were blatantly conspicuous in their multicoloured leathers, as they made their way to their waiting bikes and mechanics.

Their familiar actions made Charlotte think of her father. He'd been a fan of speedway during its heyday in the 1950s, and he'd been eager to introduce his young daughter to it as soon as possible. She'd loved it. She didn't get on particularly well with her stepmother, and consequently, speedway became her special time when she could be alone with her father. It was like a secret, elite club that they attended together, every Friday evening in summer. Unlike a lot of other sports, the competitors were always accessible and were keen to interact with the young fans. Those speedway riders had etched themselves into the psyche of many a child, and unbeknown to them, they had become childhood heroes, up there with the best rock stars and footballers of the day.

Charlotte missed her father. His sudden death had been devastating to her, a fact not helped by her stepmother remarrying so shortly after. Instead of accepting her stepmother's new husband, Charlotte had focused all her grief and discontent on the couple. Once she'd finished school, she had left home and moved alone to Willsby. Perhaps it had been the memories of her father and the speedway track that had influenced her choice of residence, or perhaps it was simply a good place to find employment, being a tourist resort beside the sea.

She had found a job easily, as a waitress in the restaurant of a local guesthouse, and was renting a small flat just off the seafront.

As Charlotte sat thinking about how her life had changed since her last visit, her thoughts were interrupted by a loud shout.

"Charlie. Is that you?"

Charlotte recognised the voice instantly. There had to be something to taint her memories; a rotten apple in the barrel, you might say. This apple was named Graham.

"Graham," she acknowledged casually. "Are you still coming here?"

"Either that or I've got a just as handsome double," he laughed loudly.

Graham was pleased to see Charlotte again and somewhat surprised by how attractive she had grown. Mind you, she had probably always been attractive, but in the past her old man's presence had curtailed any lascivious thoughts that might have been bubbling inside him. Graham was glad that she was now alone, but fearing that the old bugger might appear at any minute, asked enquiringly:

"Where's the old boy then?"

Charlotte's eyes looked to the ground.

"He died," she answered quietly, after a short pause.

Graham felt unusually awkward. His wide smile dropped. That had hardly been his best chat-up line of the week, had it? He tried to think of something sensible to say. Graham found sensible things exceedingly difficult.

"That's tough," he consoled.

He watched as the girl bit her lower lip, saying nothing in response.

"So, what have you been doing with yourself then?" he asked brightly, rapidly trying to change the subject after the awkward silence, hoping that he could perhaps salvage some of her earlier interest in him.

Charlotte explained about her move to Willsby, her flat, and her job in the guesthouse. Graham knew the guesthouse well. It was opposite The Druids: a public house that was one of his favourites. He also knew the Esplanade where she lived, and it surprised him that she had a flat in that area of town. She had always struck him as being rather well-bred, not like all the other girls he'd known from the Esplanade, if you get his drift.

Charlotte remembered Graham well too. He had befriended her father one evening and had, after that, considered it his right to come and chat with him during every race meeting. Now, it seemed, she had inherited the legacy. He was just as repellent as she remembered too. His lank, style-less hair hung around his pitted face. He spoke very loudly, and every sentence was followed by an annoying spurt of laughter resembling the sound of a rapid pneumatic-drill. Despite all this, he seemed convinced that he was the life and soul of the stadium. Admittedly, he did always seem to attract a lot of attention, but that was certainly more due to his idiocy than popularity. Charlotte felt uncomfortable with him in one sense, but at the same time, it was actually quite reassuring to see a familiar face.

Before long, the commentator's voice crackled across the public address system. The riders appeared from the pits, crammed into the back of a pickup truck. They were slowly paraded around the track on an introductory lap. Charlotte watched them, scanning their faces for the familiar Kevin McCray; the only name in the event programme that she remembered from her previous visits. He'd been an up-and-coming rider then, and judging by the low average score next to his name in her programme, he hadn't up-and-comed much further. She spotted him stood at the rear of the truck, waving enthusiastically. Graham, true to form, shouted abuse as the vehicle passed. The riders enthused on, not hearing, or perhaps just ignoring, his derogatory banter. Charlotte felt embarrassed. She kept her head bowed to the ground until the truck had disappeared back into the pits, Graham's abuse finally ceased, and the pneumatic-drill laughter relented.

"Give us a look at your programme, Charlie," he demanded, leering over her shoulder.

"Still too tight to buy your own?" she scorned. "I expect you even still climb over the back fence to avoid paying the entry fee, don't you?"

Graham had. He smiled, unsure if she was reprimanding him or merely teasing and, settling for the latter, replied, "Only a mug would pay to watch these losers."

Charlotte looked offended.

"Well, it's a good job there's one mug here, or you wouldn't get a look at the programme, would you?" she quipped.

Graham sighed. Women were a complex breed, weren't they? He'd never meant that *she* was a mug, just everyone else who'd wasted their money on the entrance fee, when there was the alternative of a perfectly easy-to-scale fence. Feeling the rebuke, he stood, quietly looking at the pictures in her programme, before handing it back to her with a polite smile.

As the sun set, and the floodlights gently eased into life, the eagerly awaited racing began. Four bikes appeared from the pits onto the track. An elaborate wheelie introduced the top Willsby rider as he accelerated down the back straight, on his way to the starting line. The riders lined up beside one another. Attempting to position themselves for the best possible start, they dug around in the dirt with their boots and manoeuvred their bikes' wheels into the freshly made crevices. Once in position, and with their eyes focused on the starting tapes, they waited. Suddenly, the tapes sprung up, and the four riders shot from the start. They hurled themselves into the first bend, inches apart, amazingly avoiding a collision as they flung their weight into the slide sideways. A mass of multicoloured leathers and machinery grouped at the corner, and a leader emerged. As the race progressed, they would separate, then bunch again, with the Willsby rider somehow managing to come out in front each time. After four laps, the bikes crossed the finishing line to the wave of the chequered flag. Charlotte watched as the riders appeared on track for the second heat. These were the lower scoring team members, and Kevin McCray would be among them.

Strangely, however, it was not Kevin McCray who caught her attention. Instead, her eyes were drawn to the other Willsby rider as he accelerated along the back straight. His plain black leathers, adorned only by a yellow stripe down each leg, made him, rather ironically, distinctive against the colourful, sponsor-emblazoned leathers of his opponents and teammate.

Charlotte watched him. Something was captivating about this mystery rider and she just couldn't take her eyes off of him. She had a strange feeling of anticipation in her stomach. It wasn't the first time in her life that she'd had this type of feeling either. It was a sensation that events were outside of her control: a sense that Fate was somehow playing a hand in her destiny. It felt as though she were caught in the tide of time, ebbing and flowing in events over which she had no control. It was as if a script were being written for her life, and all she could do was act it out, and wait to see what the author had in store for her. It was an unsettling, yet strangely exciting, feeling, and here it was happening again, as she watched the mystery young man take his place in the starting line-up for heat two of that Willsby speedway meeting.

Graham had been completely thrown by the new rider. He had wanted to impress Charlotte with his knowledge, and his not knowing the name of this new team member was not helping. He laughed loudly and nervously as he bluffed his way out of his embarrassment. Charlotte didn't notice him squirming. She was not listening to Graham, nor was she interested in the humiliation engulfing him. She was instead mesmerised by the rider in the black and yellow leathers as he took his place at the start with the other three competitors.

The tapes shot up. With a flurry of throttle, he shot forward. Charlotte watched as he slid into the first bend of the track. Her eyes were transfixed on him. He emerged in second place, just behind the leader. Charlotte watched. He looked uncomfortable on the bike. His movements seemed disjointed and uneasy when compared to the smoothness of the more experienced riders. Charlotte was watching him intently. She was so wrapped up, that she didn't even notice the battle taking place behind him, between Kevin McCray and the third-placed man. She watched her mystery rider take the chequered flag in second position, just behind the winner. Kevin McCray finished at the rear of the field.

"Bloody useless McCray," riled Graham. "That novice has made you look like a girl."

Charlotte turned her attention to her programme. Graham's novice was named Anthony Myers, and he was riding at reserve for Willsby. She looked down the remaining heats for his future races; heat seven would be his next outing. She felt unusually excited by the prospect.

The next four races were entertaining with an exciting mixture of all the best ingredients from speedway: close racing, skilful passing, and the occasional spill. The crowd loved every minute. Graham, too, was in his element: heckling, shouting insults, with his boring laughter piercing through the still evening air. Charlotte could hardly concentrate on the racing though, as prominent in her mind was the thought of Anthony Myers. Just what was going on? This was getting so weird. Why couldn't she get him out of her head? The sense that Fate was concocting something was growing stronger, and her anticipation and nervous excitement deepened.

Finally, her patience paid off as the riders for heat seven appeared on track. Charlotte's vision focused on the now-familiar black and yellow leathers of Anthony as he made his way to the start. As the commentator announced the riders, a tingle shot down Charlotte's spine; Anthony's name seemed to take on a new, deeper significance on her hearing it spoken out loud. She watched attentively as the race began. Charlotte fought intently with Anthony. He finished third in the race. The four laps had only lasted a minute, but they had seemed to take so much longer. Charlotte had felt Anthony's determination every inch of the way. She waited until he had returned to the pits before filling in the score in her race card. Her preoccupation had meant that she'd failed to realise just how close the match had become.

The next few races were won by the opposition. Willsby desperately needed to pull some points back to retain their lead. Anthony was out in heat eleven, and it was so important that Willsby didn't drop any points from the race. The crowd fell noticeably quieter as Anthony made his way to the start. Charlotte felt apprehensive. Her heart fluttered as the race began. Despite all his obvious effort, Anthony was at the back of the field. Suddenly, as they entered the third lap, Anthony's machine appeared to falter. He ventured off the racing line and into the deeper dirt at the track edge. He spun around, and his bike slid to the ground. The other riders shot off into the distance. They shot from Charlotte's thoughts too, into a dust of indifference, as she instead watched the figure sliding to the ground.

"Get up you bloody loser," shouted Graham.

The other Willsby rider was in the lead, a placing that couldn't be guaranteed were the race stopped and rerun due to Anthony's fall. Anthony didn't need Graham's lecture; he knew exactly what to do. He jumped to his feet. Charlotte watched him as he hurriedly collected his bike and pushed it onto the centre green, obviously in discomfort after his fall. Eventually, the roar of engines faded, and the lone figure of Anthony returned to the pits. Charlotte, intrigued by the feeling of familiarity she was experiencing, turned to follow in the direction of the mystery rider.

"You going now then, Charlie?"

Charlotte had been so preoccupied that she had clean forgotten Graham was still standing beside her.

"See you next week then?" he asked optimistically.

Charlotte shrugged, dismissing his question, as she walked away. She didn't notice the pained expression on his face as his hopeful smile slipped from his lips. Graham was disappointed. He'd been hoping to ask her for a drink up in the clubhouse, and then maybe pop back home with her to the Esplanade. He watched her as she walked towards the pits. Still, there was always next time. Now that the old man was out of the way, there would be nothing to stop him, would there?

Charlotte stood on the grass bank, looking down at the commotion in the pit area. Her gloved hands clutched the tips of the wooden fence stakes that divided her from the steep drop below as she watched Anthony Myers.

"Hard luck, Ant," said a rather condescending voice as a suave-looking man patted the rider on his back. Anthony removed his gloves, unstrapped his helmet, and levered it from his head. Charlotte was nervous with anticipation for a glimpse of his face. This all felt so weird. As he removed his helmet, Anthony leant forward and shook his black hair. Anthony Myers looked exactly as she had hoped. His hair was thick and quite long. His eyes were a deep brown that gradated subtly into his black pupils. This impression of continuous colour made them appear very piercing, even from this distance.

Anthony sat on a bench at the rear of the pits, his head in his hands, and his hair spilling through his cradling fingers. The suave man was talking to him. Charlotte stood above them, intoxicated throughout by the sight. She felt a tingle of excitement, wondering just what was in store for her with this man. Did Fate intend him to be her boyfriend? She had no objection there. A speedway rider for a boyfriend? How cool would that be? She watched the two men as they talked. The noise in the pits drowned out their conversation, but Charlotte could make out that Anthony wasn't happy. The other man, however, didn't seem concerned and smiled almost derisively. When the man finally left, Anthony's dark eyes watched him, burning into his blue-overalled back as he disappeared into the distance towards the clubhouse. Charlotte watched as Anthony too left the pits and began his walk to the changing rooms. As he grew smaller in the distance, Charlotte's preoccupation was eventually interrupted by a voice.

"Time you were going now, Love."

A hand grasped her shoulder. Charlotte looked up with a start. She glanced behind her and saw the stadium emptying. Obediently, she followed the marshal's direction, glancing back for one last look at Anthony as he disappeared, beneath the canopy of the clubhouse, into the changing rooms.

Charlotte looked up through the darkness at that clubhouse. She recalled having stood in this same spot several years before, but back then having been jolted from her fantasy by her father's stern voice. Tonight, however, it wasn't her father's voice that she heard but the more enthusiastic voice of Fate. Perhaps Anthony Myers would be in the bar later? If she went up there, she'd be able to give Fate a helping hand with her plan, wouldn't she? What did she have to lose? Without any further hesitation, she made her way over to the immaculately-dressed doorman.

"Good evening, Madam," he welcomed.

His blue-suited arm held open the door as she handed him her entrance money. Charlotte glanced at his gleaming name badge: 'Peter, Head Steward'.

The steps to the bar area were steep. Charlotte climbed them slowly, her heart beating rapidly with excitement. She pushed open the door, and the warmth of the room engulfed her.

The room was smaller than she had imagined and crammed full of white plastic furniture. Groups of people sat huddled in circles around the edges, clutching drinks in plastic tumblers. A buffet table stretched out through the centre of the room. Its pitiful remnants of curled sandwiches, sausage rolls, and egg vol-au-vents looked far from appetising. A blue cloud hung over the room; the smog of the cigarette smoke tickled her throat as she breathed in.

Two women served behind the bar. They looked flustered as money was waved in front of their faces by impatient hands. The customers were all talking in raised voices, trying to make themselves heard above the blurred din. Charlotte looked around her.

The man who had earlier been with Anthony, sat at the bar. He had changed out of his blue overalls and now wore a crisp, black shirt, unbuttoned at the neck, revealing a large gold medallion that nestled among his chest hair. His neatly-trimmed moustache twitched as he spoke, just as it had done while he had been talking with Anthony in the pits. A shiver ran down her spine; there was something rather disconcerting about this man.

Charlotte was planning to stay. Perhaps Anthony would join this man soon? She could maybe introduce herself to them and then hand matters over to Fate, whatever it was that Fate had in store for her? Charlotte's idea, however, was short-lived as she heard the familiar noise. The laughter bore into her head. She looked around and spotted Graham. She couldn't risk him seeing her and ruining her plan, could she? Luckily, he hadn't noticed her yet, and she had time to make a hasty retreat to the door. Peter seemed surprised by her rapid departure as she descended the stairs.

"That was quick," he said quizzically. "Were you looking for one of the riders in particular?" Charlotte's cheeks flushed, but her embarrassment at the question went unnoticed as a string of further supporters filed in. Peter's attention was diverted, and Charlotte crept out quietly behind him before making her way to the stadium's gates.

* * *

Lucy, on the other hand, had not left the stadium. She was walking, against the tide of departing fans, on her way to the pits. She arrived just in time; Willsby's top rider, Dave Chapman, was about to leave for the changing rooms.

"Dave," she called out, leaning over the partitioning fence.

He squinted, seemingly trying to recognise her face as he walked across the track towards her. Lucy stared coolly at him. A baseball cap had replaced his helmet, and his once colourful leathers were now encrusted with dust. Although drained of that earlier enthusiasm, which Lucy had noticed as he was paraded around the track before the racing, he was still politely amenable. His tired, dark eyes looked to the ground as he approached.

"Sorry to bother you, Dave. I know you must be exhausted," said Lucy as he reached the trackside where she stood. "But I was wondering if I could ask you a favour?"

She noticed his gaze shift to her hands, no doubt looking for a pen to sign an autograph.

"Yeah. Sure," he replied enthusiastically before he paused, looked at her quizzically, and added: "What?"

Lucy was smiling to herself, amused that he had agreed to her proposition without even knowing what she wanted. She stared at him, teasing his curiosity. She waited until his inquisitiveness began to falter towards annoyance, before continuing.

"I'm writing a book and could do with some technical advice."

"You're writing a book about speedway?"

He seemed surprised and instantly intrigued by the idea. He smiled, revealing a row of small, uneven teeth.

"Sort of," said Lucy, a teasing uncertainty in her voice as she grinned impishly to herself. Dave was looking at her, captivated, and awaiting further explanation. It didn't come. He looked puzzled. Lucy sensed his confusion and took the opportunity to play on his uncertainty.

"I'd understand if you didn't want to," she sighed, sounding disappointed. "I'll have to ask someone else."

"No" he interrupted, an impulsive remorse overcoming him. "I'd like to. What do you need to know?"

"Well, it's a bit in-depth, and I'm sure you've got better things to do right now," she said as she regained his interest. "Could we meet somewhere tomorrow?"

Dave looked rather concerned by the suggestion. It was one thing spending five minutes having a chat with a stranger at the trackside, but to meet her tomorrow? Lucy recognised his apprehension as his thoughts panicked at the idea. She interrupted the process before he had a chance to think about it too hard.

"Do you live local?" she asked.

Dave nodded; his train of thought having been sent hurtling from its original tracks.

"There's a pub called The Druids. Near the bridge. Shall we say about four?" asked Lucy quickly, hardly pausing for breath.

As planned, Dave had been tricked by the distraction. He knew The Druids well. He liked it in there.

"Er," he answered in his confusion.

"Great. Thanks. This is so helpful," said Lucy. "I'll see you tomorrow then."

She turned and quickly walked away. She wanted to escape before Dave had the opportunity to reply.

Dave paused for a second, wondering why on earth he'd just agreed to meet a total stranger in The Druids on his only free day of the week.

Lucy smiled confidently to herself as she hurried to the stadium's exit. This was going to be easier than she'd imagined.

*　*　*

Charlotte had arrived home and Barnaby came running to greet her.

"I saw the most wonderful man at speedway tonight, Barnaby," she said as she opened a tin of cat food and emptied it into a bowl.

Barnaby's green eyes looked up with interest.

"I guess I'll just have to go back again next week now, won't I?"

Barnaby purred emphatically in agreement, excited by the prospect, and then gulped a mouthful of food as the bowl touched the floor.

Chapter Two

Mrs Shield glanced through the doorway into the dining room and looked at her watch. It was ten to four; the restaurant was supposedly shut. However, the customer, sitting at the window table, seemed reluctant to leave.

Lucy was also conscious of the time. She took another sip of her tea, which had long since turned cold, and glanced through the window at the public house opposite: The Druids. Dave Chapman should be arriving shortly. It was time to make her move. She stood up, slowly replacing her chair under the table, and adjusting her miniskirt. She hated wearing such short skirts but knew Dave Chapman went for the leggy women, so why not show off her assets. Her assets took her to the till.

"May I have my bill now, Waitress?"

Mrs Shield had already prepared it. She handed the piece of paper to the woman whose eyes scanned the figure work.

"Just one thing," said Lucy rather condescendingly. "The cake was stale."

Her eyes looked up from the bill.

"I'll just pay you for the tea, thank you."

Mrs Shield was taken aback. The cake hadn't been stale, and even if it were, did the woman really have to eat the whole thing before realising it? She couldn't say anything though, could she? She had to remain professional, and anyhow, she wanted to close the restaurant and get home, not have an argument with the impertinent customer.

"Very well, Madam, I'll take it off your bill," she answered begrudgingly, as Lucy placed her coins onto the counter.

* * *

Mrs Shield sighed in disbelief as she watched the obnoxious woman leave. She cleared the table and returned to the kitchen.

"How about a cup of tea?" she suggested to her young colleague who was just finishing washing the dishes.

Charlotte nodded in agreement.

Charlotte had been working with Mrs Shield at the guesthouse for a few months now. Despite this, Mrs Shield knew very little about her young colleague. She was a conscientious worker but was very shy and seemed almost quite childlike at times. She had been rather reticent to divulge much information about herself and hadn't mentioned any friends or hobbies. All Mrs Shield really knew about her was that she was new to Willsby, and that she was living alone in a rented flat on the seafront. It had come as a surprise, therefore, when Charlotte had mentioned, the previous day, that she was intending to visit the Willsby speedway stadium. Mrs Shield had been intrigued as she had hardly imagined the quiet, unassuming girl would be interested in motorbikes.

Mrs Shield lived in the road just behind the speedway stadium and, with her windows open and the wind blowing in the right direction, she could just about hear the horrendous noise of the bikes every Friday night. She'd even happily added her signature to the petition, which her property-developer neighbour had brought around, attempting to get the dreadful place closed and turned into a more agreeable new housing estate. She thought it wise to keep this detail to herself though, and as Charlotte had seemed unusually cheerful that afternoon, Mrs Shield decided to ask about her previous evening's visit.

"Did you have a good time at the speedway last night?" she enquired brightly.

Mrs Shield noticed the girl's enthusiasm, but slight embarrassment, at the question. She noticed her pale cheeks flushing as her eyes looked to the floor. Of course, Mrs Shield understood now: Charlotte must have been to the speedway with a boyfriend, hence her sudden interest in motorbike racing. She grinned at the girl and looked her in the eyes knowingly.

"What's his name?" she asked with that confidence that older people seem to portray over their younger counterparts.

Charlotte smiled, and her eyes rolled in a bashful hesitance.

"Anthony," she whispered.

Mrs Shield's smile widened, partly in praise of her own acuteness in her deductions, and partly from her pleasure in learning that Charlotte was, at last, making some friends in Willsby.

* * *

Lucy had arrived at The Druids and had walked over to the bar.

The barman smiled.

"What can I get you?"

Lucy scanned the optics.

"A Courvoisier. No ice," she demanded.

The barman was surprised by her request. She'd obviously carefully studied the available brandies: Courvoisier wasn't one of them.

"I'm sorry, no Courvoisier. Just the ones here," he replied politely, gesturing to the optics.

Lucy raised her eyes and let out a loud, irritated sigh.

"Very well, give me one of *them*," she said, pointing to one of the upturned bottles.

The barman obliged, although somewhat confused by the woman's odd behaviour. He waited patiently as she counted out her loose change onto the bar.

Lucy took her drink and walked over to a table in the corner where she sat down. She watched the uncanny lights of the fruit machine beside her as they danced, randomly spelling out messages, endeavouring to seduce passing punters. There were, however, very few punters in The Druids to be seduced: a group of middle-aged men discussed the afternoon's football matches with the barman; two older men sat silently by the door, gazing into their pints, grunting occasionally as if confirming a telepathic conversation; and a young couple sat awkwardly in the opposite corner, probably tourists, they appeared eager to finish their drinks and leave without seeming too impolite. Lucy watched inconspicuously, confident that Dave would arrive soon.

It was twenty past four when he finally walked in. He noticed Lucy straight away and headed over to join her.

"I was worried that you weren't coming," she said coolly.

Dave felt gently reprimanded by the comment. He felt the need to justify his late arrival.

"Got caught up in traffic," he lied unconvincingly. "Can I get you a drink?"

Lucy had a drink in front of her, and Dave had assumed, incorrectly, that she would refuse his offer. He had already turned to walk away when she spoke.

"Yes. Thanks. I'll have a double Courvoisier. No ice, of course."

Dave turned around in surprise. He smiled again in an attempt to hide his inconsiderate thoughtlessness. Lucy seemed unperturbed. Dave was relieved.

As there were very few customers in the pub, Dave felt a little annoyed that the barman seemed so reluctant to pause his conversation and come over to serve him. He eventually wandered over to Dave.

"What can I get you?"

"A pint of bitter and a," he paused as he tried to remember what Lucy had asked for. "A double cor-vosy-er."

The barman stifled a laugh.

Was the man sniggering at his pronunciation? Dave felt irritated by the ridicule.

"No Courvoisier, the ladies drinking this one," said the barman, an impatience to his tone as he pointed to the optics.

"That's okay. Whatever," said Dave sharply, not sure of the difference anyway and annoyed by the barman's blatant mockery.

He begrudgingly paid for the drinks and returned to the corner where Lucy sat waiting.

"That barman was a bit rude," commented Dave as he pulled out the stool from under the table and sat down opposite her.

"I'm glad you say that. I thought the same but wondered if I was just being a bit oversensitive?" said Lucy as she reached into her bag, which she'd positioned on the table next to her companion.

Dave shook his head and shot a contemptuous look in the direction of the bar. Who did that man think he was?

"Can we make a start on the questions then, Dave?" began Lucy. "I don't have all that much time."

"Yeah. Sorry," apologised Dave, momentarily forgetting that it was actually *him* doing *her* the favour.

Lucy pulled out a pen and notebook from her bag and placed them on the table in front of her. She took a sip of her drink. Dave noticed her flinch. She said nothing, but he could tell she had noticed that it wasn't the drink she had asked for. He felt guilty and lowered his eyes.

She was wearing a black, mini-skirted suit. He looked at her slim, shapely legs and, becoming conscious of his stare, averted his gaze back to her face. Lucy's eyes were fixed on him patiently, her pen poised in her hand. He looked across apologetically.

"Right, if you're ready, I need a bit of information," she began. "You know the sort of stuff: How did you get into speedway? How much does it cost you? How long have you been racing? Do you have another job? Do you make a living from racing? Have you got a girlfriend? What does she think about your racing?"

Dave was happy to talk about his career. He explained how he'd been riding speedway since he was a boy. He told her that several riders either had other jobs or earned their money by riding for other clubs beside Willsby. He explained that although he rode for two clubs, he did it out of his love for the sport. He didn't need to worry about money as he had other provisions for an income. He described how he had just split with a girlfriend, and that women were always resentful that speedway took up so much of his time: all that travelling, all those plane flights, all those young, adoring, female fans. He really couldn't be bothered with all that jealousy and nagging. Why couldn't women behave more like men? Why were they so complicated? If women weren't so good looking, he didn't think he'd even bother with them. He wished he could just meet a woman who would accept that his racing came first. Was that too much to ask?

Dave had felt apprehensive at first. He was revealing some rather intimate information to this stranger, but as their conversation progressed, he felt more at ease. He liked her, and he was also growing increasingly aware of how attractive she was, for an older woman, that is. Her legs were especially shapely. He'd caught flashes of her thighs as she'd crossed and uncrossed her legs throughout their conversation. He was worried she might be offended by his stares. He tried to avoid keep looking at the woman's hemline, but whenever he thought he'd achieved it, she'd cross or uncross those legs, and he just couldn't stop his eyes shooting back in that direction.

He had thought they were getting on well, so it came as quite a shock to him when she suddenly looked at her watch, stood up, and replaced the pen and notepad into her bag.

"Thank you, Dave. That's about all I need. I've got to get off now. I'll see you around."

She smiled, clutched her bag, and hurriedly walked away.

Dave opened his mouth to call after her, but no words came out. Instead, he watched her leave, his gaze fixed on the swing of her hips, and those amazing long legs. As she disappeared through the doorway, Dave suddenly felt guilty. Had he said something wrong? Had he upset her in some way? Perhaps she had noticed him constantly staring at her legs? Surely that wouldn't have upset her? That was a compliment, wasn't it? He stood up and walked to the door.

Dave was concerned. Had he offended her? Was Lucy insulted? He hurried outside, hoping to catch her before she left. He was unlucky: there was no sign of her. He cursed himself. Why had he let her go without arranging to meet her again? I mean, she was a bit older than him, but she wasn't bad looking, and he had nothing else in the pipeline, so why not?

* * *

Charlotte had finally settled into her job. It hadn't been as easy as she'd expected, and her older colleague, Mrs Shield, was a little bossy. Despite this, she was a friendly enough woman who was happy to talk to Charlotte without prying too deeply. Charlotte had been a little embarrassed when Mrs Shield had asked her about Friday's speedway meeting. The old lady was perceptive and had guessed instantly that Charlotte had met somebody special. Charlotte wasn't sure how she'd known, but she had. She seemed interested to learn more about the speedway rider who had captivated Charlotte. There seemed little reason for Charlotte not to confide in her companion. She had described Anthony to Mrs Shield, telling her about his dark hair and his striking, brown eyes. She told her about his racing, how he had come second, and then how he'd had that terrible fall. She even confided that Anthony made her feel special, and that she knew they were destined to be together. Charlotte was glad that she finally had somebody to talk to.

That week, the guesthouse had been busy, which coupled with Mrs Shield's regular chats, meant that the days passed quickly. Charlotte was grateful. She was looking forward to the weekend when she could see Anthony again. Even Mrs Shield seemed excited to hear the next chapter of Fate's story.

* * *

The Willsby race meeting had come around quickly. Dave was tired, and he just didn't feel at his fittest as he left the changing rooms. He was making his way across to the pits when he noticed Lucy in the crowd. A lot of things had happened since their meeting but seeing her brought it back to him. He walked over to the trackside and called out her name. The fact that he'd actually remembered her name was a surprise to him. He was pleased that he had seen her. He had been wondering why she had left so suddenly from The Druids. He had tried to pinpoint what it was that he had said or done that may have upset her. He was anxious to make amends.

"Hi," he said as he approached her. "How's the book going?"

"Fine."

He sensed the reproach in her simple, abrupt reply. There was an awkward silence. Dave noticed that her usual smile was missing.

"Was I any help to you?" he asked, seeking reassurance.

"Yes, thank you."

There was another silence. Dave felt really uncomfortable now.

"I was sorry that you had to leave so quickly on Saturday," he said impulsively. "Perhaps I could buy you a drink in the bar later, you know, to make up for it?"

Dave felt consoled by his offer. He looked at her expectantly.

"Perhaps," she answered.

Her voice was unemotional. Her expression remained unchanged.

"I'll see what happens."

Dave was worried. Her nonchalance disturbed him. His mechanic was calling him from the pits, but he pretended not to hear. He stood rooted to the spot, staring at Lucy, urging her forgiveness. His mechanic called again.

"I think you're wanted," said Lucy, with a nod of her head in the direction of the irate voice. Dave glanced across to the pits. The man waved and shouted out Dave's name. His irritation was obvious. Dave looked at Lucy, reluctant to leave.

"You'd better go," she said. "I'll see you later."

The familiar impish grin returned to her lips.

"In the bar," she clarified with a laugh. "If your invitation still stands?"

The comment and smile consoled Dave.

"Yes, of course," he said. "See you up there later then."

He felt confident that he had made amends. For a minute there, he'd thought the Chapman charisma may be faltering. He walked away towards the pits and his now rather annoyed mechanic.

* * *

Travis Fengar, what a strange name, thought Charlotte as she read about the new Willsby team member in her programme. He was an American, thirty-two years old and single. It was his first year in England, and he was keen to establish himself in the Willsby team. His favourite food was chicken curry, and he enjoyed water sports in his spare time. His blond-haired photograph smiled up at Charlotte from beside the short biography.

Charlotte closed her programme and looked across the track. The riders, Anthony among them, had disappeared to the changing rooms to prepare for the evening's racing. Charlotte saw her chance to put her well thought out plan into action. She intended to give Fate a hand with her script by getting herself noticed by Anthony. She entered the pit area and mingled with the other spectators who were looking at the bikes and chatting to the mechanics. Deliberately, she had positioned herself alongside Anthony's bike, next to the suave man whom she recognised from the week before.

"Are you Anthony's mechanic?" she asked, smiling at the man.

He turned to her.

His face looked a little weathered but that hardly distracted from his almost clichéd, rugged features.

"Mechanic, brother, and bodyguard," he smirked.

Charlotte smiled enthusiastically.

"He did well last week," she commented.

"Thanks to his miracle-working brother," grinned the man, as he grabbed the handlebars and pushed the bike away.

He glanced back at Charlotte and winked. Charlotte stared at him. He was Anthony's brother? She could hardly believe it. They certainly didn't look like brothers.

As the riders began to make their way to the pits, Charlotte returned to her usual viewing spot. Graham had noticed her arrive

33

and keenly walked over to join her.

It was not long before Anthony appeared from the changing rooms. Charlotte recognised the face beside him; Travis Fengar looked just as flamboyant in real life as he did in the photograph.

As the two men walked across the centre green towards the pits, Charlotte's stomach churned. Anthony looked wonderful in his yellow and black leathers. Her stare was fixed on him throughout his entire walk from the changing rooms, a fact that he could not have been unaware of. As he passed, he glanced across in her direction. As if he were trying to place a name to an unfamiliar face, his eyes skimmed across her. They were certainly very piercing eyes. Charlotte felt comforted. Anthony had finally noticed her.

Graham looked at the two riders. He squinted, seemingly believing that this would help him recognise the stranger. Charlotte noticed his bemused expression as he looked at the blond newcomer.

"That's Travis Fengar," she said confidently. "He's the new signing."

Graham smiled in surprise.

"We have been doing our homework, haven't we, Charlie?" he laughed loudly. "Any good is he, this 'Finger' bloke?"

"I don't know about that, but he likes chicken curry and surfing," said Charlotte, pointing to the write up in her programme.

Graham laughed again, staggering around dramatically, holding his stomach as he did so.

"Give us a look, Darling. The programme seller wasn't there when I came in."

"No, he was at the entrance, not the back fence where you climbed over," she mocked as she handed it across.

Charlotte pointed to the picture of the American.

"I bet he'll get a shock surfing on Willsby beach," said Graham, reading the article. "It's hardly California, is it?"

He stuck his arms out to the side, imitating a surfer, moving robotically in unison with his erratic laughter. Charlotte smiled politely.

Graham was pleased that they were now getting along so well again.

It wasn't long before the riders had been introduced to the crowd, and the evening's racing began. Charlotte watched Anthony intently on each of his outings. She had been surprised by how well he was racing, and she proudly filled in the score in her programme. However, her surprise at his skill on the track was minimal, when compared to that which she felt with the events that unfolded next.

It was during one of the races. Anthony, as if Fate were controlling his actions, had walked into the crowd to talk to a man stood just yards away from Charlotte and Graham. Now, what were the chances of that happening? How could anybody say that such an action was a mere coincidence? This was Fate and her cunning plan, wasn't it? Anthony had passed just a few feet in front of her. As he passed, he'd glanced up at her and smiled. Charlotte had been too shocked to respond. She stared at him in disbelief and then looked away sheepishly. She felt her cheeks flush and her stomach flutter.

The episode had not escaped the notice of Graham. He found it all rather amusing and teased Charlotte loudly.

"Someone's got a crush going on there haven't they, Charlie?"

He laughed and tapped the old man next to him on the shoulder.

"Can't take the missus anywhere," he exclaimed.

The stranger smiled sympathetically. Graham was laughing loudly;

far too loudly. The reverberation of the sound echoed around the stadium. Everybody in the proximity turned around to look at him, wondering what the commotion was. Charlotte felt both embarrassed and annoyed. Had Anthony heard him? Everyone else had heard him. How could Anthony not have? She froze in embarrassment and stared coldly at Graham, willing him to shut up. Graham, however, only played on her obvious embarrassment by persisting with his behaviour.

"Chats up anything in leathers."

He nudged the elderly man next to him and laughed again loudly. The sound penetrated Charlotte's head and her heart sank. She could picture Anthony watching them. She could almost feel his brown eyes looking on with condemnation. She felt the tears rising in her eyes as the humiliation seeped through her body. She knew that she couldn't hold them back much longer, and in her desperation, she pushed past Graham and began to run towards the exit.

Graham shouted after her.

"Charlie, Baby. Did I say something wrong?"

Charlotte tried to ignore him, but his voice and laughter burrowed in her head.

"Charlie, only having a laugh, Darling."

Jeez, thought Graham, blown it again!

Charlotte pushed her way through the crowd to the gates, her vision blurred by the tears massing in her eyes. Graham had ruined everything, hadn't he?

* * *

Lucy watched the young girl pass her and, noticing the tears in her eyes, wondered what could have possibly upset the young stranger so much. She shrugged as the girl went from view, and then walked up the steps to the clubhouse.

A uniformed man stood in the doorway.

"Have you got your pass?" he asked expectantly.

Lucy looked at him blankly.

"You need a pass until after the meeting, Love."

His voice was polite but emphatic.

"Oh," said Lucy, calmly running her fingers slowly through her long hair. "Dave didn't mention a pass."

She met the man's gaze and smiled before turning away, motioning her intention to leave. "Dave Chapman?" the man enquired sheepishly.

Lucy turned back to face the reddening cheeks beside her.

"Yes. I'm his, er, friend."

The man looked embarrassed.

"I'm sorry, Love. I didn't recognise you."

He stood to one side, leaving room for her to pass.

"Are you sure that's okay? I could ask Dave for a pass if it's needed," said Lucy sarcastically.

"No problem," said the man apologetically.

"Thank you," she mouthed before climbing the stairs to the bar.

Peter watched her go, reflecting on how difficult his job as a doorman could be at times. Some of the riders seemed to get through more girlfriends than they did visor tear-offs. The young ladies would come flouncing in, expecting him to recognise them, and then took offence when he failed to do so. Dave Chapman's women were usually the biggest culprits, so it was hardly surprising that this woman was one of them. Another girlfriend? How did he do it? He wondered

37

what had become of the hairdresser from last season.

Lucy ordered a drink at the bar and then sat at an empty table on the balcony. She looked down at the four riders gathered at the starting tapes. All clad in multicoloured leathers, their faces concealed behind their helmets and goggles, they all looked remarkably similar. The rider, with the red helmet colour in gate one, could have been anyone as he sat eagerly waiting on his bike, his head tilted to one side, watching the tapes, and anticipating the start. It was only the stars down each leg of his leathers that identified him, to Lucy, as Dave Chapman.

She watched him shoot from the start as the tapes sprung up. His star-striped legs seemed to dangle behind his body as he pushed his weight forward. He thrust sideways into the first bend, holding second place. He slid across the track, looking for a way past the leader, throwing his bike into the developing gaps, then trying to force his opponent wide. It worked. As he entered the second lap, Dave switched to the inside of the track and slipped past his rival. The crowd was cheering him enthusiastically.

Dave was a hard, determined rider. His less devoted followers, however, could have been forgiven for instead labelling his actions as reckless and foolhardy. Whichever school one chose, there was no denying that Dave Chapman won races. He romped home to gain his fourth victory of the evening to masses of applause and the enthusiastic chorus of air horns.

Once the meeting had finished, several of the junior riders took advantage of the empty track to practice their racing skills. Lucy watched them, keeping one eye on the clubhouse door. It was not long before Dave walked in. He joined a group of people at the bar, two men and a rather plain-looking, plump woman. After a couple of minutes, he noticed Lucy, and walked over to her.

"I thought you'd gone home," he said, looking at her expectantly.

She gestured for him to sit down. Naturally, he did.

"I've been watching the young riders," she enthused. "They make it look so difficult."

"It is difficult!" laughed Dave as he moved his seat closer to Lucy.

Dave found himself staring at her, just as he had done in The Druids the week before. Lucy this time, however, seemed to enjoy the attention.

"I was really impressed by your racing," she said. "Another maximum, wasn't it?"

Dave did not have the chance to answer, before they were interrupted by the plain woman and her companions.

"Who's your friend?" asked the woman, her suspicion obvious.

"This is Lucy," introduced Dave. "I'm helping her with a book she's writing."

He turned to Lucy.

"This is Travis from the team, my mechanic Mick and his sister, Jane."

Without any further invite, the three friends sat down at the table. Lucy recognised Mick; she remembered seeing him tinkering with Dave's bikes earlier. She also knew the American rider. She couldn't, however, recall ever having seen the plain-looking woman before.

Dave and Travis began discussing the meeting. They had been the main spearhead of the team, scoring the vital points which had led to their team's victory. They were naturally eager to talk about their performance. The other three sat in an awkward silence, avoiding eye contact. Lucy sipped her drink, feeling uneasy in the presence of the strangers. The plain woman looked across at her. She said nothing, but her distrustful gaze was intimidating. Mick seemed to notice the expression on his sister's face too, and seemingly uncomfortable, turned to Lucy.

"So, what's your book about?"

"It's a thriller."

Mick nodded attentively. Jane's venomous glare was unrelenting.

"Why do you need Dave to help then?" she asked suspiciously.

Lucy thought for a moment before replying.

"Well, he is a thriller himself, isn't he?" she chuckled.

Mick laughed politely, but the joke was wasted on Jane, her disapproval obvious in her humourless stare. Mick again seemed embarrassed.

"How do you get ideas to write about?" he asked, no doubt more out of awkwardness than interest.

"I watch people," explained Lucy. "I see how they react to different situations. I tend to shape all my characters out of the people I meet."

"We'd better look out then, or we'll be in your next book," laughed Mick.

Jane's expression remained unemotional.

"And you make a living out of writing, do you?" she asked cynically.

Lucy smiled politely.

"I do okay."

Her voice was calm, but inwardly Lucy could feel her pulse racing. How dare this woman talk to her so condescendingly? She glanced over to Dave for reassurance but found him deep in conversation with Travis, oblivious to her predicament.

"Don't you have a proper job?" continued the interrogation.

Lucy sat still, not sure how to reply. She raised her glass to her lips and took a sip of her brandy. Inside her head, her thoughts raced confused, but it was Mick who showed the outward distress at Jane's prying question.

"Give it a rest, Sis," he interrupted assertively.

Lucy was grateful for his intervention.

"My sister's got a soft spot for Dave," he explained. "She likes to vet all his friends."

Mick had tried to make light of his sister's behaviour, but Lucy sensed that the woman had taken a dislike to her. Jane sat back in her seat, still staring at Lucy with an almost intimidating glare.

"So, what do you both do for a living?" asked Lucy, trying to diffuse the situation.

Mick answered quickly, obviously preventing his sister from replying first with yet another cutting comment.

"I'm a mechanic. Cars mainly, but I do some work for Dave. Jane's an accountant."

"No wonder she is so interested in my finances then," said Lucy, smiling coyly.

Mick looked uneasy again, concerned no doubt that the comment would reignite the earlier friction. He needn't have worried; Jane had tactfully shut up.

The private conversation between Dave and Travis continued. There were squeals of delight coming from the American as he relived one of the race heats. Dave was obviously in awe of his new friend as he too enthused at their racing prowess. Lucy was inwardly growing rather annoyed that they were ignoring her.

"What do you think could be so important, that they can't include us in their conversation?" said Lucy loudly to Mick.

There was a cheeky smile on her face as she spoke. Travis had heard the comment. He stopped talking and looked across, his huge, white teeth breaking from between his lips into a smile.

"Well, I think we've got a jealous little lady here, Davy," he teased.

Lucy recognised the mockery in his comment, instead of irritating her however, she felt an affinity with the handsome American. Let's face it, Travis could get away with anything: he just had that air about him.

Lucy was beginning to feel uncomfortable. Jane's stony glare was unrelenting.

"Dave," she prompted, resting her hand on his arm. "I really think that I should be going."

As she stood up, Dave followed.

"Nice meeting you," said Mick as Lucy turned to leave.

Jane was silent, and Travis smiled knowingly.

Lucy said her farewells, and Dave led her to the doorway. They walked together down the stairs and out to the car park.

"Can I give you a lift home?" he asked as they stood outside.

Dave's desperation was clear in his voice. The vague attraction that he had first felt towards the woman had now escalated. He was reluctant to let her go, without arranging to see her again, not wanting a repeat of the episode at The Druids.

"I've got my car. Thanks anyway," she answered.

The reply was calm; too calm to reassure him. Instead, it merely emphasised the urgency of the situation.

"Will you be coming here next week?" he asked.

Lucy was silent as she pondered over his question. Dave felt uneasy, willing her to confirm that he would see her again.

"Maybe."

The reply was slow and noncommittal. Dave felt a panic encroaching. The urgency seized him as he suddenly grabbed her arm.

The action seemed to surprise her, she flinched back, her unsmiling face staring at him in disapproval. The gentle reproach made him conscious of the intensity of his grip on her arm. He eased it slightly as he recoiled from the reprimand. The look on her face showed her disapproval, yet her hands were now gently creeping up his arms. Her small fingers tightened as they reached his shoulders. An impish, almost pouting, smile crept across her lips.

Her coquetry was the signal Dave had wanted, and he kissed her.

Slowly, Lucy pulled away from Dave's embrace, meeting his gaze as his hungry, glazed eyes opened.

"I really ought to be going."

Dave tried to control the feeling of desperation that had overcome him. The feeling fought, unsuccessfully, against his conscience as he eased his grip on her.

"Can I see you in the week?" he asked before finally relinquishing his grip. "I'm racing on Wednesday. Would you like to come along?"

As soon as he had asked the question, he regretted it. How presumptuous to think that she would want to watch him race. No doubt, she would rather they had a proper date. The other women he'd known had hated accompanying him to meetings; all that travelling in a dirty van and having to stand out in the cold watching him race.

Her response surprised Dave.

"I'd love to," she whispered as she handed him a small piece of paper. "I really must go now. I'll see you on Wednesday. Ring me."

Dave watched her go as he turned the telephone number in his fingers. He closed his eyes briefly and smiled to himself, before collecting his thoughts and returning to the clubhouse.

"New lady friend, I see? I don't know how you do it," said Peter as Dave approached.

Dave smiled.

Peter was surprised by the lack of a whimsical reply. Perhaps he was serious about this one, he thought to himself as he watched Dave climb the stairs. Funny really, she was quite a bit older than the other ones, and he certainly wouldn't have put her down as Dave's type.

Jane and Mick were still sat in the corner as Dave walked towards them.

"There's just something unsettling about her. I don't trust her. My intuition tells me," said Jane to her brother.

"She seems okay to me," replied Mick.

"Well, you're just as much of a sucker for a pair of legs as Dave then, aren't you? Believe me, Mick, that woman is trouble."

Mick's eyes gestured towards the approaching Dave, and Jane obediently shut up.

Chapter Three

Mrs Shield flinched as the customer suddenly stood up.

"You clumsy cow," he bawled as he stood staring down at the wet stain. "Do you know how much this shirt cost me?"

Charlotte's red face stared at him defiantly as the rest of the diners looked on. Mrs Shield hurried over to the commotion.

"He knocked my arm," muttered her young colleague stubbornly.

Mrs Shield saw the tears forming in her companion's eyes and gestured for her to leave the room, which she did in a grudging acceptance.

"See what your stupid waitress has done," shouted the customer unrelentingly, her senior years leading him to presume Mrs Shield's authority.

He stood with his hands outstretched pitifully to each side. The blushing, blonde woman beside him tried to calm his temper.

"Honey," she whispered, hardly moving her lips and, rather like an experienced ventriloquist, tugging inconspicuously at his sleeve.

Her puppet stood unrelentingly, and in the manner of the best comedy performers, continued defiantly.

"I said, do you know how much this shirt cost?"

Mrs Shield looked at it. She had bought an identical one for her husband from the local market the week before. It had been quite a bargain. She hid her facetiousness though as she spoke.

"I'm terribly sorry, Sir," she said politely. "Here."

She passed a handful of napkins to the man, who began to soak up the stain.

"You can be assured that we will reimburse your dry-cleaning costs, Sir."

The man calmed slightly.

"And, naturally, your meal is on the house."

He sat down quietly.

A whisper replaced the silence in the dining room. Mrs Shield picked up the offending bowl from the floor and walked to the door. She paused as she passed the stairs, fearing the guesthouse owner may have heard the fracas. Thankfully, there was only silence from the proprietor's flat above. She breathed a sigh of relief as she pushed open the kitchen door. Charlotte sat at the table, looking awfully upset.

"He's calmed down now," reassured Mrs Shield.

She had guessed there was something bothering Charlotte. Her overreaction to this accident confirmed her assumption. The girl had seemed very glum all week. She'd been reluctant to talk, especially when Mrs Shield had mentioned the new boyfriend, Anthony. No doubt, she'd had a fallout with him. It seemed like the obvious explanation. Mrs Shield looked at the girl and, having had plenty of experience with her own teenage daughter, thought it best just to leave her be so as not to aggravate the matter further. She left the girl in the kitchen while she tended to the diners. The puppet and his young companion seemed content as they ate their way through the most expensive items on the menu. They grinned victoriously as they left without having to pay a penny.

Charlotte sat alone in the kitchen. She had wanted to confide in Mrs Shield. She longed to tell her how Graham had made her look so foolish in front of Anthony. She had wanted somebody to talk to about the humiliating incident and how embarrassed she had felt. Graham had ruined everything. Anthony wouldn't want to know her now, would he? She had hoped that Mrs Shield would understand. The older woman, however, had been reluctant to talk. She hadn't even bothered to ask about Anthony or the speedway visit so it was obvious that she didn't care, wasn't it? Today's incident would only make that animosity worse, wouldn't it? Admittedly, Mrs Shield had seemed to put a brave face on the accident, but Charlotte was sure she would be annoyed. She would, no doubt, tell the guesthouse owner. Charlotte would likely be subjected to a humiliating dressing down. She'd probably have the dry-cleaning costs, and the expense of the meal, deducted from her wages. Charlotte felt so alone. She desperately wanted to talk to somebody about her problems, but Mrs Shield, the one person she thought that she could confide in, no longer wanted to know.

* * *

Dave pulled the crumpled piece of paper from his pocket and stared thoughtfully at the telephone number. He had wanted to ring Lucy all weekend, and the fact that he found it so difficult unnerved him. What was wrong with him? He'd rung numerous women in the past without this feeling of anxiety. There was something different about this woman though, and his fear of offending her only fed his uncertainty. He was unsure how she would react to his call, and for the first time in his life, it seemed to actually matter.

He picked up the telephone receiver and dialled the number. Each digit bleeped on his touch, questioning the sincerity of his conviction. The telephone rang twice before she answered.

"Hello."

It was good to hear her voice again. Dave felt reassured. Her voice was calm, but her curiosity as to who was calling was obvious in her tone. Dave took a subconscious, deep breath as he answered.

"Hi."

There was a short silence before he continued.

"It's Dave."

"I know. I was wondering when you'd ring."

Dave felt relieved. She was wondering when he would ring? She had obviously been waiting for his call then? The thought made him feel confident. However, his relief quickly progressed to guilt in the split second that it took him to digest her comment. Had he let her down by not ringing earlier? A desperation to make amends crept over him.

"I'm going up north tomorrow. You know, racing. You could come along if you like?" he blurted.

There was a short silence again as Dave nervously awaited her response. He closed his eyes in relief as she spoke.

"I'd love to come. What time are you leaving?"

Dave felt comforted.

"That's great," he enthused. "We'll be leaving about two. I'll pick you up then if that's okay?"

There was another short silence, which Lucy broke with a laugh.

"I guess you'll want to know where I live then, won't you?"

Dave felt stupid at his omission of not asking the obvious question.

"It would help, wouldn't it?" he laughed nervously.

Lucy gave him directions to her flat and enthusiastically asked about the trip. Surprisingly, she was especially interested in whether a couple of particular riders would be racing for the opposition. Dave was impressed by her interest. He felt flattered that she had taken the trouble to learn so much about his sport in such a short space of time. It must mean that she liked him. He would have been happy to talk more, but their conversation was brought to an abrupt end by Lucy's interjection.

"I'll have to be going now, Dave. I'll see you tomorrow."

Dave was shocked by the sudden announcement.

"Yeah," he muttered in his surprise. "I look forward to it."

"Bye, Dave."

He had no time to reply as she hung up.

Dave sat staring at his phone for a moment. He was relieved that she had agreed to the trip. He wondered, however, how his mechanic, Mick, would react once he learnt of the impromptu addition to their entourage the following day.

* * *

Charlotte sat beside Barnaby in front of the electric fire. It had been a busy day at the guesthouse, but she was feeling more relaxed now. She had been expecting a summons to her employer's office following the incident with the soup of the previous day. The summons had not as yet materialised. Perhaps Mrs Shield hadn't said anything after all?

Charlotte realised now just how irrational she'd been. She had upset herself so much. She'd been dwelling on the episode at the speedway stadium with Graham. Her reaction seemed rather foolish now. Perhaps Anthony hadn't even noticed? Even if he had, surely everyone there knew about Graham? Would anyone really take any notice of him? Charlotte had resolved not to think about the matter anymore. Instead, she would continue with her plan. Obviously, Fate meant her to be with Anthony. As long as she steered as far as possible away from Graham, everything would be fine, wouldn't it?

* * *

"It's the next turning on the right," said Dave as Mick drove along the Esplanade.

The news of their short detour had not been that surprising to Mick, after all, it was not the first time that one of Dave's girlfriends had accompanied them on a trip. He did, however, feel quite jealous on this occasion. Lucy was older than Dave and much nearer Mick's age. He really wouldn't have put her down as Dave's type, and what on earth she saw in him, he didn't have a clue. They pulled up outside of the large, Victorian house. It would no doubt once have been a prestigious residence but now, converted into a number of flats, it had fallen into disrepair. Mick sounded the horn as he looked up at the building. The dark, crumbling bricks and flaking paintwork surprised him. Did Lucy really live there? He had admittedly only met the woman once, but he had imagined that she would live somewhere a little more befitting of her stature. The flats on the Esplanade were notorious for housing reprobates and prostitutes. You could barely open the Willsby Gazette without reading about the antics of the residents. Mick looked across to Dave expecting to see a similar bemusement, but his friend seemed preoccupied as he gazed expectantly at the front door.

Lucy appeared. She was dressed in tight black leggings, emphasising her shapely legs. She skipped across to the van like an eloping schoolgirl. It was a marked contrast to the hairdresser, Dave's last girlfriend, who had tottered around on her stiletto heels, stretching her miniskirt over that inch of bare thigh, which was the border of decency, and dragging a huge body bag of accessories behind her.

Dave jumped out of the passenger seat and kissed her instinctively.

"I'll get in the back," he offered, sliding the side door of the van open and climbing in among the bikes. Lucy climbed into the front seat, throwing a small holdall in front of her.

"Hi, Mick."

Lucy smiled up at him from beneath her ruffled fringe. Although dressed casually, she still looked striking. Mick's eyes crawled over her. He turned away hesitantly as he started the engine. Dave leant forward between the two front seats, resting his chin on Lucy's shoulder. He had noticed Mick eyeing his girlfriend. He felt no annoyance though. He was almost proud that Mick had shown the interest. After all, it was him she was interested in, wasn't it?

It was a long journey, but the three of them remained in high spirits as they played their way through Dave's music collection. Remarkably, Lucy had an almost identical taste in music to Dave.

"Do you like the Thompson Twins?" Dave had asked as he reached into his pocket for his recently-purchased cassette tape.

"What team do they ride for?" asked Mick naively.

Dave laughed.

"They're a band, you idiot!" he mocked, handing the tape across to Lucy who placed it into the cassette player.

Lucy, amazingly, loved them too. She was keen to play the new album several times.

It was on the third rendition of 'Doctor! Doctor!' that they eventually turned off the motorway.

"Can you have a look at the map Dave," asked Mick. "The road layout's changed a bit. Do I take a left here?"

Dave grunted as he opened the Ordnance Survey map.

"Why is reading these things so difficult?" he sighed as he turned the huge sheet of paper and tried to figure out exactly where they were.

"One day you won't need maps," said Lucy. "I saw it on a television program last month. In a few years' time, maps will become obsolete, and instead we'll all be guided around by millions of satellites encircling the Earth."

"What, you mean aliens will control where we go?" asked Dave, with a bemused expression, as he looked up from his map.

Lucy looked at him. He really wasn't joking, was he?

"Something like that," answered Mick, raising his eyebrows, and smiling as he glanced across to Lucy.

They eventually arrived at the stadium, more by luck than as a result of Dave's navigational skills. A man walked towards them as they pulled up outside of the gates. He waved a hand in recognition as he let them inside. Mick drove in. As they passed, the man peered into the van, scowling as he tried to get a better look at Lucy. She seemed a little distressed by the attention and hid her face behind her hand. Dave was annoyed. He glared over Lucy's shoulder at the bulbous-nosed official. How dare he! What was he thinking?

They drove around to the pits. Lucy helped them unload the van (a feat beyond the capabilities of the hairdresser, Mick recalled) before kissing Dave as he left for the changing rooms. Mick watched them; a hint of jealousy crept over him.

Lucy could have gone to the hospitality suite, but she chose instead to watch the racing from the trackside. Dave was impressed at how keen she was to experience his racing up close. He recalled the first time that the hairdresser had chosen that particular viewpoint. He smiled to himself as he recalled her, picking grit out of her permed hairdo, and complaining that nobody had warned her about the spray from the bikes' back wheels. Thank goodness Lucy wasn't like that.

As the racing progressed, Dave became absorbed by the adrenaline of the evening. His concentration only faltered on the odd occasion that he glanced across to check that Lucy was still in the same spot. Of course, she was.

Willsby lost the meeting despite Dave having ridden well. Travis's night, however, had been disastrous; he'd had a very nasty looking crash in his first race. Lucy was surprised, therefore, to see him in such a jovial mood when she eventually joined the others in the hospitality suite after the racing. It seemed nothing could dampen his spirits. He stood at the bar, smiling broadly as if he were advertising a new brand of toothpaste. He accepted drinks from a small group of Willsby supporters who had travelled to see their team. He left shortly afterwards, inviting everyone present back to the hotel for one of his infamous parties. Lucy was aware that he liked to party after a race meeting, and she was rather looking forward to it herself.

There had, of course, been lots of drinks for Dave during the evening too. The Willsby fans were keen to reward their top-scoring rider. Dave accepted them readily until Mick suggested they make their way back to the hotel. It had been a good idea; Dave seemed to be feeling the effects of the excess alcohol.

The Yorkshire accent of the receptionist acknowledged them as the telephone rang. She seemed relieved by the interruption, as she waved her free hand, indicating the direction of the lounge bar. It had not been necessary; the noise from the adjoining room had made the party's location obvious. Lucy had changed into a rather well-fitted, yet still respectable, black dress, which Mick found exceptionally befitting. Dave's hands, like a child sidestepping to avoid cracks in the pavement, gingerly avoided any improper contact with his new girlfriend, as he placed his arm around her waist. Mick watched jealously.

Dave had already drunk a lot at the speedway stadium, and Mick was beginning to question the sense behind their attending the party. He knew how easily led Dave could be, especially by Travis Fengar, and wondered what Lucy would make of one of the American's notorious parties. She didn't seem to be the type of lady who would appreciate his wild behaviour.

Travis was certainly an extravagant character and had an insatiable hunger for fun. He had an inexplicable ability to survive on vast quantities of alcohol and extraordinarily little sleep. Prudent onlookers would probably warn Travis about his excessive lifestyle, but such advice was wasted on him. He lived for the day. Becoming an old man was an alien concept to the American, so why did he need to concern himself beyond tomorrow? Now was what mattered, and Travis had an unquenchable hunger for thrills. He took every opportunity that presented itself to him. It was probably this devil-may-care attitude that made him such a good speedway rider. There was no room for fear or hesitation in his line of business.

Mick wasn't too sure that he agreed entirely with that philosophy. Anyhow, his concern was not with Travis, but with Dave, who wasn't blessed with the same stamina as his new friend. Since the American had joined the Willsby team, Dave had tried to keep up with his teammate, both on the track and off. Mick was growing increasingly worried about the influence. He was about to suggest that they skip the party and get an early night instead. Travis, however, had noticed them arrive, and he had other plans. He appeared at the door and made a beeline for his friend. He reminded Mick of a clichéd used-car salesman with his perfect hair, pearl white teeth, and uncanny ability to orate his point of view with a persuasive sincerity.

"Hi Dave. Party time," he enthused, raising his right hand in the air.

Dave chameleoned into the role, palm slapping avidly, and matching the wide grin with his not so perfect teeth. Travis embraced his friend and led him into the lounge. Dave looked around tentatively at Lucy. She smiled reassuringly as she followed. Dave relaxed instantly, accepting the drink thrust at him as he was bundled towards the seat beside Travis.

Mick bought drinks for himself and Lucy. It was not necessary to include Dave for whom the supply of alcohol from the travelling fans seemed endless.

The room filled with a muffled revelry that drowned out the hotel's struggling piped music. Empty glasses paddled in puddles of warm beer on the tabletops. A smoky smog hung over the revellers, mixing with the smell of alcohol, creating a noxious, yet strangely appealing, environment. Mick now saw the sense behind the tacky, plastic plants dotted around the room, which stretched out defiantly into the air as the toxic cocktail leached fruitlessly at their bright, green leaves.

The bar shut at eleven but Travis, reluctant to end the party, invited everyone back to his hotel room.

The numbers had dwindled slightly by the time that they reached room 208. There were, however, still plenty of bodies to fill Travis's hotel room as he flung open the door, revealing a huge supply of beer bottles, and a massive pot of room-service chicken curry. The partygoers entered the room. Mick didn't know who most of the people there were, and he was pretty sure that Travis didn't either. Bottle tops flipped, and a sweet inviting smoke crept around the room, engulfing the revelry, as phase two of the evening began.

It was still dark when Dave woke up. His mouth and throat were dry, crying out for water, but his heavy head refused to move from the pillow. He lay for a while, his muddled thoughts trying to remember the events of the evening before. He remembered the party in the bar but had no recollection of anything else after that. He could feel Lucy in the bed beside him and cursed himself. What had happened? He really had no idea. Had he made a fool of himself? Had he been acting the idiot in front of her? No doubt, she would be annoyed just like all his other girlfriends had been. He'd worry about that tomorrow though. For now, he found thinking far too demanding on his aching head, so he turned over and slipped back into a heavy sleep.

He woke up again a couple of hours later.

Dave's mouth was stale and dry, and his head was thumping. The sound of the shower teaming in the adjoining bathroom wasn't helping matters. As he slowly gained his senses, he became conscious of the light streaming through the gap in the curtains. His eyelids reluctantly fought to face the daylight. The noise from the bathroom stopped, and Lucy walked into the room, a small towel wrapped around her middle. Her wet hair cascaded around her shoulders. She smiled.

"You look awful," she commented.

Dave did not need to be told. He felt awful too. He sat up. His head was pounding uncontrollably. He glanced at the clock. They had missed breakfast. Mick would probably already be waiting downstairs for them. He climbed out of bed and stumbled to the bathroom.

* * *

Charlotte had timed her arrival at the stadium to ensure that Anthony would be in the changing rooms. She walked purposefully to the pits, her heart thumping nervously with anticipation as she spotted Anthony's brother. He recognised her immediately.

"Hi there, Sexy," he grinned.

Charlotte glanced at the row of crowned white teeth in front of her as she mulled over her plan.

"Hi. How are you doing?" she acknowledged.

The man was obviously flattered by the attention.

"All the better for seeing you, Babe," he continued.

He placed his arm around Charlotte's shoulder as he introduced her to a passer-by.

"Hey, have you met my little friend?"

The man smiled politely at Charlotte before continuing on his way. Anthony's brother seemed to know everybody. He introduced each one in turn to Charlotte. She was not particularly impressed but feigned enthusiasm, adding to the already overinflated ego of her companion.

After a while, Anthony approached them from the changing rooms. Charlotte watched him as he walked slowly across the centre green, stopping occasionally to sign autographs at the trackside. As he entered the pits, he stared distractedly at Charlotte, before turning his eyes to his bike. Charlotte had not been this close to Anthony before. She'd felt a slight chill pass through her body as their eyes met. Anthony stared doggedly at his bike despite his brother's attempts to distract him.

"Hey, Bruv. This is Terry's little friend, er…"

Terry paused, placed his arm around her shoulder, and pulled her towards him. The smell of his aftershave was overpowering as he looked at her expectantly.

"Charlotte," she said, finishing his sentence. "My name is Charlotte."

"Yeah, Charlie, my little mate Charlie," enthused Terry.

Anthony did not react. His eyes stayed fixed on his bike and he said nothing. Charlotte could tell that he was keen to get on with his work. She had done enough for now anyhow. She had given Fate a helping hand; Anthony now knew her name, and she had befriended his brother. She pulled herself free from the man's grip and turned to walk away.

"Catch you later, Gorgeous," said Terry with a wink.

Charlotte left the pits and made her way to the grass bank overlooking the second bend. She could see Graham, in the crowd, across the track from where she stood. As usual, he was trying to make conversation with the people standing next to him. The other fans seemed reluctant to talk and, from this distant viewpoint, she could see that they were visibly edging away from him. It looked as if there was an invisible force field around him. Charlotte felt relieved that she had decided not to stand with him this evening. At least there could be no repeat of the previous week's events now.

* * *

Lucy walked towards the clubhouse. The familiar doorman was standing at the entrance as she approached.

"Hello again," she said.

He held the door open and stepped to one side, allowing her to pass.

"Hello, Love. You're becoming quite a regular here now, aren't you?" he remarked.

"Yes. I've really got into speedway in the last few weeks since I met Dave. And to think that this time last year, I didn't even know what speedway was."

The doorman looked puzzled.

"But I saw you here last year, didn't I?"

"No," said Lucy firmly. "As I said, I didn't even know what speedway was last year."

Lucy's answer was blunt but positive. The doorman did not pursue the matter further, although he was almost certain that he'd seen her face before.

"I must be mistaken," he murmured apologetically.

"Yes, you must be," smiled Lucy, as she walked past him and up the stairs to the bar.

As she entered the room, Lucy noticed Jane sat alone at a table on the veranda. Jane had also noticed her as the apathetic glare confirmed. Lucy, not particularly wanting to confront the woman so early in the evening, took a seat at the opposite end of the balcony.

* * *

Anthony was scheduled to race in heat two. The other three riders had made their way to the start but there was, as yet, no sign of Anthony Myers. A siren sounded. It was the indication that the referee had placed a two-minute time warning on him. He had just two minutes to take his place in the starting line-up or face disqualification. There was a flurry of activity around him as he waited in the pits. Voices shouted, fingers pointed, and arms waved as his brother knelt beside the bike making frantic adjustments. Suddenly, he stood back, Anthony climbed aboard, and the bike was rapidly pushed into motion. He sped onto the track and made his way around to the start to join the other three riders.

Charlotte felt uneasy, the pressure had unsettled her. Anthony looked uncomfortable as he took his place in the line-up. Within seconds the race had begun. Anthony launched himself into the first bend spiritedly, but to no avail, emerging only in last place. He trailed behind the other competitors until the second lap when, entering the second bend, his machine seemed to inexplicably accelerate, lurching him out of control and into the bike in front. Both riders slid to the track after the impact. Anthony seemed to come off worse. Momentarily tangled with his bike, he skimmed the shale, was flung around like an unloved doll, and collided headfirst with the fence at high speed. Charlotte's heart sank as the red stoplights around the track lit up, and the officials frantically waved flags to alert the other competitors.

The grounded opponent sprung to his feet, cursing his luck, as he strutted back to the pits. Charlotte stared in disbelief at the scene ahead. Anthony lay still, surrounded by the first aid staff that now crouched beside him. A group of young spectators had rushed to the trackside and were jostling for a view over the mangled fence. Charlotte looked on; her view obscured by the surrounding crowd. Anthony was still motionless. She stood paralysed on the grass bank as a hush descended over the spectators. The commentator's microphone crackled expectantly over the public address system. He said nothing. Charlotte shivered as she looked on. She felt useless and sick inside. There was frantic movement all around Anthony, but he remained unnaturally still. The track officials picked up the mutilated ruin of his bike, which lay on the track several yards away from his body.

The crowd had fallen silent as a rather inappropriate, cheery song played across the public address system. Anthony still hadn't moved, and a larger group of people now knelt around him. Charlotte struggled to maintain her view of the leather-clad body through the commotion. Her heart was beating rapidly.

It was some time before Charlotte felt the tension in her body subside slightly, and Anthony slowly sat up. His helmet was eased off with the help of a first aider. He was holding his left arm. He sat for a couple of minutes before being helped to his feet. To a trickle of applause, Anthony was led back to the pits in obvious discomfort.

Charlotte glanced across at Graham. He did not applaud with the rest of the crowd. He would, no doubt, be joking about the accident. Charlotte hated him for his insensitivity. She hurried to the pits for a glimpse of Anthony, but by the time she arrived, he was nowhere to be seen. There was an ambulance behind the pits.

Charlotte returned to the grass bank as the commentator announced that Anthony would be taken to hospital. He had a suspected broken wrist and concussion. He promised to keep them informed of any developments. Charlotte wanted to go home, but she was desperate to hear how Anthony was. She could no longer retain any enthusiasm for the racing. Her thoughts were constantly with Anthony. It was a long hour before the meeting ended. The promised update on Anthony had not materialised, and she finally made her way home.

* * *

After the racing had finished, Lucy decided to speak to Jane. She walked over to the woman and, on catching her eye, smiled.

"Hi there. I didn't notice you over here."

Jane did not look convinced by the white lie. She said nothing.

"Can I get you a drink, Janey?" offered Lucy.

"No thank you," Jane replied coldly.

Her eyes reverted to her programme. Lucy was unperturbed as she sat down beside her. Eager to share the details with Jane of her trip to

Yorkshire, Lucy continued enthusiastically.

"I've got a surprise for you later, Janey, you will be delighted."

Jane ignored her and continued to read her programme. Lucy took the hint and turned her attention to watch the young riders on the track below.

It was a long, hostile twenty minutes before Dave and Mick finally arrived. Lucy stood up and smiled as Dave approached. He slipped his arm around her waist, pulling her towards him as they kissed.

Jane was clearly shocked by the show of affection. Mick obviously hadn't mentioned the events of their trip to Yorkshire in the week. Her huge, grey eyes stared at the couple in condemnation. Dave caught the glare. He smiled at her reassuringly, but she showed no remorse, her stare only penetrating deeper. Lucy pretended not to notice. Dave was disturbed by the disapproving looks from his friend. Lucy, sensing his apprehension, rubbed his thigh with her hand and kissed him.

"Is something wrong, Dave?" she asked.

He was still looking at Jane nervously.

"No, of course not."

Lucy gently turned his head to face her. Dave's eyes moved reluctantly from Jane. Lucy kissed him again. She could feel the stony glare of Jane's eyes on them but refused to be intimidated by the hostility.

Mick had been watching. He had not thought to tell his sister about the growing intimacy between Lucy and Dave. He knew that Jane was fond of his friend. She had always been a little uncomfortable with Dave's girlfriends, but never obnoxious like she was being tonight. It shocked him, especially as it was such an unprovoked response; Lucy had been exceptionally friendly. The atmosphere had grown tense, and Mick felt the need to diffuse the situation.

"I want to get back early tonight," he said, looking towards his sister.

"That's okay, Mick. I don't particularly want to hang around here much longer either." Jane's reply was antagonistic. With her eyes still burning into Dave and Lucy, she stood up and grabbed her handbag. There was a short pause before she looked expectantly at her brother. He stood up obediently.

"I'll take Jane and the gear home then come back for you," suggested Mick.

Dave nodded.

"It's okay. I'll take him home later," offered Lucy.

Mick looked to Dave for confirmation.

"Are you sure you don't mind?" he asked Lucy.

"It's no problem at all."

The reply had not helped to calm Jane. She strutted to the door, saying nothing as she left.

"I'll see you tomorrow then," said Mick as he followed his sister from the bar.

"See you again soon then, Jane," shouted Lucy after the departing woman.

There was no reply as the chubby figure flounced from view.

Lucy turned to Dave once they were alone.

"Jane doesn't seem too keen on me. Have I done something to upset her?"

Dave felt ashamed of his friend's behaviour. Lucy sounded sincerely disappointed.

"I'm sorry," he said. "I just don't know what's wrong with her. She isn't usually like this."

Dave's defence was hollow, even he wasn't entirely sure that his friend's behaviour warranted the apology.

Lucy smiled.

"Do you mind if we make a move too?" she suggested.

"Sure," replied Dave, standing up and leading her towards the door.

Travis Fengar stood by the bar.

"Hey, Dave," he shouted as they passed. "What was all that business with Janey? Is she jealous of your new lady friend?"

His American accent sounded flamboyantly false as he grabbed Dave's arm. Dave paused, and Travis tried to draw him into a conversation. Dave, however, was not listening. He was watching as Lucy slipped out of the door.

"Look, Travis. I've got to go."

The American looked upset. His big, blue eyes watched as Dave stared at the doorway where the woman had now vanished from view. Dave had noticed his friend's expression and felt guilty. He didn't want to ignore Travis but what else could he do? How ever much he would have liked to stay with his friend, he couldn't risk Lucy leaving without him. He hurried to the door and down to the bottom of the stairs, where she stood in an uncomfortable silence with the doorman.

"Did Peter say something to upset you?" he asked, once they were out of earshot of the man.

"No, not really. He just wasn't all that friendly," said Lucy.

Dave wasn't surprised. The doorman had a unique way of saying the wrong thing. It wouldn't have been the first time that he'd upset one of Dave's girlfriends.

"It's still quite early," said Lucy.

She put the key in the ignition.

"We could get something to eat and go back to my flat. I'll run you home later."

The idea appealed to Dave. He nodded.

"Just as long as it's not a chicken curry. That's all I seem to have been eating with Travis lately," he laughed.

Lucy smiled, started the car, and drove slowly over the uneven road to the stadium's exit.

"Do you get on well with Peter?"

Lucy's question had come out of the blue and had surprised Dave. Perhaps the doorman had said something to upset her after all?

"He's okay. Can be a bit interfering at times," he reassured.

"You're not close then? You know, you're not friends or anything?"

They pulled onto the smooth tarmac of the main road. The car's suspension seemed to breathe a sigh of relief as they left the uneven track.

"No, he's just the doorman."

"You don't take anything he says seriously then?"

Lucy sounded a little worried as they stopped at the red traffic lights.

"No, he says some stupid things. Why? Has he said something to you?"

She looked across at him and smiled, seemingly comforted by his answer as she slipped the car into first gear and pulled away into the Willsby High Street.

The town centre was busy as they drove around the one-way system. It was a mild evening, and people ambled along the pavements. Revelry spilled through the open windows and doors of the public houses. They followed the road to the seafront and turned onto the Esplanade. Lucy stopped the car outside of a brightly-lit takeaway restaurant. The shop window was covered with star-shaped, handwritten notices of the high cholesterol meals on offer inside.

"Really fancy some fish and chips," enthused Dave as he peered through the celestial mesh into the shop.

Lucy searched through her handbag.

"Could you lend me some money? I must have left my purse at home," she asked.

Dave pulled out his wallet and slipped her a couple of notes from the large wodge. Lucy climbed out of the car and made her way into the shop.

The fast-food chef, dressed in a grubby white apron, stood behind the counter. His huge, black moustache twitched as he greeted Lucy and took her order. Dave watched her from the car as she paced up and down in the small shop. She did have a great figure. He looked at her shapely legs as she took the change and placed it in her back jeans pocket.

Once served, Lucy returned to the car and handed Dave the warm paper parcel. She'd appeared to have forgotten about his change; he'd have to remind her about it later.

The aroma of the food filled the car as they drove to Lucy's flat. Dave remembered the flat from his previous visit. He had not, however, noticed before just how rundown the building had been. It was dark, but the streetlights illuminated the peeling paintwork and crumbling bricks as he climbed from the car. He followed Lucy to the door.

As he stepped inside the small hallway, he felt instantly uncomfortable. A musty smell hung in the cold, damp air. Lucy flicked on the electric light. Dave looked up at the dull bulb hanging among cobwebs from the ceiling. A door led off to the right; a hand-painted letter 'A' had been scrawled on the unvarnished wood.

Lucy led him up a long flight of stairs. His boots crunched on the filthy carpet as he climbed. His hand slid uncomfortably up the worm-eaten banister. They reached another landing. A further staircase led up beside them to the floor above, but Lucy had stopped. She searched through her key ring and placed a key in the lock. The door was stiff. Lucy kicked it at foot level. It relented.

The musty smell had at least disappeared as she led him into the flat and along a corridor to a bedsitting room. Dave stood looking around as Lucy went into the adjoining kitchen.

"Any chance of a beer?" he shouted after her.

He was in luck. Lucy had, by chance, stocked up on his favourite brand earlier that day.

As he waited for his beer, his eyes followed the blank walls around the room. There was a typewriter on a table by the door and piles of paperwork next to it. He walked over, casting an eye over the manuscripts. Lucy returned to the room and handed him a can of beer.

"Is this the story that you're writing about me?" he asked as he picked up a sheet of paper.

"No!" exclaimed Lucy. "You don't want to read that."

Dave was quite taken aback by her sharp reaction.

"It's just an article for a woman's magazine," she explained as she eased the paper from his hand.

"You're right there then," laughed Dave, as Lucy hid the sheet under the mountain of papers. "I don't want anything to do with women's stuff, that's for sure."

"I'll just get your dinner," announced Lucy as she once again left the room.

Dave tried to hide his shock at the dilapidated state of the flat; a feat made easier for him by the, somewhat unwelcome, distraction of a black cat that followed his mistress into the room.

"Sorry about the annoying animal," said Lucy as she handed Dave his plate.

Dave smiled awkwardly. He didn't like cats, but they always seemed to make a beeline for him for some strange reason. He didn't like their aloofness. They freaked him out, the way that they stared through him. This one was really sinister as it was completely black with big, green eyes.

"I don't really like cats," announced Dave.

"Don't worry, he's pretty harmless," reassured Lucy.

"I'm not sure about that. It looks like one of those that witches have, being all black and all," said Dave as he opened his beer can.

"They're called familiars," explained Lucy.

Dave looked puzzled.

"That's a funny name for a cat," he laughed. "Why did you call it that?"

Lucy looked at Dave, hoping for a sign that he was joking, but not finding it, simply handed him a knife and fork.

Dave was hungry, he placed the cutlery on the table next to him and began to eat at once, picking up the battered cod with his fingers. The crispy batter was delicious. His greasy fingers scooped the chips into his mouth as his taste buds and grumbling stomach revelled in their feast.

"Aren't you eating yours?" he asked, glancing across at Lucy's plate as he cleared his own.

Lucy handed her uneaten food to him, and he began to devour her portion too.

"I'm not sure beer with fish and chips is really the sort of diet that an athlete like you should be eating," smiled Lucy, watching as Dave ravenously devoured the food.

Dave found her comment amusing.

"I'm a speedway rider, not Steve Cram!" he exclaimed between mouthfuls.

Lucy laughed; maybe one day these guys would start taking their diet a little more seriously.

As the meal began to satisfy Dave's pent-up hunger, he gradually became more aware of his surroundings. The rather dank room, and the intimidating stare of the cat that was watching every mouthful he took, made Dave feel slightly ill at ease.

They finished their meal and Lucy switched on the small electric fire.

"It's cold in here, isn't it?" she said, rubbing her arms as she shivered.

Dave placed his arm around her shoulder and pulled her closer to him. He felt more at ease instantly as he kissed her.

* * *

Charlotte sat on the edge of her bed as visions of the accident flooded into her head. She recalled Anthony lying motionless on the track. She could picture Graham heckling. She could see the crowds of bloodthirsty spectators hanging over the safety fence behind Anthony. She wondered if he was all right. Was his wrist badly broken? Did he have any other injuries? She walked over to the window. Perhaps she should go over to the telephone box and ring the hospital? She could maybe find out how he was, or if he'd been discharged? The darkness, however, was intimidating and made up her mind for her to stay put. The Esplanade wasn't the most pleasant or safest of places after dark. If only she could afford to have a home telephone connected, or maybe even buy one of those new portable ones like they had in America? She smiled to herself. They would never take off, would they? It was easier to walk to the nearest telephone box than to carry one of those ludicrously huge things around, wasn't it? She closed the curtains and returned to sit on the bed, picking up her photograph of Anthony as she did so. She pictured him sat up in a hospital bed. She imagined herself sitting at his bedside, plumping up his pillows, and holding his hand. Was he going to be all right?

Barnaby jumped onto the bed beside her. His purrs did little to reassure her. She stared at the photograph grasped firmly in her hand. She had bought it from the souvenir kiosk: a picture of Anthony and his brother together. Anthony looked up at her as Charlotte's eyes turned to the image of his brother. She stared at the photograph for a while, trying to see a resemblance between the two men. There was none.

* * *

The sound of traffic hurtling past outside woke Dave. He was so accustomed to the tranquillity of his own home, nestled in the countryside, that the bustle of the seafront was alien to him. The constant noise from the road and the waves beating against the shore had disrupted his night's sleep. The fidgeting tomcat on the bottom of the bed hadn't helped much either. He rolled over and looked at Lucy. Her ruffled hair sprawled across the pillow as she lay asleep. Dave felt sorry for her. She shouldn't be living in a place like this, should she? She had explained last night that it was the only flat she could find at short notice. Of course, she'd be finding something more suitable once she'd settled into Willsby.

Lucy looked so sophisticated and so out of place in the dreary room. He wondered about her past. What had happened to her to make her move to Willsby and to this glorified bedsit? She had obviously known better times and, if Dave had anything to do with it, she would know better again.

Dave's thoughts were dwelling on the matter when the two of them stepped out into the street later that day. Heavy, grey clouds moved slowly across the sky as they crossed the wide road to the sea. Lucy shivered slightly. Dave placed his arm around her shoulder as they stood for a moment, staring out across the water. A murky, grey lather reared with each wave, licking at the shore. The pebbles seemed to squeal as the tide trickled through them on its retreat. Dave felt uncomfortable as they stood mesmerised by the waves.

"Let's walk into town," he said. "How about we go to The Druids?"

"Okay," she smiled. "That's a really nice idea."

They walked slowly along the Esplanade. Huge buildings towered above them on the opposite side of the road. A couple of whitewashed hotels held out a little hope for the row of otherwise rundown buildings. Those two hotels stood like proud old men, reminiscing their war days while the ugly present crept around them. The rows of forgotten dosshouses cowered, in contrast, behind their flaking paintwork, trying desperately to hide their undignified demise. Lines of grey clothes littered the small balconies as nameless faces looked out from the murky windows. The cluster of bell pushes on each door gave an indication of the hidden multi-occupancy within. Each resident locked inside their solitary, tiny pen, like fattening calves, ignorant of life behind the adjoining wall. Dave looked up at the buildings and tightened his grip around Lucy's shoulder, wanting somehow to shield her from the surroundings. She wasn't like the other occupants here. She deserved better.

The concrete pathway continued, hugging the beach on one side and rows of flower beds on the other. The flowers, laid in masses by council workmen, looked bedraggled as they sat among the discarded empty tin cans and fast-food wrappers. The beach too offered little to the aesthete: drifts of seaweed, fast-food wrappers, and rusty metal cans cluttered the pebbles. Lucy was surrounded by ugliness.

As they approached the town, the slums disappeared, and the condition of the beach seemed to improve slightly. This was the area that the tourists saw, and that the council street cleaners concentrated their attention on. Rows of amusement arcades now adorned the seafront. The electronic buzz and clatter of coins spilled out onto the pavement. Youths stood in small groups, ensnared by flashing lights and whirring sounds as their hands moved levers and buttons in a robotic obedience. The artificial darkness swallowed up the battery gameplayers as they stood outwitted by the ruthless machines.

"How long did you say you've lived on the Esplanade?" Dave asked.

Lucy guessed what he was thinking.

"I know it's not a nice place. I didn't quite realise what the area was like until I moved in," she explained.

"Sorry, I didn't mean..." began Dave.

"It's only temporary," she interrupted. "In fact, I'm looking for somewhere else. The sooner I can get out the better, but it's hard finding somewhere."

Now Dave felt really uncomfortable. He submerged himself even deeper in thought. As they entered the public house, he was feeling almost guilty. There he was living in that big house. It had been a month now since the hairdresser had moved out. He didn't like rattling around in there on his own. And here was Lucy, living in that tiny flat in the roughest part of town. It just didn't seem right.

Lucy walked instinctively to the table where they had sat before, and Dave bought the drinks. It was the same unfriendly barman as on their last visit. Dave said only the minimum words necessary when ordering the drinks and then joined Lucy in the corner. He sat down beside her.

"Lucy."

His voice sounded firm as she looked across to him, waiting apprehensively for him to continue. Dave thought hard about what he was going to say. He took a deep breath.

"Why don't you come and live with me for a while? I think you'd like my house, there's plenty of room for us both."

It was an impulsive question. It had seemed like a good idea. Just temporary of course. It made sense, she needed somewhere to stay. It would be fun and imagine the jealousy of Travis and Mick. They'd be impressed that he had pulled Lucy so quickly. He also wasn't that keen on being seen visiting the Esplanade. Imagine if word got around about that at the stadium? He'd be the butt of all their jokes, wouldn't he? The walk from her flat had only made the situation seem even more pressing. She deserved so much more. He had that huge house. It was far too big just for him. He felt almost as if it were his duty to ask her to move in. He looked across at the woman expectantly but was not prepared for the answer which came.

"Are you proposing to me?"

Of course, he wasn't. How ridiculous! He was about to explain himself, to laugh at her presumption. She was of course joking, wasn't she? He looked across at her as the veil of melancholy, which had surrounded her all morning, was suddenly lifted. She stared at him eagerly. Had he misled her? Surely not? He felt guilty. His thoughts struggled helplessly in his mind. What should he say? How could he explain that it wasn't a proposal of marriage? The idea was ludicrous, wasn't it? His eyes skimmed nervously around the room. He knew that he had to say something but didn't know what. He didn't want to let her down or make a fool of himself.

"Dave," she whispered enthusiastically. "Of course, I'll marry you."

Dave regretted his silence immediately and could not imagine why he hadn't said something. He had to explain himself quickly.

"I didn't..." he began soberly.

Lucy raised her fingers to his lips.

"Shhh. It's okay, Dave. You don't need to say anything. I knew you were going to ask me to marry you. I had this feeling while we were walking here. Intuition I guess," she said. "We have something magical between us, don't we?"

"Well yes," stuttered Dave. "But I didn't mean..."

Dave had to say something. He was just about to shout at her, to

75

tell her she had got it all wrong, when Lucy turned to face the bar.

"Dave's just proposed to me. We're getting married," she announced loudly.

"Congratulations!" said the barman, followed by a round of applause from the customers at the bar.

"Get the couple a drink," enthused an elderly man, and within minutes the barman had placed refills on the bar, complete with cocktail parasols and 'congratulations' emblazed heart-shaped stirrers. Lucy walked over to collect them, beaming as she returned.

"I want us to get married as quickly as possible. Just a quick wedding. Nothing flash. One that will fit in with your racing schedule," said Lucy, placing the drinks on the table. "That is the most important thing, of course."

Dave stared silently.

"We won't have many people there. Just our close friends, like Travis, Jane and Mick," continued Lucy.

Dave sat silently.

"That is what you want too isn't it, Dave?"

Dave was silent. He removed the parasol from his pint and took a sip. Lucy continued.

"I'm so pleased that you feel the same as me."

With each new sentence that emanated from Lucy's enthusiastic tongue, he felt deeper and deeper trapped. He couldn't bring himself to say anything. She looked so happy. How could he shatter her joy now? And in public too? He said nothing, just nodded. He'd explain himself later when they were alone. He could hardly say something now, could he? Not in front of everyone in the pub. He'd look a right idiot, wouldn't he?

Dave did not sleep well that night. He'd planned on going home but wanted to set the record straight with Lucy, so he'd stayed another night with her. Unfortunately, they'd had a few too many in The Druids. He didn't think that he'd drunk that much, but it had sure knocked him out. Things had just sort of developed, and he hadn't got around to saying anything about her misunderstanding. He'd woken early and lay there trying desperately to think of a way out of his predicament. Sure, he wanted Lucy to move in with him, but marriage? That was just ridiculous. How had he got into this mess? How could he let Lucy down lightly? He had to be careful. He knew that both Mick and Travis had their eye on her, and he certainly wasn't going to give up his latest conquest to let either of them muscle in. If he couldn't find a way of letting her down gently, he'd no doubt lose her altogether. He couldn't face that humiliation. He'd look stupid, wouldn't he? The thought was frightening. He'd have to think of something. Perhaps if he just went along with it for a while he could back out before it got too serious?

He glanced across at Lucy, who lay asleep next to him. She looked so peaceful. A relaxed, contented smile graced her lips. Dave ran his fingers over her shoulder. She stirred and, taking a slow, deep breath, opened her eyes.

"What time is it?" he asked.

Lucy leant over to the floor beside her to look at the clock.

"Nine-forty," she answered as she stretched and sat upright.

Dave collapsed back onto his pillow with an irritated sigh.

Lucy looked puzzled by his reaction.

"It's deceptive in here, isn't it? Doesn't feel that late," said Lucy, assuming that he'd thought it was earlier.

"I'm supposed to be meeting Jane at ten," said Dave, his voice agitated.

Lucy looked surprised.

"What for?"

The question had sounded uncharacteristically abrupt but the smile, which subsequently crept over her lips, seemed to apologise for the unintentional inconsistency in her composure. Perhaps she just wasn't a morning person? He could understand that.

"I don't know," said Dave. "She just asked to see me. I think she's having a few problems with her husband. I promised I'd go there today for a chat."

"I see. Yes, you must go then. I'll run you over there straight away," reassured Lucy as she climbed from the bed. "I'll get dressed now. I'd hate to think that you were late for Jane because of me."

Crikey, this was going to be hard. Lucy was so considerate, even to Jane who'd made her dislike of his girlfriend obvious. He'd have to be so careful how he let Lucy down. He was in a rush now though. He'd speak to Lucy later and put the record straight.

It was ten-thirty when they pulled up outside of Jane's house. Lucy waited until Jane had opened the front door, before waving to them both and driving away.

"Sorry I'm late, Jane," said Dave as he walked into the lounge. "I overslept at Lucy's."

Jane did not look impressed. They both sat down and stared across the room at one another as Dave waited for Jane to speak. He felt a little irritated by her summons and hoped that she appreciated the sacrifice that he was making in coming. He did, after all, have his own problem to worry about, didn't he?

"Dave. There's something I want to say to you."

"Sure. Is it him again?"

Dave was referring to Jane's husband. They had spoken about him several times before. Dave had always been so supportive, and Jane appreciated his concern. He was indeed right again on this occasion, Jane was having problems with her husband, but that was not what she wanted to talk about.

"No," she answered soberly. "It's Lucy."

Dave looked at her. His expression mixed intrigue with defiance as she continued.

"There's something not right about her, Dave. I don't want you to take this the wrong way but…"

She bit her lip before continuing, worried that Dave would take offence.

"Do you not think that she might be after your money?"

Despite the real feasibility of the suggestion, Dave seemed amused.

"And I thought she was only after my body," he joked.

Jane smiled at him. He could always make her laugh, even in the most adverse of situations.

This time though, she was genuinely concerned, and her smile soon disappeared.

"I'm serious Dave. There's something very strange about her, and I'm sure I recognise her from somewhere."

Dave was surprised that his joviality had not quenched her suspicion. He looked at her reassuringly.

"You've got Lucy all wrong," he smiled.

Jane's tone changed. Her eyebrows knit together, and her voice was firm.

"Dave, she's up to no good. I just know it," she urged. "You mustn't trust the woman. You must stop seeing her at once. She's after your money, I just know it."

Dave felt angry. How dare his friend lecture him like this.

"That's not fair, Jane. What's up with you? Are you jealous? There will never be anything between you and me, you know."

Jane was fuming. Dave was unjustified with his presumptions. She slapped him across the cheek.

Dave reeled from the outburst. Jane was out of order. What business was it of hers who he went out with? Bloody women. Why were they so complicated? What was it with them? Thank goodness Lucy wasn't like the rest of them. He could make his own decisions. He didn't have to do what his jealous friend told him to do. His anger at Jane was seething inside him. He felt like slapping her back. He couldn't hit a woman though, could he? He wanted to get his own back. He had an idea.

"Guess you won't be happy to learn that I'm marrying her then, will you?" he announced vindictively.

Dave had shocked himself by his statement. Had he really just said that? He hadn't of course meant it, but it had the desired effect on Jane. She looked horrified. She raised her fingertips to her hastily greying lips.

"Dave," she whispered in disbelief. "You've asked her to marry you? That's a bit sudden, isn't it? You hardly know her. What made you ask her to marry you? What the hell are you thinking of? She really has got her claws into you, hasn't she?"

"Well, I didn't actually plan it. It just sort of happened."

"Just sort of happened!"

"Well yes. I was planning on asking her to move in with me, and she misunderstood."

"Misunderstood! You really are gullible, aren't you? You idiot, you're being tricked into this," said Jane sternly.

Dave looked angered by the remark.

"Of course, I'm not being tricked," he snapped, almost convincing himself of his sincerity.

Jane flinched at the uncharacteristic outburst from her friend. Dave noticed and tried to regain his composure.

"Jane. She's okay, I'm sure. Ever since I got the money, and what with all that business with Sam Orpin I had last year, I've always felt reluctant to trust anyone. Lucy's different though. She hasn't even mentioned the money. I'm sure she doesn't even know about it, how could she? She's never seen me or had anything to do with speedway until this year. Give her a chance, Jane. She's really trying to be nice to you. She's a genuinely nice person."

Jane was touched by his speech, but she realised how gullible Dave could be. It wasn't that long ago, after all, that he had nearly lost his money to that Sam Orpin. A right dodgy character he had been. If it hadn't been for that murder around the same time, Dave would have had his fingers seriously burnt.

"You are making a huge mistake, Dave. That woman is trouble," yelled Jane.

Dave said nothing. He'd had enough of all this. He left the room, slamming the door behind him, determined to prove her wrong.

Chapter Four

Charlotte made her way around the stadium to her new viewing spot, away from the prying attentions of Graham, overlooking the second bend of the track. She had been watching the racing from this new position since the embarrassing episode with him some five weeks earlier.

She could still see Graham across the track. He bounced around, out of synchronisation with the movements of the rest of the crowd, as he waved his arms and shouted. The distance between them muted his obscenities and that hideous laugh, but Charlotte could imagine exactly what he would be saying. He'd be shouting abuse at the riders. He was so uncouth and predictable.

Charlotte turned her eyes to her programme as she sought to push Graham from her thoughts. She turned over the glossy page: Anthony smiled up at her.

Although the picture in the programme was in black and white, she recognised it instantly as having been taken at the same time as the colour photograph that she'd purchased from the souvenir kiosk. The short paragraph beneath the picture announced Anthony's imminent return to the Willsby team. It quoted him: he was keen to race again, his wrist was still giving him some pain, but he hoped to be fit enough to return the following week. Charlotte looked at the picture as he explained his disappointment at having missed so much of the racing season, and his eagerness to make up for lost time. Charlotte could hardly wait. Anthony had been away for what seemed like an eternity, and she was missing him desperately. She had a lot of catching up to do.

* * *

"What am I doing, Travis?" asked Dave as he stared into his chicken curry.

Dave had been particularly busy. It was the height of the speedway season, and he'd been jetting off to race meetings both at home and abroad. Lucy had moved most of her belongings into his house, and she made a point of being there, waiting for him, when he got home from his trips. It was great not having to come home to an empty house. His food cupboards were always restocked, and his bills were always paid. She seemed to think of everything. He liked having her around, and he was looking forward to her moving in properly once the tenancy ended on her flat. She kept him grounded. She looked after the house, organised his trips, and dealt with all that annoying paperwork that he just didn't have time to do normally. His problem, though, was that he hadn't actually got around to talking to her about that misunderstanding over the marriage proposal. He'd put it to the back of his mind, but as he sat in that Indian restaurant with his friend Travis, he started thinking about the dilemma.

"I thought it had all blown over," explained Dave. "But now

she's arranged an appointment at the registry office. Some sort of paperwork stuff. I think she really intends to go ahead with it. What should I do, Travis?"

Travis took a sip of his beer; boy, that vindaloo was particularly spicy tonight.

"I think deep down that's what you want, Buddy," said Travis, wiping his brow.

"You do?" asked Dave, sounding puzzled.

Travis called the waiter over and ordered more beer.

"Don't you think that if you didn't want to marry her, you'd have said something by now?" explained Travis.

His friend was right. Dave was rather perplexed as to how he'd gotten into this mix-up.

"Trust me," continued Travis. "It's your subconscious mind taking control. It must be what you want, Buddy. I mean, you like having her around, don't you?"

"Well, yes," stuttered Dave.

"I've noticed a massive change in you since she came on the scene. Your racing has improved too, hasn't it? You're scoring more points now, aren't you?"

Dave thought for a moment. Yes, Travis was right. He was able to concentrate more on his racing now that Lucy was organising everything else for him.

"And she's pretty efficient with all your finances, isn't she?" continued Travis, pausing his meal as he spoke.

"She's brilliant at that stuff, pays all the bills, and totally looks after my bank account," replied Dave.

Travis took another gulp of his beer, leant back in his seat, and let out a long, flagging, deep breath.

"You don't know how lucky you are then," continued Travis. "I'd give my right arm to have all that done for me. Don't know how you managed to find her, right under my nose like that. It might have been a different story if I'd got there first, you know."

Travis winked at his friend, before starting a final onslaught on his dinner.

Dave felt flattered. So, Travis was jealous of him? That was a first. And of course, he was right, wasn't he? Lucy was good for him.

"I reckon you should go for it, Davy. Go with the flow. You don't want to lose all that, do you? Maybe it's all a bit quicker than you'd expected, but sometimes you have to take the bull by the horns, don't you?"

Yes, Travis's words did make sense. Dave had always planned to get married one day and why shouldn't that be now rather than later?

"You two make a great pairing. I reckon you were made for each other," continued Travis.

It was the first time anyone had said that to Dave. Most people he'd spoken to were rather deprecating about his and Lucy's suitability to one another.

"Do you really think so?" he asked.

Travis nodded his head in agreement. That mouthful of vindaloo was extra hot. He took another slug of beer.

"Don't you think she's a bit old for me though?" blurted Dave, maybe a result of his subconscious mind still looking for excuses.

"Careful!" exclaimed Travis, almost spitting out his dinner. "She's not that much older than me. You're not calling me old, are you?"

"Course not, Granddad," laughed Dave as Travis continued.

"Women reach their prime in their thirties, you know. I can vouch for that. More mature. Don't nag and moan like the younger ones."

Travis did have a point.

"Anyway, you've got to get married now. I've already bought my best man's suit, so you can't back out," laughed Travis as he wiped his naan bread around the curry residue on his plate.

"Yes, Lucy was pretty insistent that you'd be the best man," smiled Dave.

Thinking about it, Lucy had been rather keen for Travis to be at the wedding. He did think that was a bit odd. Yes, they were friends, but he had only known the American for a few months. It was strange that Lucy was so keen for him to be there, but she didn't want to invite any family members. You know, Lucy did seem to have a soft spot for Travis. He didn't want to risk losing her and have Travis jump in to take his place, did he? Marriage though? That was rather a big step, wasn't it?

"Don't you think she might get fed up with me being away all the time though?" asked Dave, as his doubt niggled at his thoughts again.

"I think she's happy for the time alone, to be honest, Bud. She does all that writing, doesn't she? Probably likes the peace and quiet to concentrate on that," reassured Travis.

"You're right there, Travis," agreed Dave. "She's always working on that book."

"Ever read any of it, Buddy?" enquired Travis.

Dave smirked.

"Yeah, I guess that was a stupid question, wasn't it?" laughed Travis, knowing full well that Dave would have no interest in ever reading a book.

Dave watched his friend finish his meal. How he managed to eat anything that hot was beyond him. He thought about Lucy. Maybe Travis was right? They did make a good pair, didn't they? She organised everything for him and never complained about his racing. Perhaps he should go ahead with the wedding? If a confirmed bachelor like Travis thought it was a good idea, then it had to be a good idea, didn't it? Why had he ever doubted himself? He could always get divorced if it didn't work out, couldn't he?

Travis downed his beer as the waiter came over with the bill. He handed the slip of paper to Dave.

"Great curry as usual," complimented Travis as he sat back in his seat, rubbing his belly.

The waiter looked on expectantly.

Travis glanced restlessly across to Dave as the waiter coughed quietly.

"Just got to pop to the bathroom. Sort that check out Buddy, can you?" said Travis as he made a beeline for the door.

Dave pulled out his wallet. He seemed to be getting the bill quite a bit lately.

* * *

Charlotte woke up to the sound of heavy rain on the windowpane. She opened her eyes. The room seemed even darker than usual. Barnaby poked his head out from behind the curtains. He looked over at her from the windowsill, and Charlotte could tell from her cat's expression that the news was not good.

It had been raining all night. If the downpour continued, the prospect of the speedway meeting that evening going ahead looked bleak. Charlotte got up, slipped her feet into her slippers, and walked to the window. Barnaby mewed, his tail in the air and his ears pricked up, his green eyes looked anxious as Charlotte approached.

"It's all right, Barnaby. I know it's raining," she reassured as she opened the curtains.

Barnaby had been right to be concerned. The guttering above was overflowing. A constant stream of water bounced from the outside sill. The road was patched with puddles, the persistent raindrops scarring them as they fell. Charlotte could hear the cars splash past on the main road, behind the trees opposite her window. She sighed as she trudged to the bathroom.

It was still raining later that day when Charlotte finished her shift at the guesthouse.

"Miserable, isn't it?" said Mrs Shield, catching her colleague staring out of the window at the downpour.

"I just wish it would stop."

Charlotte sounded irritated as she spoke. Mrs Shield smiled.

"At least we haven't had to water the garden."

"I don't care about gardens. I just wish it would stop raining," said Charlotte angrily. Charlotte sat down at the table, her head in her hands. Mrs Shield sensed her frustration.

"Got something special going on then, have you?"

"It's speedway tonight!" said Charlotte, surprised that Mrs Shield hadn't already worked that one out.

Mrs Shield was surprised too. Charlotte hadn't mentioned her boyfriend since he had broken his wrist, several weeks earlier. She had been under the impression that Charlotte's relationship with the mysterious Anthony had petered out, and that her enthusiasm for speedway had similarly cooled. She tried to hide her ignorance.

"Oh, of course, it's Friday, isn't it?"

She thought that she had sounded quite convincing.

"How is Anthony? How is his wrist?"

"Better now," replied Charlotte shyly. "He's racing again tonight for the first time since the accident. He's very keen to get back into the team."

"How long was he in hospital for?" asked Mrs Shield, trying to show some interest and make up for her earlier insensitivity.

Charlotte was silent.

"Did he have to have surgery on it?" asked Mrs Shield.

Charlotte still said nothing as she bit her lower lip.

"Still, if the meeting is called off, you could have a romantic evening in instead, couldn't you?" said Mrs Shield.

She sat looking at Charlotte expectantly, but the girl was quiet and seemed a little uncomfortable as she wrung her hands. After a further silence, Charlotte spoke.

"He's keen to race again. His wrist is still giving him some pain, but he thinks he'll be fit enough to race tonight."

Mrs Shield smiled sweetly. This girl didn't make conversation easy, did she? She looked at her watch.

"My, is that the time. I really ought to go and lock up."

Charlotte had her coat on when Mrs Shield returned to the kitchen.

"See you tomorrow then, Charlotte."

The girl pulled her hood up over her head as she stepped into the open doorway.

"I hope it stops raining soon," called out Mrs Shield as her colleague left. "And give my love to Anthony. I hope it all goes well for him."

Mrs Shield watched her colleague leave. She was a strange one, wasn't she? In her opinion, the girl spent far too much time on her own. It wasn't good for someone that young. She needed some friends. Hopefully, this Anthony character would be able to bring Charlotte out of her shell.

Charlotte was in a happier mood when she arrived home. She felt optimistic too. The rain had eased, and the sky was noticeably brighter. Despite the forecast being for more, heavy rain, there was at least a little hope that the race meeting would go ahead.

Tonight, it was Anthony's first night back since his accident. It had seemed like an eternity, and Charlotte had missed him. As she stared out at the brightening skies, Charlotte felt confident that her long wait would soon be over.

The skies were still bright as Charlotte left her flat on her walk to the stadium. There was, however, an ominous breeze that blew a succession of dark clouds across the struggling sun.

As she arrived at the stadium, the skies had darkened once again. The officials stared hopelessly at the waterlogged track, whilst optimistic fans filed through the gates. The usually-cheerful, old man selling programmes seemed to be dispensing despondency and gloom with each programme sold. Charlotte bought hers and made her way around to the first bend of the track. She would have a better chance of catching Anthony's attention from there, and she had decided that was worth the risk of bumping into Graham.

Graham was already there when she arrived. He smiled at her as she approached but said nothing about her absence over the previous weeks. Perhaps it was his way of apologising?

"Want some coffee?" he offered, holding out a plastic cup.

"No, thank you," said Charlotte harshly.

She strained her eyes as she peered into the pits. Yes, Anthony was there. After a short time, he noticed her looking and smiled. He pointed to the sky and shrugged his shoulders before turning to his brother. Charlotte understood. Anthony was disappointed by the weather too. Still, he had at least noticed her, and he had even remembered her.

Charlotte stood looking out over the track. Gulls darted in the darkening sky, their cry cutting through the air, warning perhaps of the impending downpour?

It was not long before the black clouds finally relinquished, and the first huge, wet drops of rain fell. Around the stadium, umbrellas opened like sprouting mushrooms, and Charlotte retreated to the shelter of her hood. Graham, too, pulled his jacket over his head. A tag, complete with washing instructions, popped out from the back and hung conspicuously over his forehead. He seemed unaware as it flapped around in the wind.

Charlotte watched as the spectators ran to shelter, their coats pulled up over their heads. She was holding onto the hope that the gulls had been wrong, but her grip slackened as more black clouds crept towards the stadium. She watched the ink smudge on her programme.

Two of the riders appeared from the changing rooms. Instead of their usual colourful leathers, they were clad in dark jeans and jackets. Almost simultaneously with their arrival, the rain began to fall heavier.

Charlotte felt the cold wetness seeping into her body. Beads of rain gathered on Graham's tag, until a steady procession of drips fell in unison with those from the strands of wet hair, which hung over his eyes. He looked at her through the curtain of droplets.

"Sod this, Charlie, I'm going home. I'll see you next week."

He hurried away as the downpour continued. The ground beneath squelched as Charlotte moved her feet. Graham's discarded plastic cup blew around in the wet grass.

There was a short crackle, before the commentator's voice announced solemnly that the meeting had been abandoned. The few remaining spectators looked up at the sky disappointedly before trudging to the exit. Charlotte glanced towards the pits; Anthony had gone. She turned and followed the other fans wearily to the gates.

* * *

Lucy watched the sodden mass of spectators as they filed through the turnstiles and out of the stadium.

"Why do you think they still bother coming in this sort of weather?"

"Beats me," said Travis, who was sat beside her in the warmth of the clubhouse. "Perhaps they just love me so much that they can't keep away."

"There's only one person in love with egotistical Travis," teased Lucy.

"And I guess you'd know all about that, wouldn't you, Lucy?" retorted the American.

They smiled at one another as Dave and Mick approached. Travis stood up keenly.

"Anyone fancy a curry?"

Dave smiled enthusiastically at his friend before glancing across to Mick. His eagerness diminished swiftly as Mick spoke.

"Not tonight, Travis. We're off home."

Travis looked disappointed, his wide grin faltered slightly as he glanced across to Dave, his bright, blue eyes almost begging a change of heart. Dave looked to the ground in a remorseful determination. Travis turned to Lucy with a last desperate pleading gaze. She was, however, just as baffled by their rapid departure and shrugged as she stood up dutifully.

"See you later then," said Travis in a frustrated acceptance as he sauntered towards another group of his friends at the bar.

Lucy followed as Dave and Mick walked silently down the stairs to the car park. It was raining hard as they dashed to the van, and the downpour had left them drenched after the short sprint.

Dave and Mick were both in a solemn mood, and Lucy sensed that the harsh weather wasn't the only cause. Having noticed the obvious absence of Mick's sister, she assumed the explanation was plainly Jane linked. She leant over between the two front seats where the two men were sat.

"Where's Jane tonight?"

There was an uneasy silence. Both men looked at one another for the explanation. Dave spoke.

"She left her husband this morning."

The silence returned momentarily as Mick started the engine and pulled away.

"She's staying at my house at the moment," he eventually continued

"I'm so sorry about that," said Lucy sympathetically.

"She's done the right thing," said Mick. "I've never liked him. He's had a gambling problem for some time. We knew, but none of us realised the extent of it."

"How terrible," said Lucy fervently.

Mick fell silent.

Lucy had only met Jane's husband once. He had been just as she had expected: middle-aged, fat and arrogant. Perfectly suited to Jane, she had thought.

They pulled into a service station, stopping beside a fuel pump. Dave paused for a moment, considering the task ahead, before jumping out into the cold wind and rain. He filled the fuel tank. Rain blew towards him, the roof over the pumps offering little protection against the horizontal deluge. Lucy and Mick watched him from the van as he darted across to the brightly-lit shop to pay. He pushed open the glass door and, passing buckets of bedraggled flowers, he entered the shop.

Lucy looked at the flowers, obviously past their best and struggling to keep up appearances in the storm. An idea entered her head. She smiled.

"Hey, Mick. I might go and buy some of those lovely flowers for Jane, to cheer her up?"

Mick smiled. He found the irony of the suggestion amusing. He realised that Lucy had meant well but knew that Jane would be far from cheered up by the gift. Jane had a dislike of flowers. Their sister had suffered a cot death and Jane, being only a small child herself at the time, had unfortunately been the one to find the body. She had, naturally, found the whole thing disturbing. The funeral had been especially difficult. The masses of flowers around the tiny coffin seemed to be a particularly disturbing sight. The subconscious link had stayed with Jane into adulthood. It was not something that she liked people to know about, so Mick was reluctant to explain further.

"Jane doesn't like flowers."

Lucy looked bemused by his comment. There was an uneasy silence as they both watched Dave queuing in the shop, and then Lucy spoke again.

"If Jane needs somewhere to live, I've got an idea that might help."

Mick looked intrigued.

"Naturally, I'll be giving up my flat when I marry Dave. Perhaps Jane could take it over? I'll have a word with my landlord. I'm sure it will be okay."

The idea appealed to Mick. He'd not been looking forward to having to share his small home with Jane for too long. How ever much he loved his sister, they did tend to argue rather a lot lately. At the same time as finding the idea appealing, Mick also felt a sense of shame. Jane had made no secret of the fact that she disliked Lucy. She had even told both himself and Dave the very same to their faces. He felt ashamed of his sister. Here was Lucy, trying to help her, even after the way that Jane had treated her. Lucy's thoughtfulness touched him.

"That's really good of you, and it's a brilliant idea. I'll mention it to her later. I'm sure she'll be thrilled."

Mick wasn't entirely convinced that his sister's reaction would be quite so favourable, but he was determined to make her see sense. They needed to have their own space again, and this was the ideal solution.

Dave returned to the van. A cold gush of damp air blew into the vehicle as he opened the door and climbed inside.

"That's horrible out there," he said as Mick started the engine.

They arrived at Mick's just after ten-thirty. Jane was sat in her dressing-gown, watching the television. She looked up as they entered the room, discreetly pulling her towelling robe over her chubby thighs. It was obvious that she had been crying, her eyes were red and puffy. Lucy walked over to her, oozing sympathy as she sat down. She reached out, cupping Jane's hand in her own.

"I was so sorry to hear about your husband. If there's anything I can do?"

Jane's distrusting glare stabbed at her comforter. Her reply was unconvincing as she pulled her hand abruptly away from Lucy's.

"Thank you. I can manage myself."

Mick had been watching. He sighed conspicuously at his sister's ungrateful reaction. He walked over and sat alongside the women.

"Jane," he began with a serious tone to his voice. "Lucy's had an idea."

His voice was firm. Jane glanced at him lethargically. She looked drained, and her suspicion about what he was about to say was obvious in her voice.

"What?"

"Well, they're getting married soon, aren't they?"

Jane raised her eyebrows in a reluctant acknowledgement as her brother continued.

"That means that Lucy will be leaving her flat on the seafront empty. She thinks she could persuade the landlord to agree that you take the tenancy over. You could move in there. I mean, we are a bit cramped in here, aren't we? It would be good for you to have your own place, wouldn't it?"

Dave, ignorant of his fiancée's suggestion until that point, looked up, a surprised but pleased expression on his face.

"What a brilliant idea."

Jane's gaze was fixed on her brother. She said nothing, but her expression showed her aversion to the idea. Mick was annoyed by her ungratefulness. Lucy, surprisingly, did not seem intimidated.

"It's a lovely flat," said Lucy. "It's just right for someone on their own."

"And it's handy for town," encouraged Dave.

"You'd be doing Dave a favour too," added Lucy.

Jane showed no intrigue at Lucy's comment, but Lucy explained herself all the same:

"It's my cat, you see. He's getting rather old now. I don't really want to have to move him, he's settled in the flat. I'd be so worried about him if I took him to Dave's house. And of course, Dave's not keen on cats, is he? If you moved into the flat, you could look after him. Dave would be so grateful."

"Hey, you like cats don't you, Jane?" said Dave. "I must admit I wasn't especially looking forward to having it move in with us. It keeps staring at me."

Jane remained unconvinced. She was reluctant to accept any favours from Lucy. She found it difficult to believe that the woman would do anybody a good turn, she no doubt had ulterior motives. The pressure from her three companions, however, continued.

"It's an ideal opportunity, Jane," said Mick, his voice had grown firm. "You'd be stupid not to accept."

"It seems everything is working out brilliantly," added Dave.

Jane was reluctant. The last thing she wanted was Lucy's grubby little flat in that notorious part of town, but Mick was right. She couldn't stay with him forever, she had to find her own place eventually. She realised that if she refused Lucy's offer, Dave and Mick would turn against her. That was the last thing she wanted. Leaving her husband had been difficult, she needed the support of her family and friends.

"Okay. But only temporarily, until I find somewhere myself."

* * *

Charlotte put her hand into her jacket pocket and pulled out the programme from Friday's speedway meeting. It had dried out, but the crumpled paper and smudged print was a reminder of the evening's torrential downpour. She smiled to herself as she looked at the team photograph on the back. Anthony crouched beside Travis Fengar who sat on the bike in the centre of the picture. She sat holding the programme as she looked out of the train window.

The fields of sheep rolled past in the afternoon sunshine. Graham had once mentioned that the Willsby team used a remote dirt track for practice sessions on a Sunday afternoon. The track was located, twenty miles out of town, on ground owned by a local farmer. Charlotte had considered going there before but, as it was a good four-mile walk from the nearest station, she'd felt a little nervous at the prospect of the journey. After Friday's setback however, when the meeting was rained off, Charlotte had decided to pay the practice site a visit. According to Graham, all the riders used it, including Anthony Myers.

The train pulled into the unmanned station as Charlotte opened the carriage door. The station was small and consisted solely of a short platform and a couple of red-painted, iron benches. It resembled a conventional station so little that, for a moment, she wondered whether the train had merely stopped at signals. A door opened further up the carriage, reassuring her that this was indeed her destination.

She descended the train onto the concrete platform. As the train pulled away, Charlotte walked behind a young fisherman. They trudged down the steps to the main road. He headed towards the marshlands of the river edge, and Charlotte paused, looking at the barren farmland around her. She watched as the fisherman left, his footsteps getting quieter as he faded into the distance.

Now she was entirely alone. She looked at her map before crossing the road and heading up a country lane in the apparent direction of the track.

The afternoon sun filtered through the tall trees as Charlotte made her way along the road. The birdsong became more prominent as she grew further from the main road and into the countryside's calm. She had walked a long way and paused to look back over her route. She hadn't seen a soul on the entire walk, and there was still no sign of human life anywhere.

She continued walking, and eventually, the reassuring sound of speedway bikes could be heard in the distance. Charlotte followed the sound until she arrived at the farm. As she opened the gate, two dogs barked viciously from behind the window of the adjoining farmhouse, jostling for a view of the intruder. Charlotte closed the gate behind her nervously, as a figure appeared at the window, yelling at the confined animals.

Charlotte followed the muddy path between two barns to the racing area. The shale track was much smaller than the one at Willsby and encircled a grass mound. There were no facilities for either the riders or spectators. Most of the people present appeared to be with the riders; she felt quite self-conscious. Cars and vans were scattered around the muddy field and young men changed into their racing leathers in the backs of the vans. A queue of young riders waited with their bikes for their turn on the track. She recognised some of the lads from Willsby. Anthony, however, wasn't there.

After watching a couple of practice laps, Charlotte retreated from the harsh wind, sheltering behind one of the barns. She sat amongst the long grass and sighed.

Trust Graham to get it wrong, she thought as she looked at the figures in the distance.

It had been a long walk from the station, and it would take a good hour to walk back. The prospect seemed daunting, and it had all been pointless. She sat, running her fingers through the grass, as she pondered her long journey home. Her thoughts were interrupted by an unexpected voice.

"What are you doing down here then?"

Charlotte startled and stood up instinctively.

"Anthony!" she exclaimed.

"Got bored watching the racing, did you?" he asked.

Anthony was dressed in a black sweatshirt and jeans. He seemed smaller than she remembered and looked so *normal* out of his racing leathers. He seemed more relaxed and approachable away from the confinement of the Willsby stadium. Charlotte stood, nervously brushing grass seeds from her clothes. This had all come as such a shock that she floundered, trying to think of what she should say or do. Anthony watched her; his long fringe hung down above his dark eyes. Charlotte met the gaze of his piercing stare.

"You could say that," she replied.

She smiled nervously and continued to brush the grass seeds from her jacket.

"I thought I spotted you arrive earlier," said Anthony. "Didn't think you'd be that interested in a practice session though."

He was still looking directly at her. His dark eyes seemed to penetrate inside her as she felt her stomach roil.

"Well actually, I came because I hoped you'd be racing," she said timidly.

As soon as she'd spoken, she regretted it. She suddenly felt very vulnerable.

"Wanted a sneak preview before next Friday, did you?" he laughed. "Well sorry to disappoint you."

Charlotte felt belittled by the comment. She looked sheepishly away. As her eyes fell to the ground, Anthony reached out to her and brushed the few remaining grass seeds from her jacket.

"I'm sorry. I didn't mean to sound rude. I'm giving my wrist another week," he said quietly.

Anthony had not taken his eyes off her. Charlotte felt self-conscious and remained looking at the ground bashfully. Anthony hadn't moved his hand from her arm. He leant forward. His fringe tickled her forehead. She looked up and their eyes once again met.

He smiled reassuringly.

The moment was interrupted by a voice.

"Anthony, can we get off now?"

A small group of people stood a few yards from them. Anthony took a step back, obviously unaware until then that his friends had followed him.

"Sorry, but I've got to go now," he said.

He smiled, quickly leant towards her, and kissed her on the cheek. Charlotte was taken aback.

"Will you be at Willsby on Friday?" she asked.

Her voice had sounded almost desperate, Anthony had not failed to notice.

"Of course I will. I'm in the team, aren't I?" he replied as he rejoined his friends and disappeared behind the barn among a murmur of laughing voices.

Charlotte sat down on the grass and collected her thoughts. She could hardly believe what had happened. She raised her hand to her cheek, still reeling from that kiss. Had that really just happened? She smiled to herself. It was more than she could ever have hoped to achieve. This hadn't been a mere coincidence, had it? This was Fate steaming ahead with her plan, wasn't it? She sat there, recalling their conversation and collecting her thoughts. She felt so much more optimistic as she finally stood up and made her way out of the farm.

The restrained dogs barked as she passed the farmhouse, but Charlotte was not frightened this time. She was so wrapped up in her triumph of the day that she hardly noticed them, nor the tiring walk back to the station.

That night, Charlotte lay in bed. She could picture those dark eyes looking into her soul. She remembered Anthony's touch and imagined that he was there beside her. It seemed that the more her mind dwelt on the thoughts, the more realistic the images became. She could almost sense Anthony's presence as Barnaby stretched out and chattered in his stupor at the foot of the bed. Charlotte reached under her pillow; her hand felt for the reassuring touch of the photograph. She smiled, comforted as she held the picture of Anthony. Soon he would be here with her. She just knew that he would. It was Fate for them to be together, after all, wasn't it?

Chapter Five

The wedding had been kept low key; only Jane and Mick the two witnesses, and Travis had been invited. Dave would perhaps have liked a few more of his friends and family to come along, but Lucy was adamant in her decision to keep it a simple, personal affair. She had been reluctant to introduce Dave to any members of her family, and she hadn't wanted to meet any of his either. It seemed unusual to Dave, but he just assumed that she wasn't a family orientated person. Dave didn't mind. He was so busy jetting around with his racing that sorting out a wedding was the last thing on his mind. He certainly didn't want his mother and sister making a fuss about it all, so it was probably best that they didn't know. There wasn't anything for him to do anyhow: Lucy seemed to have it all under control.

Dave had been pleased when Lucy had suggested that Jane attend the wedding and be a witness. He had hoped that the gesture, together with the offer of the flat, would help to sweeten his friend towards his new wife. He was, however, to be disappointed.

Lucy looked stunning in her white miniskirt suit. That familiar, impish smile spread across her face as the two of them stood outside of the registry office. Dave looked at his watch; Jane and Mick were late.

"Don't worry," urged Travis, sensing his apprehension. "There's plenty of people here who can sign papers."

Dave smiled at him. He was right, of course, but there was more to Jane's being there than merely signing papers. Jane had been a good friend to him over the years, and he had wanted her to be a part of the ceremony. Anyhow, if he had to live with only having three guests at his wedding, he would at least like them to have the graciousness to turn up.

"Yeah. I know. I'd just like it if they were here," he said as he leant against the wall.

Dave looked smart, dressed in the suit that Lucy had hired for him, although he did seem somewhat overshadowed by the handsome Travis, who looked like he had just stepped out of the pages of a fashion magazine.

Dave breathed a huge sigh of relief when he spotted the familiar car pull into the car park. The relief, however, soon turned into trepidation as Mick and Jane climbed from the vehicle. Jane's face was as long as the pleated skirt that hid her dumpy legs. Mick looked uncomfortable; he was obviously annoyed by his sister's blatant hostility. Jane glanced at Dave. It was a look of disapproval. It angered him.

"Are we ready then?" urged Jane.

She sounded stern. She turned her back, walking towards the entrance to the registry office without even acknowledging Lucy's presence.

"I'm sorry," whispered Mick. "She's been in this mood all morning. She even said that she wasn't coming at one point. I really had a lot of trouble persuading her."

"Perhaps you shouldn't have bothered," said Dave sharply.

Dave felt ashamed of his friend's behaviour. Lucy, however, kept smiling. Either she had not noticed Jane's rebuff or, most likely, she was bravely ignoring it. That was one of the things that Dave liked about Lucy: her ability to keep smiling, even under this sort of antagonisation.

"You look great," said Mick, obviously trying to make up for his sister's rudeness.

"Thank you," said Lucy politely. "And isn't Jane's outfit, well, befitting of her?"

Jane showed no emotion. Dave smiled to himself. Jane's outfit was hardly flattering. Her yellow blouse was far from fashionable, and the contour of her round belly showed beneath her too tight, navy blue, pleated skirt. Even so, it was nice of Lucy to compliment her.

Lucy followed Jane and Mick into the building. Her slim legs elegantly climbing the steps. Dave watched her as he followed. He appreciated how she had tried to encourage Jane to be a part of the wedding. It was a challenging task, and he was proud of her.

The five were ushered into the marriage room. They were late, and the staff members were seemingly keen to get on with things. The ceremony was short. Dave reflected on how scarily quick and easy it had been to get married. Lucy had selected the shortest ceremony possible. All he had to do was repeat what the bespectacled registrar said. It was like a game of 'Simon Says'. He didn't even notice what he was saying as he concentrated on getting his lines right. He knew that Travis would be waiting for him to slip up. He was careful to repeat it all exactly, or he'd never be allowed to forget it, would he? It was all over in a few minutes, and the event passed smoothly, despite

Jane's long, elliptical glances.

Mick took some photographs outside of the registry office.

"Take a picture of Jane. She looks so different in that pertinent choice of outfit," enthused Lucy.

Jane posed reluctantly, the forced smile on her face clearly hiding her true emotions. Once his camera film was used up, Mick congratulated Dave, whilst Lucy walked over to Jane, who was standing by her car. Lucy held out her bouquet, as an obvious gesture of friendship, and smiled. Of course, both Dave and Mick knew that Jane, having as she did an aversion for flowers, would not accept them, but neither was prepared for her reaction. She lunged forward at Lucy, knocking the bouquet from her hand, and sending the flowers flying across the tarmac.

"You malicious bitch," she screamed as she climbed into the car and slammed the door.

"Jane!" shouted Mick in annoyance.

He turned to his friend, apologised, and ran after his sister. Dave looked at Lucy. She looked hurt as she gazed at the flowers scattered across the concrete. Her brown eyes were glazed with imminent tears.

"Jane doesn't like flowers," he explained apologetically.

"How was I to know that? I was only trying to be friendly."

She looked up at him resiliently. She was trying to put a brave face on the incident, but Dave could tell that she was upset. He held her close to him, kissed her on the nose, and gently pulled her head to his shoulder. He could hear her sniffling, no doubt crying, as Jane and Mick drove away.

Travis looked at the flowers, a broad smile still on his face.

"We can still go for the curry, can't we?" he said insensitively.

Dave glared at him as Lucy once again stifled her sniffles into her husband's shoulder.

* * *

Charlotte had been planning this day for some time. She left a large bowl of food for Barnaby and headed for the stadium; her overnight bag slung over her shoulder. By the time she arrived, Anthony's brother was already there. Anthony was, as she'd expected, out of sight, no doubt in the changing rooms. Purposefully, she walked over to the pit area.

"Hi there, Sexy," grinned Anthony's brother. "Long time, no see. I thought for a while there that you'd gone off me."

"Well, Anthony hasn't been racing, has he?" she responded quickly. The man laughed.

"You're here early this evening?" he continued.

"I've had to leave my flat, my landlord's having some work done on it. I can't go back until tomorrow."

"What, you've had to move out? Where are you staying then?"

"I was hoping you might be able to help there. Do you know of any bed and breakfast places around here?"

"You'll be lucky," laughed the man. "They get full up at this time of year. You could try the one in town, opposite The Druids. Do you know it?"

"I've already asked. They are full up," said Charlotte, trying to hide her amusement at the irony of his suggestion. "I don't know what to do. I don't know anyone in Willsby who I could ask to put me up, and I can't go back to the flat tonight."

She had realised that her plan was a long shot, but having previously overheard him talking about his wife, she was confident that he would not think that she was angling to stay with him for the night. Her confidence however appeared misguided.

"You could stay with me, Babe. I wouldn't mind at all," he smiled.

Charlotte's heart sank. She tried not to show her horror at his suggestion as she tried to think of something to say.

"Wife wouldn't be quite so keen though," continued the man, with a teasing grin.

There was silence as Charlotte revelled in her relief, and the man pondered her dilemma. "Hmm. I suppose there's always Ant's," he said suddenly.

Charlotte could hardly believe her luck. She had never really expected her plan to work this easily. She tried to sound calm as she spoke.

"Do you think he'd mind? It would really help."

"Leave it with Uncle Terry, Babe. Can't have a pretty thing like you sleeping on a park bench, can we?"

He grinned and patted her on the bum.

Terry walked away, chuckling to himself as he knelt next to Anthony's bike. Charlotte smiled, partially through self-appraisal and partly at Terry's gullibility. Fate was finally helping her out, wasn't she?

She returned to her spot in the crowd where she stood, looking out over the track.

The racing began, but Charlotte was finding it difficult to concentrate. Graham had noticed her inattentiveness.

"Penny for them?" he said suddenly.

"What?"

"Penny for your thoughts," clarified Graham.

"You'll have to offer me more than that, Graham," she joked.

Graham looked confused. It wasn't like her to be quite so candid. It also surprised him that she didn't seem to be embarrassed by his fooling around. He gave up his attempts at trying to make her blush; the fun had gone from the game since she'd stopped responding. He hoped that she wasn't losing interest in him.

It was the penultimate race of the evening and Charlotte had grown concerned that Terry had not yet spoken to Anthony. She approached him. He looked up and smiled but said nothing.

"Any luck with Anthony?" she prompted.

"Ah yeah," said Terry hesitantly. "Meet him 'round the back of the changing rooms in half an hour."

Charlotte felt relief as she returned to the crowd to watch the last race. Willsby had won the meeting easily, everyone seemed to be in high spirits.

"You coming?" asked Graham quizzically as he was about to leave.

"Not yet. I've got someone to see."

Graham was puzzled.

"See you next week then," he said as he left.

The stadium was slowly emptying. Charlotte sat on the grass bank looking at her watch as anticipation churned in her stomach. At last, something was going right for her. She waited for twenty minutes and then made her way around to the changing rooms. The pathway was dark. The only light illuminating her route came from the row of small windows along the top of the changing room walls. Condensation dripped from the glass of the open windows. The sound of someone singing broke the otherwise silent atmosphere. The door opened, and one of the riders from the team appeared, a holdall slung over his shoulder.

"See you in the week," he shouted back into the building.

He startled as he noticed Charlotte, who stood in the shadows. He nodded in a polite acknowledgement as he passed her. Six more men came out of the building over the next ten minutes, but there was no sign of Anthony. It was now half an hour past the time that Terry had told her to meet his brother.

* * *

Dave had changed out of his racing leathers already.

"I'm really sorry about Jane's behaviour at the wedding," said Mick as they loaded the bikes into the van. "I think she's still upset by her own marriage breakup."

"That's okay, Mick," said Lucy. "I realise that. I don't feel any animosity. Dave explained to me about the inappropriateness of my offering her my bouquet. I don't suppose that went down too well, did it?"

"You can say that again," laughed Mick.

"Did she move into my flat okay this afternoon?" asked Lucy.

"Eventually, after a bit of persuasion. She's going to be really grateful to you one day for helping her out like that."

"Don't worry about it, Mick. I do understand how upset she is."

Dave was not quite so optimistic.

"I hope you're both right," he sighed. "I've never seen Jane like this before."

* * *

Charlotte was beginning to think that Anthony had already left. The door opened again. She looked towards it, hoping to see Anthony, but Kevin McCray appeared with another man.

"Excuse me. I'm waiting for Anthony Myers. Is he still in there?"

"Washing his hair, Darling."

Kevin's reply was derisive. His friend sniggered as they walked away indifferently towards the clubhouse.

The silent darkness descended again. The noise from within the changing rooms had ceased. She had been waiting for almost an hour and was about to leave when the door suddenly swung open. Anthony stood in the doorway with Travis Fengar. The sight rather surprised Charlotte. Travis was well known in speedway circles for being a little hot-tempered, both on and off the track. He was hardly the sort of person she would have imagined Anthony would be friends with. She looked across at Anthony. Just as he had done at the practice track the previous week, he looked so *normal* again. It reassured her.

"Got time for a curry?" asked Travis as they approached.

"Not tonight, Travis. I've got to get back."

Anthony paused as they reached Charlotte. Travis looked confused for a moment, before spotting her.

"See what you mean. Have a good night. Enjoy."

He sniggered to himself as he walked away, mischievously kicking a discarded tin into the darkness and singing, rather oddly, Abba's *Dancing Queen*.

Anthony waited until Travis had gone then looked at her somewhat suspiciously.

112

"Terry says you need a place to stay tonight?"

Charlotte sensed his wariness but, having planned for such a response, was confident in the sincerity of her reply.

"That's right. My landlord's doing some work on my flat. I was hoping to find a guesthouse to stay in, but they are all full up. I'm really grateful to you for helping me out. Are you sure you don't mind?"

"I guess not," he replied. "The car's over here."

Anthony led her across the car park. The stadium had emptied except for a few figures that milled around in the darkness. Only the lights emanating from the clubhouse lit up their route through the night to the car. Charlotte felt a little uneasy. Anthony's reluctance to speak was not helping.

"You rode really well tonight," she said attempting to reassure herself. "It must have been difficult coming back after such a long break."

Anthony smiled but said nothing.

"Is your wrist okay now?" continued Charlotte.

Anthony's reply was dismissive.

"I suppose so."

His apathy was obvious. Charlotte felt nervous. Was this all a mistake? She was desperate to break the uneasy silence between them.

"It was a nasty fall you had. The way you hit the fence like that must have really hurt. You were knocked out as well, weren't you? It's so dangerous," she blabbed.

Anthony still didn't respond.

"I don't know why they haven't thought about using inflatable fences," continued Charlotte in her nervous waffle. "You know, something like the bouncy castles you see at fairs."

It seemed to work momentarily as Anthony sniggered at the ridiculous thought.

He stopped beside a silver-coloured car with a trailer attached to the back, into which his two speedway bikes were strapped. He opened the passenger door and walked around the vehicle to the driver's side. Charlotte climbed in.

Anthony looked tired as he started the engine. The headlights lit up the road ahead as the car pulled away gingerly, the trailer rattling behind them. Anthony still said nothing as they drove through Willsby. He seemed preoccupied. His silence was unsettling. Charlotte sat timidly, shrinking into the cold, leather seat. Her thoughts wandered in the silence, as they left the familiar sights of the town and headed out into the countryside.

The streetlights came to an end as the road narrowed. Trees arched above them, forming a long, hedgerow tunnel. It had started raining. Charlotte felt uneasy as the raindrops tapped on the roof. The perilousness of her situation plagued her thoughts. She had lost her bearings long ago. She had no idea where she was, or where she was going. She was sat in a car with a stranger. She pictured her father's face, contorted in disbelief at his little girl's stupidity, as he stared at her. She was being stupid, wasn't she? Putting herself in such a vulnerable position. After all, she didn't even know the man sat beside her, and here she was going to stay at his house for the night. All she knew about him was that he rode a brakeless motorbike around a track at sixty miles an hour; hardly the most level-headed of pastimes. Her father would have disapproved for sure. What was she doing here? Why had she put herself in such a vulnerable position? What did Fate have in store for her? She was trapped inside this stranger's conscience, a prisoner of his morality.

The rain outside had intensified. It pelted down on the windscreen, was washed aside, and then reappeared with what seemed to be a greater vengeance as the wipers clambered across the glass. A car came from the opposite direction. Its headlights blinded Charlotte as they shone through her. She felt vulnerable and scared. Anthony slowed the car as the two vehicles passed precariously. The headlights disappeared, and they were alone once again.

Anthony was concentrating on the dark road ahead. He peered out from under his fringe, his hands tortoising from the long sleeves of his jumper. Charlotte was nervous. She was scared. Had this all been a mistake? She longed to be at home, with Barnaby, in the security of her flat. She glanced across to Anthony who, at last, seemed to sense her apprehension.

"We're nearly there now," he muttered as streetlights once again appeared in the distance, and the silhouette of a small village became visible in the night sky.

The reassurance she'd felt by seeing the approaching signs of life, however, soon disappeared again as Anthony turned off the road onto an unmade track.

The unlit pathway led through the trees with only the car's headlights illuminating the route ahead. Ghostly conifers towered above them, and the darkness devoured Charlotte's senses. Where were they going? This wasn't even a proper road. Where was this stranger taking her? She felt uneasy, recoiling in her seat, her heart thumping obtrusively as they came to a stop outside of the building.

Charlotte looked up at the odd structure through the car window. Where had Anthony brought her? The building had no windows. This didn't look like a house? What was it? Where were they?

Anthony climbed out of the car.

"Are you coming then?" he said rather sharply.

His voice was firm. It did nothing to reassure Charlotte as she gingerly opened the car door and stepped out.

Once outside, Charlotte could see a door and windows in the odd building ahead of her, which reassured her that this could indeed be Anthony's home. It was an unusual, single storey house with a high sloping roof. Curiously, the windows were positioned high in the walls, just above eyelevel. They reminded Charlotte of the row of steamy windows on the changing room walls at the Willsby stadium.

Anthony unlocked the front door, and with a flick of a switch, the L-shaped hallway was ablaze with electric light. A passage ran into the darkness ahead of them. To their right, the kitchen at the front of the house, and the lounge at the rear, were visible through their open doors. Anthony gestured towards the lounge.

"Make yourself at home. I've got to put the bikes away."

He turned and left by the front door.

Charlotte watched as the door closed, before stepping gingerly towards the lounge. The light from the hallway dimly lit the room ahead. She felt around the door frame for a light switch and flicked it on.

Charlotte stared ahead of her. The room was huge. She was instantly captivated by the stylish simplicity of the decor. The walls ahead of her and to her right consisted almost entirely of full-length windows, each framed regimentally by deep green, velvet curtains.

The remaining two walls were painted in pale green and decorated with several unusual, abstract paintings. The polished wood floor was covered by a large central rug. The ceiling above her was crossed with thick wooden beams, from the centre of which hung a chandelier. A grandfather clock stood in a corner of the room; its deep pulse echoed with each swing of the pendulum.

Two large, green-checked sofas were arranged around the open fireplace. The absence of the usual home comforts, like a television or music system, was intriguing. The room looked rather like one you would expect to see in a stately home. Charlotte could almost visualise the restraining ropes, and the vigilant attendant watching sceptically from the corner. She felt rather swallowed by the grandeur of the room. She walked over to the window, her reflection following her in the glass.

She looked out into the darkness. A light was visible in the distance, illuminating a large workshop. She could see the figure of Anthony inside.

Charlotte slipped off her shoes and carried them to the nearest sofa. She stood beside the green-serge settee, still mesmerised by her surroundings. This had come as a complete surprise. She would never have imagined Anthony to live in such a characterful house. What, she wondered, would he make of her tiny flat? She stood there, captivated, holding her shoes and clutching her bag close to her body, as her eyes studied the paintings on the walls.

It was about twenty minutes later that Anthony finally returned. He walked over to the windows and closed the curtains, which fell at ease with his touch. He looked at Charlotte, stood there, peculiarly cradling her bag and clasping her shoes.

"You can sit down," he said.

"Thank you," she replied nervously, perching herself on the edge of the seat.

"Would you like a coffee?"

"Yes. That would be great."

Charlotte was aware of the tremor in her voice as she spoke and wondered whether Anthony had noticed. She watched as he left the room.

Suddenly, the room brightened as coloured light streamed through the small windows above her. She had not previously noticed the row of high windows, either side of the chimney breast, in the wall that separated the kitchen from the lounge. They were of a similar style to the ranch windows at the front of the house, but these had stained glass panels that cast colourful shapes across the lounge floor.

Charlotte placed her shoes and bag onto the rug beside the sofa and leant back in her seat. Something sharp stuck in her back. She jolted forward, reaching behind her, and pulling out the offending object. It was a key. It looked like it could be for a front door. She turned it over in her hand, wondering what it was doing stuck down the back of the sofa. She heard Anthony's footsteps approaching and, panicking, slipped the key into her pocket. Anthony entered the room and handed her the drink.

"Thank you," she said politely.

Anthony sat down on the other sofa. Charlotte clutched the scalding mug. It was hot, but she sat holding it all the same, not sure where she should put it down as there was no table. She watched Anthony for guidance as he placed his mug onto the rug at his feet. Charlotte followed his lead, doing the same with her own.

Anthony was quiet. Charlotte noticed him clenching his fingers as he leant back in his seat.

"Your wrist is still hurting, isn't it?" she commented sympathetically.

"It's ok. It could have been worse," answered Anthony.

"It's so dangerous what you do," continued Charlotte. "Aren't you scared when you are racing?"

Anthony smiled to himself.

"Don't really think about it," he answered pensively. "I just enjoy riding. It's the speed and the excitement. It makes me feel alive. It's addictive."

"I can understand that," said Charlotte. "I get an adrenaline rush just watching when those tapes go up, so it must be an amazing buzz doing it."

"You'll have to have a go sometime," enthused Anthony.

Charlotte laughed.

"Have you got another job?" enquired Charlotte. "Or do you only do speedway?"

"I wish I could just do speedway," enthused Anthony. "One day I'd like to. I'm a driver for my brother's delivery company for now though. It's okay. It fits around my racing schedule. I don't really like working for Terry, but I have to pay the bills on this place somehow."

Anthony seemed reflective again. There was a long pause before she spoke to break the awkward silence.

"This is a beautiful house. Do you own it?"

He sounded proud as he replied.

"Yeah. I fell in love with it as soon as I saw it."

"I can see why," agreed Charlotte. "It's certainly unusual. I love unusual buildings like this."

"It was in a right mess when I bought it. I've just about got things sorted out now though," smiled Anthony.

"Do you live here alone?" asked Charlotte.

She noticed Anthony wince with her question, and immediately regretted asking it.

"Yes, of course. Why did you ask?" answered Anthony rather defensively.

"It just seems like a big house for one," commented Charlotte nervously.

"I prefer it like that," he replied firmly.

An uneasy silence fell over the room again.

Charlotte sipped her coffee.

Anthony baffled her. They had seemed to be getting along marvellously, but now he appeared to be chastising her for asking too many questions. His reluctance to talk, and his abrupt reply to her question, unsettled her. She didn't like the silence, so she spoke again.

"You seem to be a lot more settled in the Willsby team now," said Charlotte.

Anthony appeared to relax once more. He was happy to talk to her about his racing. He explained how he had first got into the sport, and she told him about her visits to Willsby as a child. Anthony had been watching the team at the same time. They laughed together as they recalled the names of some of the riders from that earlier era. Anthony seemed impressed by her knowledge. They had been talking for ages. She tried to stifle a yawn as she looked at her watch.

"Am I keeping you up?" asked Anthony.

"I didn't realise how late it is," said Charlotte.

Anthony sat forward in his seat.

"Come on. I'll show you where your bedroom is."

Charlotte would have been happy to stay there talking to Anthony all night. Anthony, however, had stood up and was waiting expectantly in front of her. She stood up too, and picking up her shoes and bag, followed him from the room.

He led her out into the hallway and along the passage to the bedroom at the rear of the house.

The bedroom was similar in design to the lounge. Long windows overlooked the garden on one wall, and the familiar small, ranch-style windows adorned another. Anthony turned on the light and closed the curtains, shutting out the darkness behind the huge, cold glass panels.

A large, antique, four-poster bed seemed almost swallowed by the expansive room. Even the large Chesterfield settee in the corner didn't seem to fill any significant space. Charlotte noticed with surprise, the television, video, and hi-fi that had been missing from the lounge.

"The bathroom is just down the hall. Will you be all right in here?" asked Anthony as he paused at the door.

"I'll be fine. Thank you," said Charlotte.

"See you later then," replied Anthony as he left the room.

Charlotte looked around. A shelf above the television was full of trophies, mostly prizes for grasstrack racing as far as she could tell. She noticed too, a vast collection of videotapes. Her attention was drawn especially to the ones with handwritten labels relating to speedway meetings. She longed to take a look, but her manners got the better of her. Instead, she simply undressed and climbed into the huge bed.

The linen sheets were crisp and cool. She stretched out contently beneath them.

She had been lying in bed for about ten minutes when she heard the creak of the opening door. Charlotte looked out nervously from under the covers. Anthony's silhouette stood in the doorway. The light from the hallway spilled into the room around him.

"Anthony?" she murmured.

She shivered, and her stomach churned.

"You didn't really have to leave your flat tonight, did you?" he asked quietly.

His voice was not reprimanding, but calm. She felt relieved. The deceit had been uncharacteristic for her, and she had felt uneasy with the lie.

"No," she whispered. "I'm sorry I lied, but I just had to think of an excuse to be with you." "With me?" asked Anthony surprised. "But didn't you ask my brother if you could stay with him? I thought it was him you were interested in."

Charlotte laughed at the absurd suggestion.

"Good Lord, no," she exclaimed. "What made you think that?"

"That's Terry for you," laughed Anthony. "He thought you'd made up some excuse to spend the night with him. You've had a lucky escape. He probably would have taken you home with him, you know."

"But I thought Terry was married?"

"He is. But that wouldn't stop him, believe me. You're only here with me now because he's got too many women on the go to cope with."

Anthony laughed as he spoke, but Charlotte could tell that there was more to his comment about his brother than he was letting on.

"You don't mind me coming here tonight do you, Anthony?" asked Charlotte nervously.

"I'm really glad that you did," he reassured as he sat on the bed beside her and leant over to kiss her.

Chapter Six

It was morning when Charlotte woke up. She stretched out contentedly beneath the crisp, cotton sheets. As she opened her eyes, and looked up at the canopy of the bed, the sudden recollection of where she was, jabbed at her thoughts. She was in Anthony's house. The thought jolted her from her waking daze, and she sat up.

The room was as she remembered: the large bed, the long windows, the television, the trophies and the videotapes. The events of the previous evening were now replaying in her mind as she tentatively looked at the bed beside her. Anthony wasn't there.

She immediately began to question the realism of her memory. She had, after all, spent so many evenings with Anthony in her imagination, was this all just part of that fantasy? She carefully tried to recall the details since leaving the speedway track the evening before. It all seemed too vivid to be a dream. She recalled Anthony walking into the bedroom and sitting on the bed beside her. She looked at the pillow next to her; it was ruffled slightly. It was the confirmation she needed; Anthony really had spent the night with her. She smiled to herself as she climbed from the bed.

The hallway was quiet as she tiptoed through to the bathroom.

She called out, but there was no reply and no sign of Anthony. She quickly washed and dressed and made her way to the front of the house. She looked through to the lounge; the room was empty.

She walked into the kitchen. It too was empty but the outside door, at the opposite end, was ajar. The driveway and garden were visible through the small gap. Still there was no sign of Anthony. She walked over to the open door and called Anthony's name. There was no reply.

She walked gingerly to a wooden table and sat down, shivering slightly as the fresh draught from the open door licked at her shoulders. She rubbed her arms to keep warm and looked around the room.

The characteristic high glass windows adorned the walls at ceiling level, one row dividing the kitchen and lounge, the other on the outside of the house. A row of kitchen units, incorporating the usual appliances, spread along one wall. Next to her, mounted on the wall, was the telephone. Her eyes crept across the six digits that were printed beside the push buttons. The numbers imprinted themselves on her mind. It was Anthony's telephone number: she certainly wouldn't forget that.

The kitchen was tidy, and like the rest of the house, almost unnaturally so. It all seemed rather odd. This didn't look like a man's touch. Perhaps Anthony had a cleaner? The row of cupboards opposite her seemed almost clinically clean. She longed to open the doors, eager to see whether the orderliness extended inside, or whether they hid an unruly disorder like the ones in her flat. The very tidiness of the kitchen was, however, enough to prompt her manners. She sat instead, tentatively touching her surroundings with her gaze alone.

It was as her eyes felt their way around the room, that she noticed the bag. It was a small makeup bag, made from a cream-coloured fabric and decorated with purple and black flowers. It sat obtrusively on the white worktop. She peered at it inquisitively, noticing how the edge was stained by the carelessly smudged residue of makeup. She stood up slowly, her eyes fixed with curiosity on the unexpected object. She stared at it, urging an explanation to come into her mind as she walked towards it. What was a makeup bag doing in Anthony's kitchen? Who did it belong to? As she reached the worktop, her hands stretched out to it. Carefully, she pulled open the zip.

The two edges separated obediently as the inside gaped at her. Her fingers, dirtied by their contact with the bag, rummaged through the contents: grubby eye shadows, lipsticks, and eyeliner pencils were cluttered around a hairbrush. Thick, black hairs were entangled firmly around the brush's bristles. She stood staring at the items for a moment and then rezipped the bag. She took a step back, but remained staring at it in disgust, as she rubbed the contamination from her fingertips.

Suddenly she heard footsteps approaching outside. She quickly sat back down at the table.

The back door opened and a chill crept across her body as Anthony entered.

"Good morning," he said cheerfully, running his fingers through his long fringe and walking towards her. "Have you been up for long?"

Charlotte tried to ignore the piercing gaze of the bag beside him as she raised her eyes to meet his.

"No. I've only just woken up," she answered coolly, her eyes looking through him.

Anthony leant forward as if to kiss her. She turned her face away. She glanced at the bag and then back at Anthony. No wonder he had been hesitant when she had asked him, the night before, whether he lived here alone. Perhaps he had a girlfriend who lived here as well? Was that who owned that bag? She also recalled how he had laughed when he'd mentioned his brother's infidelity the night before. Was that because he was doing the same? Let's face it, they were brothers: they were cast from the same mould, weren't they? She tried to control the distraught feeling that twisted in her stomach. Surely, there could only be one explanation, couldn't there? Anthony must have a girlfriend.

"Sorry to have left you. I had to get the bike cleaned up. Should really have done it last night," he said. "Before the mud dried on."

"I see," said Charlotte, glaring at the bag on the worktop beside him.

She could not muster a smile as she turned her attention back to Anthony.

"Do you want some breakfast?" he asked.

Charlotte felt sick inside, amazed by his complacency, as the bag stared at them ruthlessly. How could Anthony be so callous? He had dared to ask her if she wanted breakfast as if there was nothing wrong. She had been so gullible and so foolish.

Anthony looked at her, prompting an answer to his question.

"Just coffee," she answered reticently.

She felt stupid. Of course, it had been absurd to expect Anthony to conform to her dreams, hadn't it? She watched as he silently poured her coffee and stirred in the sugar. He placed the mug on the table in front of her and sat down opposite, holding his head in his hands.

He looked up at her and opened his mouth as if to speak. Charlotte could not bear to listen. She did not want to hear what he was about to say. He was bound to mention the bag, which glared at them so obtrusively from across the room. Perhaps he would make up some excuse about it? Or would he admit to it belonging to a girlfriend? Charlotte interrupted his impending words, not wanting to hear his rejection.

"I ought to get back soon."

Anthony leant back in his chair. He sounded almost disappointed as he spoke.

"Do you have to go so soon?"

Charlotte was taken aback by his audacity.

"Yes, I do," she said sternly.

"Okay. I'll run you home when you're ready then," he said calmly.

Charlotte stood up.

"Thanks. I'll go get my things now if that's okay."

She walked silently from the kitchen, holding back the tears as she went. She felt weak and sick inside as her thoughts dwelt on her shattered dreams. She had made a fool of herself, hadn't she? She had tricked her way into Anthony's house, and now she was paying for her stupidity. She returned to the bedroom. The memories of her night in the room viciously jibed her thoughts as she packed her belongings. Her eyes glazed by the impending tears, she took a last look around the room. Fate could be so cruel. She took a deep breath and returned to the kitchen.

Anthony was waiting with his car keys.

"Have you got everything?" he asked as she entered the room.

She nodded. Her eyes glanced over at the worktop. The bag had disappeared. She stared at the space where it had been. Why had he moved it? Guilt perhaps? He must have been trying to hide it. Maybe he had hoped she hadn't noticed it? Hoped that she hadn't seen through his deceit? It was too late for that now. She had seen it, hadn't she? She felt almost insulted by his deviousness. Did he really think that she was that gullible?

"Are you sure you can't stay a bit longer?" he asked.

His nerve irritated her.

"No, I said I want to go home," she answered coldly.

Anthony looked at her. He seemed quite surprised by her aloofness.

"Okay," he answered quietly as he led her out to the car.

As she climbed into the car, and took a look back at the house, everything seemed so ordinary. It had been misleading the night before, under the shroud of darkness, when the house had seemed so unique and mystical. The truth, however, was that it was semi-detached and shared a driveway with an almost identical cottage next door.

There was an uncomfortable silence in the car as they headed back towards Willsby. Anthony said nothing as they meandered through the country roads. He seemed rather aloof. Perhaps he now realised that she'd seen through his deception? It was not until they reached Willsby that he finally spoke:

"Which way do I go?" he asked as they pulled onto the High Street.

Charlotte directed him, through the town centre, to the Esplanade. He stopped in the cul-de-sac outside of the flats.

Charlotte looked up at the tall, friendly building beside her. Barnaby was sat at the window looking out expectantly, unaware as yet of her return. Anthony looked across at Charlotte.

"I'll bring your bag in if you like," he offered.

"No," she replied abruptly. "I can manage on my own."

She just wanted to get inside and hide from her foolishness. She just wanted to forget, as quickly as possible, about the events of the last twelve hours.

Anthony turned away. Charlotte's reprimand had scolded him. His gaze was fixed on his hands as he gripped the steering wheel. Charlotte opened the car door.

"I guess I'll see you around then," said Anthony, leaning towards her.

She flinched, hurriedly pushed open the car door, and climbed out. Comforted by her escape, she remembered her manners as she looked back into the car.

"Thanks for letting me stay," she whispered, before turning and walking to the front door.

She felt Anthony's dark eyes on her back as she calmly turned the key in the lock and entered the building without looking back. Once inside, the tears broke through her resistance as she heard the car pull away outside. She wrenched the heavy door open again in her desperation and watched as Anthony drove out of the cul-de-sac. He did not look back. Her pleading stare followed him out of sight. She hurried upstairs to her flat, unlocked the door, and ran inside where she collapsed onto her bed, sobbing.

She had been lying there for some time before her tears finally stopped. She composed herself and made her way into the kitchen. Barnaby was waiting patiently. He mewed as she opened a tin of cat food and emptied the contents into his bowl. He chewed ravenously on the food as she began to tell him what had happened. She told him about Anthony's callousness. She told him about the makeup bag and how Anthony had tried to hide it from her. Barnaby looked up and nonchalantly licked his lips. He refused to sympathise with her as he turned his attention back to the bowl in front of him.

Charlotte watched him. Perhaps he was right? Perhaps she had been hasty? Maybe she should have allowed Anthony to explain? Perhaps she had jumped to conclusions? She began to feel guilty. Had she acted unreasonably? Perhaps the bag belonged to a relative? His cleaner? There were, after all, several explanations. She felt so confused. Why had she jumped to conclusions?

Anthony had been so kind to her. They had gotten on so well. She should have just asked him directly who the bag had belonged to, shouldn't she? She should at least have allowed him to explain. She had to see him again. She concocted a plan; she would go to the practice track the following day. He was bound to be there, and then she could ask him directly who that bag belonged to.

* * *

Mick was deep in thought as he drove along the Esplanade. He was on his way to his sister's flat. Jane had invited him, Dave, and Lucy for dinner. The invitation had come as a surprise as today was the twentieth anniversary of their sister's death. He had thought that Jane would have been far too upset to even consider a dinner party. Perhaps, he wondered, had she forgotten the date? It was possible, although it seemed unlikely. It had been, after all, Jane who had found their sister's body all those years ago. She had always remembered the morbid anniversary before, preferring to stay at home with her husband each year. It seemed inconceivable that she would decide to hold a dinner party this year. Then again, Jane had been acting out of character a lot of late. Perhaps this was just another example of her irrational behaviour? The mystery of his sister's changed character was gnawing at his thoughts as he drove. It was Lucy's interruption that finally broke his musing.

"How's Jane settling into my flat?"

Mick glanced in the rear-view mirror at his two passengers who sat on the back seat.

"Really well," he said smiling. "It was so good of you to arrange for her to move in."

"I wish Jane could see it that way," sighed Lucy. "I do so want us all to get along."

Mick felt sorry for Lucy. Jane had taken an irrational dislike to her. Lucy had gone out of her way to be pleasant, even to the extent of arranging for Jane to take over the flat on the seafront. His sister, however, remained hostile. This was just another example of how unreasonable she was acting lately.

The smell of the cooking meal hung in the air as Jane twisted the corkscrew. She placed the bottle of wine on the table and walked to the window. Her visitors would be there soon. She looked out at the trees opposite. Their gnarled branches stretched out into the darkening sky. Jane closed the curtains and sighed as she looked around the room. It was so depressing here; she'd switched on every light in the flat, but it still seemed gloomy. The silence of her surroundings, broken only by the erratic tapping of the saucepan lid over the boiling vegetables, made her acutely conscious of her loneliness.

She had not realised just how difficult it would be living on her own. She had grown so used to her husband's company that, despite all his shortcomings, she was missing him terribly. The flat was not in a particularly nice area either. The other residents seemed so hostile. It was a very lonely place to be living. She had even wondered whether Lucy had known just how isolated she would feel here. Was that why she had been so keen for Jane to move in? Perhaps she was being paranoid? Surely, even Lucy wouldn't be that nasty? There was, nonetheless, something very unsettling about Dave's new wife. Jane was convinced that the woman was after Dave's money, but even that couldn't explain why she was being so horrible.

Jane was feeling particularly upset tonight as it was the twentieth anniversary of her sister's death. She had not wanted to spend the evening alone so had suggested a small dinner party. She would be glad of her brother's company. He would understand, better than anyone, exactly how she felt. Dave too would be sympathetic. She had, of course, been reluctant to invite Lucy. That woman's snide comments were hardly the reassurance that she needed today. Unfortunately though, Dave was besotted with his new wife, and even Mick, for some inexplicable reason, seemed to be taken in by her false charms, so Lucy had to be invited.

The guests arrived on time. Jane hurried down to the door to welcome them. They followed her up to the flat and into the bed-sitting room.

"You've got the place lovely, Jane," commented Lucy.

Jane noticed the sarcasm in her voice. It was obvious that she hadn't had time to do anything to the flat as yet. There were even boxes still dotted around the room that needed unpacking. She glanced at Lucy dismissively.

"Well, if everyone is ready, I'll go dish up the dinner," said Jane.

"Great," enthused Dave. "I'm starving."

"I'll come and give you a hand," offered Lucy as she followed her hostess into the kitchen.

Mick smiled to himself as the women left. Lucy was so obviously trying to be nice to Jane, maybe tonight would be the time when Jane would finally realise that herself.

It was not long before Lucy reappeared, carrying two plates.

"It's really hot in that kitchen," she said as she placed the dinners on the table.

Jane followed with the other two meals.

"Isn't it Jane?" continued Lucy. "It was really suffocating in there."

Jane said nothing.

The four of them sat at the table.

"Jane's quite a cook," commented Dave.

"It looks really tasty," added Mick.

"Yes, Jane's culinary skills have really taken my breath away," said Lucy as they all began eating.

Jane remained silent as she passed a contemptuous look in Lucy's direction.

Despite Mick's attempts at making conversation throughout the meal, the atmosphere remained tense.

"Well, that's just about done me in. I think I'll die if I eat anymore," said Lucy gratefully, placing her knife and fork onto her empty plate, and leaning back in her seat.

Jane's glance towards Lucy was venomous, a fact that hadn't

escaped the notice of Dave or Mick. Dave could not understand why Jane was being so hostile towards his wife. Lucy was trying her hardest to be friendly. There was another uneasy silence before Lucy, unperturbed, again tried to make conversation with their hostess.

"That wine's got a lovely bouquet Janey," she commented as she took a sip of her drink.

Both Dave and Mick were shocked by Jane's response; she sprung to her feet, lunging across the table towards Lucy who flinched back into Dave's arms.

"Why are you such an evil bitch? Is it because I can see what you're up to? Is it? Is that why you're always picking on me?"

The outburst had taken the men by surprise. Dave panicked as he tried to diffuse the situation. He quickly stood up, shielding his distressed wife as he led her out of the flat. Mick stared in disbelief at his sister.

"What's come over you, Jane? Why are you acting like this?"

"Can't you see what she's up to?" shouted Jane.

Mick looked at his sister defiantly, before following the others from the flat.

Jane sat down, her head in her hands, as the door downstairs slammed shut. She could hear the footsteps and condemning voices of her guests as they walked to the car. She knew she was right. Lucy was up to something. Why couldn't they see that?

Chapter Seven

The train had stopped again. Charlotte leant back in her seat, breathing an impatient sigh. The journey was taking longer than it had done previously. Repair works were being conducted on a stretch of the track, and the train had been rerouted. She was beginning to question the sense behind her making the journey to the practice track.

She looked out, through the grubby window, over the bleak fields. Rugged sheep munched nonchalantly at the grass, indifferent to the motionless train bordering their field.

After a long ten minutes, the train eventually lurched forward. The sudden jolt sent an empty tin can scurrying under the seat opposite. Charlotte watched it disappear into the dusty darkness. She turned her eyes back to the window as the train crept forward. The sheep progressed into more sheep as the fields rolled past. At least the train was moving now, and it wasn't long before Charlotte recognised the passing scenery.

Eventually, the train slowed and pulled into the station. Charlotte opened the door eagerly. She looked down at the platform hurtling past at her feet. It eventually came to a stop. She jumped off, slamming the door on the empty carriage behind her. The guard hung out of an open door further up the carriage, and signalled to the driver, before the train began to pull away. The train passed Charlotte, firstly traveling at the same pace as her walking, and then gradually building up speed into its rapid departure.

Charlotte looked around her. The marshy fields stretched out towards the river. A breeze blew around her as she descended the steps to the road.

There was no need for her to consult her map. She remembered the route to the practice track from her last visit and headed off along the country lanes. The farm was visible in the distance, and the sound of bikes was resonating through the still fields.

It was not too long before she arrived at the farm. She climbed over the closed gate. The dogs at the farmhouse's window failed to alarm her as they barked predictably.

The practice track was considerably busier than it had been on her last visit. She didn't, therefore, notice Anthony at first and was beginning to think that her journey had been a waste of time. Then she saw the silver car. It was definitely Anthony's car. She walked towards it, eager to speak to him. As she approached, the smile slid from her mouth and she froze in her tracks.

Two figures sat in the front seats of the car. Charlotte's eyes focused, not on Anthony, but on the woman who sat beside him.

Dyed black hair fell untidily around the woman's chubby face. Large, made-up eyes stared menacingly from behind the windscreen. Her hand rested on the frame of the open window. A cigarette burned between her fingers. Her hand rose to her mouth, a succession of cheap bracelets jangled down her arm. Her large, red lips sucked on the cigarette and blew a trail of smoke into the air.

The woman looked across at Anthony. She leant forward and kissed his cheek.

Charlotte stared at the woman. She recalled the makeup bag, the red lipstick, and the hairbrush entangled with that ugly, black, wiry hair. It all fell into place.

She stared, sickened by the sight. She had been right all along, hadn't she? The bag had belonged to Anthony's girlfriend. She turned her head, her eyes not wanting to confront the sight any longer. She felt tears welling in her eyes as she turned her back and ran impulsively back to the farmhouse.

The dogs barked angrily as she unlocked the gate. Pushing it slightly ajar, she scrambled through the gap. She hurried away along the country road. An old man shouted after her, slamming the gate shut in his annoyance.

"You bloody kids. Why can't you shut the gate?"

Charlotte was not interested in his lecture as she scurried away.

The road was quiet. It was a long walk back to the station. Charlotte felt uneasy as she hurried along the route. The tall hedgerows loomed down around her. Invisible figures seemed to be rustling in the bushes as her deceiving mind conjured up shapes in the shadows. A car approached from behind, forcing her onto the grass verge as it passed. She quickened her pace, eager to get home as soon as possible.

It was growing colder, and a breeze swept across the fields from the river as Charlotte sat alone on the platform, waiting for her train home.

Why had she been so stupid? Why had she even thought about coming here today? She had been so desperate to be wrong about

Anthony. She had hoped, so much, that she had been mistaken about the makeup bag. She had been so foolish, hadn't she? She felt vulnerable and frightened as she huddled beneath the flimsy shelter of her jacket.

* * *

Dave was walking out of the bathroom when he heard the voices. Mick had already arrived. They had a race meeting that evening, and being as sensible as always, Mick would be wanting to allow plenty of time for the journey. Dave walked into the kitchen, flinging his bag onto the table.

"Have you spoken to Jane since last night?" he heard Lucy asking Mick in the next room.

"No. I haven't."

The reply was rather sharp. Dave was not surprised; Mick was no doubt fuming about Jane's outburst of the night before. Dave had been angry too. He could only feel sympathy for his wife as he tried to make sense of Jane's odd behaviour. The only possible explanation he could conceive was that she was jealous. Dave knew that Jane was fond of him. She must be jealous that he'd got married? There couldn't be any other explanation, could there? Why were women so complicated? Thank goodness Lucy wasn't like that. He smiled to himself, happy with his conclusions, as he walked into the lounge.

"Hi Mick. Nice and early as usual I see," said Dave. "I hope Lucy's been looking after you?"

"Of course, I've been looking after him," said Lucy with a teasing smile.

Mick looked a little embarrassed.

"We'd better get off," he urged, looking at his watch. "We're a bit late already, Dave."

"Crikey Mick. What's the rush?" asked Dave casually.

"Well, the traffic could be busy. You don't want to get there late, do you?"

"I don't know, Mick," laughed Lucy. "You are a worrier."

Dave kissed his wife.

"Now are you sure you don't want to come with us?" he asked.

Lucy paused.

"You should come," continued Dave. "It will be a good meeting. Me and Travis are on top form. I can't see anyone in the league beating us at the moment."

"If she doesn't want to come, don't force her," interrupted Mick.

Dave was quite surprised by his friend's abruptness.

"I haven't said I don't want to yet," teased Lucy.

"It will be a late one," warned Mick. "I'm sure you've got other things to do."

Lucy paused pensively.

If Dave didn't know his friend better, he would have thought he was trying to put her off the trip.

"Come on, Lucy," urged Dave.

Lucy pondered the thought in a long silence.

Mick looked visibly distressed.

"Please, Lucy," urged Dave.

Finally, Lucy replied:

"No. I think I'll give it a miss."

She smiled to herself as Mick hurriedly led Dave from the house.

Dusk had descended by the time that the train pulled into the station. Charlotte watched as a succession of brightly lit, empty carriages rolled past her. The train eventually slowed to a stop. She opened the door and climbed up into the carriage.

The warmth engulfed her as she slammed the door shut and sat down. She was alone. The train began to move. She looked around the carriage. Faint graffiti stared at her from the wall opposite. Frantic scrub marks had tried to obliterate the vulgarities, but their stubborn residue remained, just like the images of Anthony and that woman in Charlotte's head.

The train was now travelling quickly. Charlotte slumped dejectedly in her seat as she looked at the window. The sheep and fields were hidden by the darkness. Her reflection stared back coldly as a light rain began to caress the glass.

After what seemed like an eternity, the train finally slowed, and the familiar sight of Willsby station appeared. She climbed from the train and walked towards the exit. The station was empty. Nobody waited at the top of the stairs to collect her ticket. She tore it in two and discarded it into the litter bin.

Pushing open the heavy station door, Charlotte walked into the night. It was raining quite hard now. She pulled her collar tightly around her neck and hurried along the station approach to the High Street. The shops were brightly lit but deserted. Prominent padlocks and metal cages protected the vulnerable windows from damage. The streets were empty as Charlotte hurried through them. She was anxious to reach the security of her home.

As she passed The Druids, Charlotte noticed a familiar face in the window. Graham had also seen her. His face lit up, almost as quickly as her heart had sunk. She sped up her pace, but it was too late. Graham had come running out of the pub and had caught up with her.

"Are you all right, Charlie?" he gasped as he grabbed her arm. "You look really upset. Has something happened?"

Charlotte shrugged him off, tears brimming in her eyes. This was the last thing she needed.

"Let me walk you home. You look like you could do with a friend," he offered.

"Leave me alone, Graham. I don't need any help from you or anyone else," she snapped at him.

She quickened her pace making it obvious that she didn't want his company. Typically though, he hadn't taken the hint. Although he had kept his distance, Charlotte was aware that he was following her. This was all she needed. What a creep Graham was!

Chapter Eight

Charlotte was relieved to reach her home. The walk through the dark streets had been both intimidating and frightening. Having Graham follow her hadn't helped her uneasiness. As she walked into the cul-de-sac, she was aware of him trying to hide behind the bushes, no doubt thinking she hadn't noticed him. The sight of her flat was reassuring as she walked up to the front door. The building was quiet as she turned the key in the lock and walked inside.

She removed her soaked jacket and hung it over the back of a chair. Her clothes were drenched. She ran her fingers through her wet hair and walked over to the window. She looked gingerly outside. She peered into the bushes at the entrance to the cul-de-sac: at least Graham had now gone.

The sound of the heavy rain outside seemed to ease slightly as she closed the blue curtains. Barnaby stirred, stretching out from his slumber among the feathered duvet. She sat beside him.

The photograph of Anthony and his brother stared at her callously from the mantelpiece opposite. She stood up and walked towards it, lifted it in her hand, and stared at it for a while. As Anthony smiled up at her, an image of the woman's menacing face returned to her thoughts. What could Anthony see in that woman? She hurled the picture across the room as tears welled in her eyes.

Why was Fate being so cruel to her? She could feel the pent-up tears inside but for some inexplicable reason, her eyes remained dry. It was as if her body was so weak that it couldn't even muster the energy to shed tears. She caught a glimpse of herself in the mirror as she picked up the photograph and replaced it on the mantel. The composure of her reflection surprised her. It stared at her coldly, distancing itself unsympathetically from her distress. The two-dimensional face that reflected from the mirror seemed detached from the person that she could feel inside her. Charlotte returned to Barnaby, stroking his head as she sat beside him. He sighed, irritated by the disturbance. Charlotte rested her hand beside his face, which he accepted in a begrudging compromise. She lay down beside him and closed her eyes as the first tears finally began to trickle down her cheeks.

* * *

Lucy was sitting on the sofa when the key turned in the front door lock. Dave was home. He was feeling guilty. It was almost three-thirty. He had stayed on after the race meeting for a few drinks and a curry with Travis. Mick had been reluctant to stay. He had made it quite clear that he felt they should get back to Lucy, but Travis had been persistent. Travis was always so persuasive, and Dave just couldn't let his friend down. Now, however, he regretted having stayed out so late. Lucy had been so upset by Jane's outburst towards her at the dinner party, and it was rather inconsiderate of him to have left her alone for so long. The thought was now playing on his conscience as he entered the house. He noticed the light filtering into the hallway from the lounge: Lucy was waiting up for him. He walked tentatively into the room as his wife's dispirited face looked up at him.

"Sorry I'm late," he said defensively. "We got caught up in traffic."

Dave was not convinced by his implausible story. It was three-thirty in the morning after all, hardly rush hour, and he could smell the alcohol on his own breath as he spoke. Surely Lucy would know he was lying? She seemed, however, to accept his story and that was enough to settle his inebriated conscience.

"Don't be silly," she reassured. "I don't mind you racing, do I? It's not you who has upset me, anyway."

Dave was relieved by his acquittal but was still concerned by his wife's obvious anguish. "Is it Jane?" he asked.

He could tell immediately from Lucy's expression that he had hit upon the problem. Lucy looked at him, sighing and bowing her head.

"I know she's said some hurtful things," he comforted. "Just give her time. She'll come 'round, I'm sure."

Lucy took hold of his hand.

"I'm trying to be nice to her, honestly I am. I know how much it means to you."

He pulled his wife gently towards him as tears formed in her eyes. Her vulnerability touched him.

"I'm upset because she rang me tonight."

The comment did not surprise Dave. He'd thought something must have happened as he'd noticed, on his way in, that the telephone receiver had been left hanging from the kitchen wall.

"She was really being vindictive. She said that I was only after your money. How could she say that? I didn't even know you had any money until after we were married, did I?"

Lucy was clearly distressed.

Dave was confused. Jane had always been so good to him in the past. Perhaps a little sour towards his girlfriends, but never malicious like this. He could not understand it. Lucy hadn't provoked the animosity, had she? It just did not make sense. Jane was out of order.

"I'll speak to her tomorrow," he reassured. "I won't let her get away with behaving like this towards you."

The comment seemed to comfort Lucy.

"Thank you, Dave," she whispered.

* * *

When Charlotte eventually woke up, it was light outside. She sat up. Her head ached. She felt awful. Barnaby was curled up on the bottom of the bed. He raised his head and reluctantly opened his eyes as she stirred.

Nothing had changed, had it? She felt no better than she had done the night before. She was still thinking about Anthony. As she climbed from the bed, she caught a glimpse of her reflection in the mirror above the fireplace. Her eyes stared at her. They were puffy and red, and encircled by smudged makeup. She looked terrible. She couldn't face having to go to work. How could she cope with all those customers after everything that had happened this weekend? She dressed, left the flat, and crossed over the road to the telephone box.

"It's Charlotte. I won't be in today, Mrs Shield. I'm not feeling very well."

Mrs Shield seemed genuinely concerned.

"Oh, my dear. Is it that 'flu bug that's going around?"

Charlotte wanted to tell her the truth, but where would she start? Mrs Shield wouldn't care anyway, would she?

"Yes, I think it must be," she answered half-heartedly.

"Well, you get yourself to bed my dear, and stay warm."

"I will. Thank you."

Charlotte hung up and stood staring at the telephone. Two schoolgirls glared impatiently into the telephone box. Should she ring back? She needed someone to talk to. The schoolgirls knocked on the window. No, Mrs Shield wouldn't be interested in listening to her problems, would she? She pushed open the heavy door. The schoolgirls giggled as they passed her into the booth.

Charlotte felt lonely that day. The doorbell had rung. Whoever the caller was, they were persistent: that was the third time it had rung in a matter of minutes. It was probably a salesman. Charlotte sat ignoring it. She didn't want to see anyone. She just wanted to be left alone.

* * *

Dave was reluctant to agree.

"I don't know, Travis, we only went out last night, didn't we?"

"C'mon Dave. You know you want to. I've just clinched an amazing sponsorship deal. It's big bucks. I want to celebrate. I told you that you'd get all boring once you were married, didn't I? I knew you'd turn into a pipe and slippers man."

Dave felt insulted by Travis's connotations, but he had promised Lucy that he would go to see Jane and sort out all that tension between them. He hadn't got around to it today; his head ached after that late night yesterday. He had planned to go tomorrow instead. He couldn't let Lucy down, could he? But Travis was right, how could he turn his invite down either? The American was unrelenting.

"Dave. I need some help in the morning stocking up for the party tomorrow. Don't let me do it all on my own, Buddy."

Lucy entered the kitchen.

"Who is it?" she asked.

Dave held his hand over the mouthpiece.

"It's Travis. He wants me to go over tomorrow. He's having a party."

Lucy smiled.

"Travis is one long party," she laughed.

His wife's jovial comment reassured him as the muffled voice on the telephone continued resolutely.

"I won't go until you've agreed. And make sure that beautiful wife of yours comes too."

"Okay. Okay," relented Dave.

"You'll come?" confirmed Travis.

"Yes, we'll come," Dave conceded.

"Right on. See you later."

The telephone quickly went dead with Travis's sudden victory. Dave replaced the handset. He realised that the American could talk him into anything, but that was Travis for you.

"Looks like we're going out tomorrow," he announced. "You will come, won't you?"

"I don't know," replied Lucy.

Dave was concerned. He didn't like the idea of leaving his wife alone again, especially as she was so upset by what Jane had said to her the night before. Lucy had noticed his anxious expression.

"It's okay," she said reassuringly. "I don't mind you going without me, you know that."

She wrapped her arms around him and kissed his cheek. His guilt disappeared.

"You go and have a good time. I've got plenty of things I can do. I've got that writing to get finished, remember?"

"What about me speaking to Jane like I promised?"

"I'm sure that can wait a while."

Dave smiled. His wife was such a considerate person.

* * *

Charlotte looked at the food in front of her. Steam rose from the meal as she stabbed at it with her fork. Why had she even prepared it? She felt so sick inside that she couldn't face eating anything. She placed the plate down beside her and glanced across at the photograph of Anthony on the mantelpiece. Why had things gone so wrong? Why couldn't she get him out of her head? She just had to speak to him. She had to tell him how she felt about him.

She had been thinking about making the call for some time. She could remember Anthony's telephone number from her stay at his house. All she had to do was ring him up and speak to him. It was simple. She had nothing to lose. It was eight-thirty when she finally mustered up the determination and crossed the Esplanade to the telephone box. The booth was empty.

As she stood inside, she could hear the roar of the waves behind her. The telephone number flashed through her head as she picked up the receiver. She dialled the number. It rang three times. Her hand was shaking as the receiver was picked up at the other end. Charlotte slipped the coin into the slot and a woman's voice answered.

It was a cheap, common voice. Charlotte pictured the face of the woman in the car. It fitted the uncouth voice on the other end of the line.

"Hello? Hello? Is that you?"

There was a long silence. Charlotte didn't know what to say. The thought of the woman sat in Anthony's kitchen repulsed her. She pictured that long black hair and those red lips.

"Look," screamed the voice." I don't have to put up with this you know. Leave me alone."

The woman hung up. The crash of the receiver momentarily deafened Charlotte. How had the woman known that it was her? Perhaps Anthony had said something? How dare she talk to her like that? She had only wanted to talk to Anthony, after all. Charlotte cringed as she recalled the voice. She felt sick inside as an angry jealousy leached through her body. The woman had no right to stop her from talking to Anthony.

Chapter Nine

Charlotte lay on her bed staring up at the ceiling, as confused thoughts washed through her head. Subconscious voices reminded her of the woman who had been in Anthony's car: the same woman who had been so rude to her over the telephone. As the voices whispered, visions began to accompany the words. Firstly, they were disjointed images: red lipstick, the makeup bag, large, black-rimmed eyes, and that thick, black hair.

The visions then grew more intense as Charlotte pictured Anthony's house. She imagined the woman sat on the green-serge settee. She pictured the woman lying in Anthony's bed, beneath those crisp, cotton sheets, just as she had done herself on her visit. She pictured the woman in Anthony's arms. She could hear the woman's voice in her head. Jealousy knotted inside her.

Charlotte's sleep that night was tortured by her confused emotions. The sight of the sun rising in the morning sky finally ended the night's torment. She felt sick inside as she sat up. Why was Fate being so cruel? Everything had been going so well. She was getting on so well with Anthony. Nothing made sense anymore. How could Anthony have been so kind to her when he had another girlfriend all along? She had to speak to him. She had to confront him. She couldn't ring again, could she? She couldn't ring again in case that woman answered. If the woman wouldn't let her speak to Anthony over the telephone, then perhaps she should go around to the house to see him?

Logic and emotion were arguing in her head. She had to see Anthony. She'd made up her mind. She would go to Anthony's house that morning. She would tell him exactly how much she thought of him, and then it would be down to him: he could then choose between her and the other woman.

Charlotte dressed and carefully applied some makeup. It was more makeup than she would normally have worn, but she wanted to hide the fact that she had been crying and anyhow, perhaps it was about time that she started to be a little bolder? Anthony obviously liked his women that way.

Once she had finished, she sat back, staring into the mirror. The uncharacteristic, black-rimmed eyes stared back from the glass. It didn't even seem like her. It was almost as if another person was looking out of the mirror. The stranger looked bolder and braver than how she felt inside. It gave her the confidence she needed to continue with her plan.

She left her flat and walked around to the bus station. It would take a while to get to Anthony's house, but her determination egged her on.

She sat on the back seat of the bus, staring out of the window. The other passengers sat quietly, avoiding one another's gaze. It was a long journey. Charlotte watched as passengers boarded and then disembarked as she sat patiently. The bus had left Willsby and was now making its way along the narrow lanes to the smaller villages. Overhanging trees scraped against the windows as the vehicle meandered through the countryside. Finally, Charlotte stood up. She had reached her stop. The road to Anthony's house led off to the right. The bus came to a halt and she alighted. She watched as the bus left. She was alone. She stood resolutely, staring up the road. There was a stillness to that summer day as she made her way towards Anthony's house. The tall imposing hedges loomed beside her on either side. Eventually, she reached the driveway. The familiar building stood ahead of her as she walked up the gravel track. There was a car parked haphazardly by the front door. It was not, however, Anthony's car.

Charlotte's gaze fixed on the vehicle as she walked closer to the house. Perhaps the car belonged to the woman? Charlotte squeezed past the vehicle, her jacket buttons scratching the paintwork as she went; she didn't try to stop them. She rang the doorbell and waited. There was no reply. She pressed the bell push again. There was silence.

She felt in her pocket for the key. It was the key that she had found down the back of the settee when she had been in Anthony's lounge. She turned it over between her fingers. Dare she? Dare she try it in the lock? Her curiosity got the better of her. She slid it into the keyhole, and the door opened easily. Should she go inside? Well, if there was nobody at home, what harm could it do? She could have a look around to see if there were any signs of the woman living there. Then she'd know for sure, wouldn't she? She pushed the door open.

The house was quiet and still. Charlotte entered. The lounge door was open ahead of her. The green curtains hung in the distance. She was walking towards them when she heard the noise. She startled, turning in the direction of the sound. It had sounded like footsteps.

There was silence again as she looked towards the door on her right. It was slightly ajar. She had previously assumed that it was a bedroom, although it was the one area of the house that she wasn't familiar with. The noise had come from inside the room. She walked curiously towards it, pushing the door slowly open.

The woman lay on the bed, her hair splayed out around her chubby, white face. Her red lipstick and black eye makeup had smudged over her face. Her eyes were closed, and the erratic movement of her breathing was clearly visible under the flimsy sheet that covered her. The empty bottle beside the bed explained her stupor.

There was a stale smell of alcohol hanging in the air. The sight and smell nauseated Charlotte. The woman looked so vulgar. She approached the bed as one of those earlier voices suddenly returned to her head.

The voice was even more forceful than before. It frightened her as this time it sounded so clear. It was almost as if her subconscious thoughts were standing in the room right behind her, talking into her ear. She could almost feel their breath on the back of her neck as they spoke. The voice summed up all the hatred and contempt that she felt towards the woman.

"I'd like to see her dead," it whispered venomously. "She's getting in the way, isn't she?"

The voice was right, of course. Charlotte nodded in agreement.

"We could get rid of her, you know. It would be so easy and then she'd be out of the way, wouldn't she?" urged the voice.

The voice had grown louder, its ferocity confirmed all the contempt and hatred that Charlotte felt for the woman.

"She deserves it all for what she's done."

There was sighing from beneath the sheets as the woman wriggled under the white, cotton membrane. Charlotte tried to blot the voice out of her head, but it only grew louder and more emphatic. The stale smell of alcohol had grown even stronger. She could almost taste it in the air passing across her lips.

"Come on then. What are we waiting for? All we've got to do is put the pillow over her face," said the voice.

Charlotte obediently lifted the pillow from beside the woman's head. Her hand, which had been resting on it, fell without resistance onto the mattress, cheap bangles rattling as it dropped.

Charlotte knew that she couldn't go through with it. She was telling herself to put the pillow down. That logical side of her conscience was fighting, however, with the other voice which grew louder and louder and more dominant. Charlotte so wanted to put the pillow down, but the voice had grown angry.

"Come on! Come on! Let's do it," it demanded furiously.

With the voice still screaming at her, Charlotte lifted the pillow above her head.

It took hardly any effort. Her subconscious resolve was so strong.

"She deserves all that she gets," continued the voice.

Before she'd had a chance to consider her actions, Charlotte felt herself launch forward, thrusting the pillow onto the woman's face. Her full body weight held the writhing mass beneath, with a strength she'd never before experienced. She knew that she should let go, but her hands seemed inexplicably pinned to the pillow, her strength stronger than her will to stop. The body squirmed beneath her. Charlotte was frightened. She wanted to stop, but she couldn't let go. The smell of alcohol had intensified. Her eyes were blurred by her tears, but she couldn't stop. She was possessed by her jealousy and hatred.

The woman jerked. Her cries were muted by the compressed pillow that smothered her face. Her legs kicked out, her arms reached out in desperation, but Charlotte held them under control with the force that had overcome her. Charlotte was crying, sobbing loudly. Her body felt so weak, but somehow an unrelenting inner strength had taken her over, and she couldn't stop the assault.

Eventually, the victim's struggle relented. The body twitched in a last weak fight, before finally relinquishing. It fell limp beneath her. Charlotte's intense grip, however, held on vehemently, draining every morsel of life from the victim. She wanted to let go, but her inner strength persisted. It was like a bad dream, she wanted to wake up, but everything seemed so horribly real. She wriggled in her desperation, but her hands refused to let go. She screamed, tears scorching her cheeks.

Then, just as suddenly as the strength had appeared, it was now gone. She was finally able to relax her grip as she collapsed on top of the lifeless mass. She was sobbing uncontrollably as the voice in her head started to laugh.

Charlotte felt so weak. Her previously discovered strength had now totally ebbed away. She felt sick, as the realisation of the horror of what she had done seeped into her head.

She mustered the little strength that she still had as she scampered from the bed, clambering across the lifeless mass, staring at the pillow. What had she done? She pictured the contorted, horror-stricken face beneath it. What had she just done?

The voice was still laughing. Charlotte held her head.

"Stop it. Stop it!" she screamed, but the laughing continued.

Charlotte backed away in her disbelief. She was shaking uncontrollably, tears streaming from her stinging eyes. She wanted to run, but her body froze in fear. The voice was still in her head, laughing victoriously as it urged her to look at their achievement. She tried desperately to block it out as she turned and ran from the house.

She ran, alone and scared, along the country road. Her vision was impaired by her constant tears and confused thoughts. She noticed the telephone box opposite and ran towards it. A car screeched and skidded. Charlotte hardly noticed it as she tugged open the door to the telephone and lifted the receiver, repeatedly pressing the digit nine.

* * *

Dave sat for a moment, his hands tightly gripping the steering wheel. The girl had run out in front of him. He had almost hit her, and he felt shaken. He should have seen her, but his mind had been wandering. He thought that perhaps he should ask her if she was all right, but she seemed unbothered as she made her phone call, so Dave instead pulled away.

* * *

A voice answered. Charlotte could hardly speak.

"She's dead. Please come quickly. Please come," she sobbed, her voice almost incoherent.

"Where are you Madam? What has happened?" said the voice

calmly.

"Grange Farm Road. Quickly please," screamed Charlotte.

"What has happened?" repeated the woman on the other end of the line.

Charlotte sobbed.

"Madam? Madam?" urged the voice.

Charlotte hung up. She panicked. She pushed her way out of the telephone box and ran along the road, scrambling through a hedge into a field.

* * *

Dave was nearly home. He glanced at his watch. He was later than he'd planned to be. He had already dropped Travis home and was now toying over his excuse for the delay. He would tell Lucy that they had got caught up in traffic. He hoped that she wouldn't be angry with him.

He pulled into the driveway. His initial surprise, at the absence of his wife's car, disappeared as he noticed it parked, unusually, at the side of the building. She didn't normally leave it there; he'd have to park around the back. He parked up, climbed out of the van, and walked into his home.

"We got caught up in traffic," he lied. "Had a bit of a near miss coming up the road too, almost hit a girl who ran across the road."

"How terrible," said Lucy.

She kissed him then sat down on the settee. Dave sensed that something was wrong.

"I know I'm late. I'll make it up to you," he reassured.

"It's not you, Dave," said Lucy. "I went to see Jane today. I wanted to sort things out. All this bickering, it's been going on too long. I just wanted to make up with her."

Dave sat down beside his wife.

"What happened?" he prompted.

"She was so nasty, Dave. I felt really frightened. Look."

She turned her face to the side.

"She hit me."

The bruise on Lucy's face looked painful.

"This is the last straw," he fumed. "I'll go 'round and see her straight away. I'm not letting anyone do that to my wife."

Lucy was reluctant for him to go, but Dave insisted. He kissed her and stormed outside. He climbed into Lucy's car. He was in a hurry. It would have taken too long to get the van out again, and Lucy's car was much more convenient. He drove away, the screech of the wheels across the gravel seemingly endorsing the urgency of his departure. He looked down at the passenger seat; the leaves and specks of pollen puzzled him.

* * *

Charlotte wandered aimlessly along the country lanes. She was hardly aware of where she was heading. Her mind was too busy reliving the horrors of the last hour. Rows of crops stretched out in the fields around her, and small birds sang in the hedgerow. The calmness did little to reassure her and instead seemed to accentuate her thoughts.

She realised now, the gravity of what she had done. She was

frightened. She had never meant to kill the girl. It had been horrible. She had felt possessed. Her jealousy had taken control of her mind and body. What was happening to her? Was she mentally ill? She'd read about voices taking over people's thoughts. That's what had happened to her. The voice had admittedly gone from her head once she had left Anthony's house, but it had been so real back there. It was as if she'd had another person in her head. She felt so confused. She wanted somebody to talk to. She wanted somebody to help her, but who could she turn to? She was alone. Who would want to know her now? It would only be a matter of time before she was caught. What would happen to her? She thought about prison. She thought about hospitals for the mentally ill. She had ruined her life in that short space of time. How had it happened? She had never meant to hurt the girl. What had come over her? She was so frightened.

She arrived in Willsby. The familiarity of the streets did little to reassure her. The town was busy. People walked past her, unaware and unsuspecting. Their indifference disturbed her. She was scared and confused. Her terrible secret haunted her.

Her mouth was dry. She spotted a refrigerated cabinet of canned drinks, just inside a shop door. She stepped inside, picked up a tin, and ran. She expected someone to notice. She expected someone to shout. She expected someone to run after her. She wanted to be caught. But there was nothing. Nobody had even noticed.

She began to cry again as she ran. She ran down the Willsby High Street and along the Esplanade to her flat.

As she stood at the door to the building, she noticed a discarded bouquet of flowers. She stared at them. They somehow seemed to encompass her own feelings of abandonment. She picked them up.

She wondered who they had been for, and why they had been left there, as she carried them into the building.

Charlotte knew what she wanted to do now. Her mind was made up. She arranged the flowers in a vase and placed them on the mantelpiece, next to the picture of Anthony. She sat on the edge of her bed staring at them. They helped her to focus her thoughts. There was only one thing she could do now, wasn't there?

She stood beside her bed, holding the knife tightly in her hands with some of that strength and determination which she had earlier felt. This time the voice was silent. She didn't need any encouragement though. She took a deep breath and, holding the weapon firmly in front of her, lunged forward. As the knife penetrated, relief spread through her body, and she was finally at peace.

Chapter Ten

It was April 1984 and the first meeting of the new speedway season. Anthony had been keen to secure a permanent place in the Willsby team, and tonight he had been given the opportunity to show what he was capable of.

The sun was setting in the crisp, evening sky as he left the changing rooms and walked across the track's central green towards the pits. The crowd was gathering in clusters around the track. As Anthony entered the pits, a small boy ran over to him thrusting a pen and autograph book towards his hands. The boy looked up expectantly. Anthony added his signature to the haphazard collection of scribbles already adorning the page. He looked at the names; they were all riders from teams across the country. He had earned his place on that page, and he wanted to prove tonight that he deserved to keep it.

Anthony made his way to the rear of the pits where his brother, Terry, knelt beside the bike. He looked up at Anthony.

"Bike's going great, Ant."

The comment had done little to settle Anthony's nerves. He sat on the makeshift bench that ran the length of the pits. He watched Terry.

Terry was eight years his senior but didn't look as old as his years would suggest. He had a classically handsome look about him: the clichéd, sculptured look of a romantic fiction character sprung to mind. His rich, brown hair was thick and cut neatly. Although, like Anthony, he had dark eyes, his somehow seemed more trustworthy, being a shade of warm chestnut as opposed to the rather piercing darkness of Anthony's almost black eyes.

Terry stood up and walked towards the rear of the pits to retrieve a fuel can. As he lifted the can, Anthony noticed that Terry's wedding ring was missing from his finger. The observation annoyed Anthony, but he wasn't surprised. Despite having a charming and attractive wife, Terry liked to play the field and had been seeing a young art student from the local college for a couple of months now. Anthony felt uncomfortable knowing about the affair and resented being sucked into the deceit against his sister-in-law. He was beginning to regret his brother's involvement in his racing too. Terry had offered to become his mechanic, and there was no doubting his ability in that field, but Anthony had been reluctant. They weren't very close and had never developed any sense of brotherly camaraderie. Terry had a compelling, charismatic character that strangers somehow seemed to warm towards. For Anthony though, his brother's blandishments did not impress. Terry rarely did anything out of the goodness of his heart; there was usually some hidden agenda behind his charitable deeds. Anthony had resisted his brother's offers of help in the past, but now that he had gained that long-awaited Willsby team place, he needed a good mechanic. Terry was available and, despite his unreliability, he knew the workings of a speedway bike inside out. Anthony, however, was concerned that an unspoken debt was slowly accruing, and one day he would be expected to pay it back. It worried him.

His thoughts were finally interrupted by the Willsby team manager. "Anthony"

Anthony looked up. The man gestured frantically to the front of the pits.

"Parade."

Anthony looked out onto the track. The other team members were climbing into the back of a pickup truck for the pre-meeting parade in front of the crowd. Anthony hurried across to join them. The manager smiled, slapping his new rider on the back as he climbed into the truck. The smile, however, was almost intimidating as it crept across that staid face.

Anthony knew that he had to impress tonight. He felt nervous, almost like an impostor, as he stood in the back of that truck. He had to prove his worthiness of the team place, and tonight was the only chance he would have to do it.

The truck progressed slowly around the track. The atmosphere in the stadium surprised Anthony. The crowd was small, but their enthusiasm was obvious. The team captain was perched beside him; he waved dutifully, almost robotically, to the spectators, hardly daunted by that sea of faces as he spoke.

"Keep your mind on the job and you'll be fine," he said, obviously sensing Anthony's apprehension.

Anthony smiled as he gave an uneasy wave to the spectators. He'd never really thought that much about them before. He just enjoyed racing. The fact that people might want to pay to watch him seemed quite bizarre really.

The truck returned to the pits, and Anthony returned to his brother. He checked the race card that he'd hung open on the pit wall behind his bike. He was confident that he could do well in his first race. He had ridden against his teammate and one of his opponents before, and he was unintimidated by the competition. His remaining opponent was more of a mystery, a useful rider by all accounts. Anthony knew that the team manager would be satisfied with his scoring a point from the outing, but he wanted to make an impressive start.

Terry wheeled the bike out onto the track. Anthony pulled on his helmet. His nerves twisted in his stomach as he followed his machine onto the shale. He climbed aboard and was pushed into motion.

As he accelerated down the back straight, his nerves ebbed. This was familiar territory. It was easy to concentrate, cocooned inside that helmet and behind those goggles, with the familiar feel of the shale track beneath him. The bike felt good too. Terry had done an excellent job.

As Anthony lined up at the starting gate, his earlier feelings of unease turned into determination. His adrenaline levels rose as rapidly as the tapes. Anthony launched himself into the first bend. The unknown opponent had made a good start and was leading the field. Anthony stuck close to his rear wheel. The bike hadn't let him down, and he managed to stay hugging second place for the full four laps. As he crossed the line, he lessened his grip. To be honest, he'd probably been holding onto the bike too tightly, he'd have to loosen up a bit for the next race. He was happy though with his performance. He'd not been outclassed and was encouraged by his ride.

Terry was waiting as he returned to the pits. Anthony pulled off his helmet. The manager smiled proudly, the menace in his earlier expression had disappeared. Anthony walked to the front of the pits to watch the next heat, as Terry started working on the bike, ready for his next race.

The Willsby team was doing well and had gained an early lead. Anthony felt optimistic as he prepared himself for heat seven. He had already beaten one of his opponents that evening, so his confidence was high. He rode well. He gained a respectable point for the team and had been impressed by the way that the bike handled. Terry had done an excellent job.

As the racing progressed, however, the opposing team members were becoming more accustomed to the track. The scores grew closer. Willsby's lead was slipping away, and there was a growing apprehension throughout the stadium. The team manager was growing agitated. His smile had disappeared again as he shouted aggressively at his two riders in heat ten. His face reddened, and his expression grew hostile, as he watched his hopes finish at the rear of the field. Anthony tried to ignore him, as he once again strapped on his helmet. He didn't need to be reminded just how important this next race was.

Anthony had been allocated the outside gate for the start of the race. It was his least favourite starting position and next to the opposing team's top rider. The task ahead was daunting. He knew that winning would be a big ask against such an experienced opponent.

The crowd had fallen silent. Anthony peered out from his goggles. The silent anticipation of the spectators unnerved him. They were worried. They wanted their team to win. To lose was unthinkable. Their team's top rider would do well, he always did. Their confidence in Anthony was, however, less optimistic. He sensed their anxiety as he made his way around the track to the starting position.

Anthony had been introduced to the sport of speedway as a child, and it had been his late father who had bought him his first bike. He'd been devastated by his father's death, and he had resolved to take up the sport in his memory. This past year, some of the club promoters had started showing an interest in him. The Willsby management had been keen to sign up the local lad before anyone else got their hands on him. There was a lot of competition between the younger riders, so it was difficult to secure a team place. Anthony had previously travelled with the team to a few of their away meetings, but it had not been until tonight that he had finally been given a permanent team place. This was the meeting that mattered, and this race was the race that mattered.

The daunting task was prominent in Anthony's mind as he lined up at the starting gate. He kicked the shale around and flattened a path in the dirt. The action was just as much down to his nervousness than to any real attempt to improve his gating.

Anthony tried to ignore the top-scoring man beside him as they lined up. As the tapes shot up, the four riders sped forward. Anthony noticed the higher standard at once as the other three riders shot ahead, beating him easily into the first bend. A bombardment of stinging grit flew from the race leaders' wheels. Anthony grappled to keep up with his opponents. His vision was impaired by the flying debris. He threw himself into each bend but just didn't seem to be able to keep up with the other racers. In a desperate attempt to make up some ground, he tried to take an outside line around the man in third position. In retrospect, it had been a rather foolish action. He hit an uneven patch on the dirt track as he ventured from the racing line.

Despite all his efforts, he lost control of the machine and slid to the ground. He skimmed across the track, into the fence.

As soon as he regained his orientation, he leapt to his feet, oblivious to his discomfort. He collected his bike and pushed it clear of the track, not wanting to cause the stoppage of the race while the other Willsby rider was in the lead. There was a trickle of applause for his gesture from the crowd.

From the centre green, he watched as his teammate maintained his lead. Anthony fidgeted nervously as he turned, watching the three riders encircling him. Willsby won the race. The points were shared. The sight of the chequered flag was a relief to Anthony. His mistake didn't seem to matter so much now as the crowd congratulated their winner, who made his way around the track on his victory lap.

Anthony returned to the pits, a numbness in his shoulder stabbed at him as he started to walk. The fall had hurt more than he had realised.

Terry was waiting for him.

"Hard luck, Ant," he said, slapping his younger brother on the back. Anthony winced: his back really did hurt from that fall.

* * *

Dave Chapman was pleased with his performance. Six points would, perhaps, have disappointed him in another meeting, but tonight the opposition had been tough. He was content that he had discharged his responsibility as a solid support behind his higher scoring teammate. He had certainly done enough to help his team to victory.

Mick, his mechanic, wheeled the bike to the van that was parked at the rear of the pits. Dave would, as usual, get changed, and then join Mick and his sister in the clubhouse for a quick drink before he headed home. He began his trek to the changing rooms. The stadium was emptying rapidly so he was surprised when he heard the voice call him.

"Dave."

It was a distinctively feminine voice. He looked up from beneath his baseball cap, trying to recognise the face of the woman calling and, failing to do so, looked to the ground as he approached her.

"Sorry to bother you, Dave. I know you must be exhausted, but I was wondering if I could ask you a favour?"

Dave looked to her hands, expecting to see a pen for the autograph. There was none. Her small fingers peered over the edge of the fence. He looked up enthusiastically.

"Yeah, sure. What?"

She wasn't unattractive. She must have been in her mid-thirties. Without the vantage of this closeness, however, he would have thought her much younger. Her small, well-shaped body and long, brown hair, coupled with her youthful dress sense, befitted a much younger woman. He looked at her inquisitively.

"I'm writing a book and could do with some technical advice," she explained.

Dave was taken aback.

"You're writing a book about speedway?"

He was intrigued. He'd never been that good at school, and the idea that somebody could actually write a book impressed him.

The woman's reply, however, sounded somewhat noncommittal.

169

"Sort of."

Dave was confused but strangely curious. His mental disorientation led the woman to believe, incorrectly, that he was reluctant to help her. She interrupted his bemusement sternly but despondently.

"I'd understand if you didn't want to. I'll have to ask someone else."

The doubt perturbed him. He answered immediately and firmly in defence.

"No. I'd love to. What do you need to know?"

The woman seemed reluctant to explain further.

"It's a bit in-depth, and I'm sure you've got better things to do right now. Could we meet somewhere tomorrow?" she asked.

Dave was unsure. Meet her? It was one thing spending five minutes talking to a fan at the trackside, but to arrange to meet the woman was an entirely different matter. He was looking forward to his day off. Why would he want to give it up for a stranger? He didn't know what to say and was just about to decline when she spoke.

"Do you live local?"

Dave's thoughts had been distracted by the question. He nodded impulsively.

The woman continued instantly, suggesting that they meet at The Druids. Dave knew the pub well. It was one of his favourites in town. The woman looked up at him hopefully.

"Shall we say about four?"

"Er," said Dave in his confusion.

"Great. Thanks. This is so helpful. See you tomorrow then," she muttered as she turned away.

Dave watched her leave. Her shapely legs carried her effortlessly up the sloping embankment that led from the track edge. He turned away and continued his walk to the changing rooms, already wondering what he had just agreed to, and why.

* * *

By the time that Anthony had changed from his racing leathers, after that first speedway meeting of the season, Terry was already in the clubhouse. Anthony, anxious for some help to load his machinery onto his car's trailer, was looking for his brother. He peered into the room and instantly spotted Terry who was sat by the bar, a glass in one hand and a lit cigarette in the other. He was chatting enthusiastically with the regulars. Terry noticed his brother and beckoned him towards his circle of friends.

"You haven't met my brother, have you?" he said loudly, putting his arm around Anthony's shoulders and enthusiastically reeling off a series of names as he pointed to each of his companions in turn. Anthony's back still hurt from his earlier fall. The drunken weight of his brother pressing on his shoulders wasn't helping.

"Can you give me a hand with the gear?" asked Anthony.

"In a bit. Have a drink first."

Terry waved his money above the bar, trying to attract the barmaid's attention.

"No thanks, Terry. I just need a hand," pressed Anthony.

It had been a mistake. Terry wasn't going to leave the clubhouse to help, was he? He was being his usual pig-headed self as he banged his fist on the bar.

"Can I get some service in here?" he shouted sarcastically at the flustered woman.

"Don't bother," snapped Anthony as he turned and walked away from the group of men.

Anthony heard his brother mutter something to his friends, and the echo of laughter which followed. He left the clubhouse.

Terry would never change, would he? Thank goodness there were still a few people in the pits to help Anthony load his bikes into his trailer. Terry could find his own way home tonight. Anthony wasn't going to wait around for him. He slammed the car door shut in his determination and drove home.

* * *

Lucy watched the young reserve rider drive recklessly out of the stadium, keeping a safe distance behind him. She turned on the radio. The rhythmic beat of the music cascaded into the dark car. She caught a glimpse of her face in the shadowed rear-view mirror, her cool smile welcomed her. She was confident that Dave would be suitably intrigued to meet her the following day.

She recalled him stood in front of her at the trackside earlier. His bright leathers encasing him in an aura of acclaim, distinguishing him from the ordinary. She recalled the trusting smile of his young, well-shaped lips. She smiled as she pictured his hair, lightened by the naivety of youthful peroxide experimentation. He was exactly as he had been described to her, and even better, he was actually quite cute.

* * *

Anthony's driving was erratic. He was angry, not just with Terry but also with himself. He had been so stupid to put his trust in his errant brother. There was, however, more to Anthony's dislike of his brother than a mere clash of personalities.

Terry was, in fact, his half-brother. They hadn't even met until Anthony was in his early teens. It had been five days after his thirteenth birthday when his father had died. It was an awkward age for any child to lose a parent, consequently Terry's appearance, just a few months beforehand, could not have been timed worse.

Terry was his father's son from a previous relationship. The ex-girlfriend had moved away after their separation, apparently pregnant with young Terrance at the time. She'd had some problems and hadn't been able to look after the young child. Terry had been adopted. He'd never managed to trace his birth mother, but his father had been another matter. Anthony's father had either been unaware of Terry or had spent thirteen years hiding his secret from his youngest son and new wife. It seems that he felt guilty, and somehow in that guilt had written a will making Terry the main beneficiary. He'd bequeathed to Terry a large sum of money and his successful delivery business. He couldn't have known he would shortly die, could he? He was, after all, a healthy man; the heart attack had come as a shock to everyone. Who knows, perhaps if he had lived longer, he may have had time to rethink and change the will? Anthony was sure that if his father had got to know the real Terry, he wouldn't have been quite so generous.

Their father had left a final wish that his wife and the two brothers looked after one another. That was hard. Anthony despised his new brother and had expected his mother to react the same. She didn't. Terry was charming, she trusted him, she felt sorry for him, and perhaps he even reminded her a little of her late husband? Terry had moved in with them, taking advantage of the grieving widow's kindness, and using his newfound wealth to treat the woman with gifts that bought her admiration and respect. Anthony had resented him from the start, and Terry had done nothing to change that since their first meeting.

Anthony arrived home and pulled into his driveway. The car's engine seemed to sigh as he turned the key in the ignition, perhaps relieved to be home safely after the rather erratic drive from the stadium? He walked to the front door, turned the key in the lock, and entered his house.

Anthony was proud of his home. It was one of only two semi-detached cottages, set back from the road in a secluded cutting among the trees. Approaching from the road, the only visible windows on the house were long, ranch-like ones that ran horizontally, just above head height. The front door was the only clue to the first-time visitor, that the building was actually a domestic residence. He'd liked the fact that it was unusual, and the huge workshop in the back garden was the deal clincher. He'd bought the house by raising a down payment from his share of his late father's money. A much smaller share than that left to Terry, of course.

As he entered the hallway, Anthony switched on the electric light and pushed open the kitchen door. The kitchen crouched in the borrowed illumination until, with a flick of a further switch, it lit up, stretching out ahead of him. He walked into the room, slinging his keys onto the table as he went. He filled the kettle and switched it on before returning to the hallway.

He entered the lounge and closed the heavy curtains. It was the largest room in the house, and Anthony kept it mainly for entertaining guests. For his personal use, he spent most of his time in the huge bedroom at the rear of the property, which he had made into a cosy bedsitting room.

The kettle clicked off automatically as Anthony returned to the kitchen. He made himself a mug of coffee and carried it through to the hallway.

He peered around the door of the spare bedroom, situated at the front of the house, across from the kitchen. It was Anthony's least favourite room in the house. Perhaps it was the lack of natural light in there that made him dislike it so much; the only windows being the characteristic, ranch-style ones at head height. He'd never felt comfortable in there. It seemed to have an uncanny stillness to it. He'd always wondered if perhaps something unpleasant had happened in there. But that was silly, wasn't it? He closed the door, dismissing the thought, and walked up the long hallway, past the bathroom, and into the main bedroom.

Placing his mug on a table next to the bed, he looked out into the darkness. The full-length windows looked out across the garden to his workshop. Anthony shut out the darkness behind the curtains and sat on the leather sofa, flicking on the remote control of the television as he did so. He would drink his coffee and then go out to the workshop to begin the task of stripping down his bikes.

Chapter Eleven

What am I doing? thought Dave as he looked at his reflection in the bathroom mirror. His hair was a mess, its bleached curls hung untidily over his forehead. His last girlfriend, a hairdresser, had dyed it for him. It had looked good at first, but now, without her attention, it stayed permanently in an unkempt state. He pulled on his customary baseball cap, hiding any need to worry about the predicament, and walked to his van.

He had initially been hesitant about meeting the woman in The Druids. He wasn't even quite sure how he had come to agree to it. The whole idea seemed so ludicrous. By Saturday morning, he had resolved not to go, but as the day progressed, he had become less convinced of that decision. He recalled the woman's face; she'd clearly been pleased that he had agreed to meet her. Although she wasn't really his type, she wasn't unattractive and was rather charismatic. Perhaps a bit more sophisticated than the normal type of woman he'd go for, but he liked a challenge. She was relying on him, and he was, after all, rather curious about the book that she was writing. He quite liked the idea of having a biography written about him. The more his thoughts dwelt on the subject, the more convinced he had become of his duty to meet her.

* * *

The relationship between Anthony and his brother had always been strained. Despite Anthony's fears though, Terry was doing an excellent job in preparing the bikes. The prevalent problem, however, was Mandy.

Mandy was an art student at the local college. She had met Terry in The Druids, Terry's favourite public house. She was a plump, short girl whose wardrobe seemed limited to a selection of black or purple outfits. Her face was always densely made up in rebellious colours. Her long, dyed black hair was backcombed and held in place by gallons of environmentally-friendly hairspray. Mandy was a typical student. She was determined and confident, knowing, or at least thinking that she knew, exactly what she wanted out of life. She claimed to be a nonconformist yet, ironically, she was simply following the lead of her peers by rebelling and dressing the way that she did. Terry seemed attracted to her strong character, not to mention her ample bosom, which seemed to make an appearance whichever purple or black outfit she chose. What she saw in Terry, who was over ten years her senior, was more of a mystery to Anthony. Maybe it had something to do with his charisma, or simply his flash car and frivolous love of spending his inheritance.

* * *

By the time that Dave climbed from his van, outside of The

Druids, he was feeling guilty that he had ever doubted coming. He walked into the pub and instantly noticed Lucy sat at a table in the corner of the room.

"I was worried that you weren't coming," she said, smiling as he approached her.

"Got caught up in traffic."

Lucy realised that he was lying but found his obvious guilt amusing.

"Can I get you a drink?" he offered.

Lucy knew that Dave had seen the glass in front of her, and that he would assume she didn't want another drink. She waited until he was about to walk away before answering:

"Yes, thanks. I'll have a double Courvoisier. No ice, of course."

Dave seemed to smile apologetically.

Lucy watched in amusement as he ordered the drinks, recalling her earlier attempts to rile the barman. Apart from a swift, contemptuous frown from the man, the whole episode passed without incident. She was disappointed. The barman hadn't bitten. That was a pity; she'd enjoyed winding him up.

When Dave returned, Lucy noticed his awkwardness.

"That barman was a bit rude," he said as he pulled out the stool from under the table.

She smiled. Perhaps the barman had been riled after all?

"I'm glad you say that. I thought the same but wondered if I was just being a bit oversensitive," said Lucy convincingly.

Dave shook his head.

Lucy took her notebook and pen from her bag. Her keyring on the bag's zip jangled. It had 'Lucy' written on it in large, black letters.

She placed the bag, with the key ring strategically visible, on the table as she spoke. Hopefully, that would help Dave remember her name.

"Can we make a start on the questions then, Dave? I don't have all that much time."

She had known that he would have second thoughts about meeting her, but she had been certain his curiosity would win through. Now that he was here, she was confident that she could sufficiently captivate him.

Lucy noticed that he was staring at her. She'd heard that Dave was a sucker for a woman with a good pair of legs, and she had deliberately chosen the suit because the skirt was cut high. She had well-shaped legs; they were her strongest *physical* feature. She crossed them flirtatiously, feeling the hemline creeping up her thigh in unison with her companion's eyes. She smiled to herself as she watched his pathetic attempts to disguise his interest. He caught her gaze. She eyed him in a teasing reprimand and then spoke sternly.

"Right, if you're ready, I need a bit of information."

The questions were all carefully thought out. She could find out whether he still had his money, and how she should behave to be different from his past girlfriends. She would be able to find out everything she needed to know, without him suspecting a thing.

As they talked, Lucy sensed that his interest was growing in her, and once certain that his fascination was sufficient, she stood up.

"Thank you, Dave. That's about all I need for now."

She smiled at him.

"I've got to get off now. I'll see you around," she said as she walked away.

The action had surprised Dave, as expected. Lucy could sense that he didn't want her to leave. Everything was going perfectly to plan. She walked to the door and quickly hurried outside, hiding around the corner until she saw that Dave had left without noticing her.

As she drove home, Lucy thought about Dave. He would be feeling guilty, no doubt sifting through his mind, trying to pinpoint what he had said to make her leave so suddenly. She laughed aloud as the thoughts spun in her head.

* * *

Anthony was finding it increasingly difficult to ignore the developing intimacy between his brother and Mandy. He was fond of his sister-in-law, Maria, and felt awkward in this situation. Anthony had been friends with Maria at college. They had spent a lot of time together working on college assignments, and it had been on one such occasion that she had first met Terry.

Terry had been captivated by her. His charlatanic charisma had gone into overdrive. Anthony had been embarrassed. He felt sure that Maria would not succumb to it and felt ashamed of Terry's behaviour. Anthony had been very wrong; Maria and Terry were married within a matter of months. Anthony could not understand what had come over her, and although she had not confided in him since her marriage, he sensed that she now realised it had all been a mistake.

Anthony walked from the changing rooms towards the pits. Travis Fengar was at his side. His colleague's American accent was droning on, something about curry, but Anthony wasn't listening.

As he approached the pits, Anthony noticed that Terry was talking to a young girl. She was a pretty thing, and he recalled how he had felt flattered the week before when he had caught her looking at him. Anthony felt a little jealous as he watched Terry joking with her.

* * *

Lucy had noticed Dave leave the changing rooms and had walked to the trackside, where she began reading her programme. Dave spotted her and called out her name. The key ring ploy had obviously worked. Lucy feigned surprise as she looked up.

"Hi. How's the book going?" he asked enthusiastically.

"Fine," she answered.

She was pleased with her response, it had sounded complacent, even more so than she had intended.

"Was I any help to you?" he asked, obviously seeking reassurance.

Lucy kept her answer simple.

"Yes. Thank you."

Lucy allowed a silence to creep between them.

"I was sorry you had to leave so quickly on Saturday," continued Dave. "Perhaps I could buy you a drink in the bar later, to make amends?"

Lucy continued with her performance.

"Perhaps, I'll see what happens."

Dave looked worried. Lucy sensed that she had teased him enough. His mechanic called out from the pits.

"I think you're wanted," she said, bringing a renewed touch of enthusiasm to her voice. "You'd better go."

Dave nodded.

"I'll see you later, in the bar. If your offer still stands?" she continued reassuringly.

She smiled, and Dave seemed happier.

"Of course. See you later then," he enthused as he headed off to join his mechanic.

* * *

His friend, Simon, had said that he might come to the meeting, so Anthony was not surprised to notice him in the crowd. He waited for a convenient break in his races and then left the pits to walk over to see him.

As Anthony made his way through the crowd, he noticed the girl that Terry had been talking to earlier. He smiled as he passed her, noticing that she was with Graham.

All the riders knew Graham. He came every week and loved to heckle and jeer the team in jest. He was quite a handful but entertaining, and essentially it was all harmless banter. In fact, he was always keen to buy drinks for the riders and track crew after the meeting, and he'd arranged a collection last year for an injured rider, so he was a good egg at heart.

Anthony reached his friend, who stood in the crowd a little way behind the girl and Graham. Simon had been impressed by his friend's performance and was keen to take a closer look at his bike. Anthony was equally enthusiastic to show it off, so they left, making their way to the pits. Anthony was surprised to find that Graham was alone as he passed. He wondered where the girl had gone. Perhaps she'd got fed up with listening to Graham's laugh? And who could really blame her for that?

Lucy had walked around to the clubhouse. She knew that it was club members only until after the meeting had finished, but she was convinced that she would be able to sweet-talk the doorman. She pushed open the door as the blue-suited attendant looked at her. She recognised him instantly as Peter, and she was relieved that the look on his face did not confirm his mutual recognition. She had seen him several times in the past and certainly did not want him to remember their previous encounters. She continued, unperturbed, with her plan. Peter obediently asked her for her pass. She coolly feigned uncertainty, mentioning Dave's name, and motioning her intention to leave. He took the bait, obviously unable to keep up with the tide of women linked to Dave Chapman. He made his apologies and urged her in. Lucy walked up the stairs to the bar.

It was good to be back again. The barmaids were different, but she did recognise a few of the sponsors and a couple of the riders' wives and girlfriends. As she walked past the group of women, Mrs McCray glanced up at her. It was obvious that she had recognised her too, although she said nothing. That was only to be expected really, given the circumstances of their last meeting.

Dave had changed from his racing leathers quickly. He wanted to catch the woman in the clubhouse. The doorman smiled at him as he walked in.

"Your lady friend's already here, Dave," he smirked.

Dave smiled. He wasn't sure he liked the man's assumption, but he felt relieved that Lucy had kept her promise to meet him.

He entered the room. His mechanic, Mick, and Mick's sister, Jane, were sat at the bar. He nodded, acknowledging them, before looking around for Lucy.

She sat alone on the balcony and had obviously not noticed him arrive. He walked over.

"I thought you'd gone home," he said, interrupting her concentration.

She gestured for him to join her.

"I've been watching the junior riders. They make it seem so difficult," she said as Dave sat down at the table.

"It is difficult," laughed Dave.

Lucy smiled at him coyly. The dim light from the bar caught his face. Lucy had been aware that all the young fans loved Dave. His photograph had sold more copies in the souvenir kiosk than any other rider; well, at least until Travis Fengar had joined the team, of course. She also knew that he had been seeing a rather good looking, although not exceptionally bright, hairdresser until very recently. As she stared at him, she thought how his naïve popularity would make things easier. His wide smile began to drop as the silence between them lengthened, his small, pointed incisors retreating behind his lips again.

"I was really impressed by your racing. Another maximum, wasn't it?" Lucy asked.

Dave did not have the chance to answer, before they were interrupted by Mick, Jane, and Travis.

"Who's your friend?" asked Jane, enthusiastically.

"This is Lucy," said Dave proudly. "I'm helping her with a book she's writing."

He turned to Lucy.

"This is Travis from the team, my mechanic, Mick and his sister, Jane."

Jane and Mick sat down as Travis pulled Dave to one side. Travis Fengar was the latest addition to the team, and he had taken a liking to Dave.

"We showed them out there tonight, didn't we? Kicked their asses," said Travis, his American accent almost squealing in delight. "I reckon you and me are going to make a great pairing. You're almost as crazy as me."

Dave smiled, taking the comment as a compliment. He was anxious to speak to Lucy, but his companion was reluctant to stop talking. Dave was therefore relieved by Lucy's cheeky interruption a few minutes later.

"What do you think could be so important that they can't include us in their conversation?"

Travis had heard the mocking question, and Dave was surprised by his calm response.

"Well, I think we've got a jealous little lady here, Davy."

Travis smiled knowingly at Lucy.

As the evening progressed, Lucy was growing concerned by the suspicious stares and comments that were coming from Jane. She decided that it may be a clever idea to make her exit.

"Dave, I really think that I should be going."

"Okay," said Dave, ending his conversation with Travis abruptly.

Lucy stood up. Dave followed obediently.

"It's been nice meeting you," said Mick as they left.

Jane was silent.

Lucy followed Dave out of the room, down the stairs, to the car park outside.

"Can I give you a lift home?"

Dave was drunk with panic as he asked the question. The light from the clubhouse crept across her face.

"I've got my car. Thanks anyway."

The answer unnerved him. He panicked.

"Will you be coming here next week?"

There was an uneasy silence as she pondered the question.

"Maybe."

Lucy was teasing her companion. She knew that he had been captivated by her calculated coolness. She feigned surprise as he grabbed her arm, reprimanding him for his impulsive and abrupt action. She noticed him flinch slightly, then slowly crept her hands gently up his arms. She stared at him and smiled as her fingers reached his shoulders, urging him to kiss her. He obliged.

"I really ought to be going," she whispered as she finally pulled away.

She was not surprised by the desperation he showed.

"Can I see you in the week? I'm racing on Wednesday. Would you like to come along?"

She played on his presumption by pausing before answering.

"I'd love to," she finally confirmed.

She slipped the pre-prepared scrap of paper holding her telephone number into his hand.

"I really must go now. I'll see you on Wednesday. Ring me," she said as she walked away to her awaiting car.

* * *

Anthony felt encouraged by the events of the evening. He'd had some excellent races and had ridden better than anyone would have expected. The team manager had obviously been delighted by the performance. Anthony felt confident and decided to join his brother in the clubhouse after the meeting. He changed from his racing leathers then made his way to the bar.

As he entered the smoke-filled room, he instantly spotted Terry sat on a stool at the bar. He was talking to a group of men. Anthony recognised very few of his brother's friends, but they, of course, all knew him. As soon as they noticed him arrive, they welcomed him enthusiastically, making room for him on a barstool beside Terry. There were endless questions for Anthony and a seemingly endless supply of drink offers. Anthony felt a little bewildered by all the attention and was quite relieved when Terry's friends began to leave.

Anthony relaxed a little once the crowd had left. Terry, having stocked up on drinks as last orders were being taken, still sat at the bar, its shutters now pulled down. The barmaids were collecting glasses and stacking the empty stools, loudly clattering them around, hinting at their impatience to close the clubhouse. A few hardened drinkers remained. Terry, one of them, sat defiantly at his seat, intent on finishing his drink. Anthony took the opportunity to ask his brother about the girl who had been with Graham. Apparently, he had been mistaken; Terry hardly knew her.

"Charlie? She's just a bird from the crowd, but she's got the hots for me," he joked crudely.

"She's friends with the troll, isn't she?" said Anthony.

Terry laughed coarsely, spitting out trails of cigarette smoke. There was no need for an explanation, he knew exactly who Anthony was referring to.

"No. She used to come here with her dad a few years back. She knows Graham from then. She's really embarrassed by him. Did you see him tonight?"

Terry launched into a long tale, explaining how Graham had taken a dislike to one of the opposing team's riders.

"I can't imagine what he'd done wrong, but when he got back to the pits, Graham ambushed him. He was swearing at him, hurling abuse. He chucked his plastic drinks cup at the poor sod, then, wait for it, his bobble hat."

Terry motioned the throwing action whilst imitating Graham's distinctive laugh. The impersonation was quite convincing.

"Poor guy didn't know what was happening, not knowing Graham like. He was shielding himself with his arms as he scampered to safety. We were all creasing up watching."

Terry was laughing loudly as he recited the story. The barmaid was growing impatient and turned off the main lights in the room.

"Come on now lads, haven't you got homes to go to?"

Terry leant over the bar, peering through the meshed shutter.

"You offering to take me back to yours?"

The woman turned away.

"You should be so lucky," she teased as she walked away, her flabby buttocks swaying beneath her miniskirt, and her stiletto heels clicking on the wooden floor.

Terry was offended by the rebuff and shouted after the woman.

"Stuck up tart."

"Come on Terry," urged Anthony quietly.

Terry stubbornly finished his drink before following his brother into the refreshing evening air.

Chapter Twelve

The doorbell rang. It was just after eight on Tuesday evening. Lucy was in two minds as to whether she should answer the door; she suspected that it may be her landlord. He normally called on a Friday evening, but she was two months in arrears with her rent, so perhaps he was making an impromptu call tonight instead? Lucy was worried. She had little chance of being able to pay, but she couldn't risk being evicted.

The doorbell rang again. Was it him? If it was, she would simply ignore it. There was another possibility though, wasn't there? It could have been Dave Chapman. It was not, after all, unfeasible that he may have followed her home after their last meeting, and he was now paying her a personal visit. If it was Dave, impatiently ringing that bell, it was important for her plan that she seized the opportunity to see him. She walked down the stairs and opened the heavy front door.

Her heart sank.

The landlord stood there menacingly, with a huge dog sitting obediently at his side.

"Ah, you are in", said the man.

Lucy looked at him timidly, letting him enjoy his moment of power. He opened a grubby little book with his stubby fingers.

"You're two months in arrears, Love, aren't you?" he said as he ran his forefinger down the column of numbers.

Lucy looked at his bowed head. There was a cluster of small scars on his bald patch. Intriguing. Perhaps they were the result of an unsuccessful hair transplant? She'd never seen anything quite like it before.

He looked up at her when she failed to respond to his last comment. Lucy quickly averted her eyes.

"I said, I need two months' rent," he reiterated firmly.

The dog noticed the change in tone of his master's voice, cocking his head as if to confirm the statement.

"I didn't realise it was that much. I'm so very sorry. I'm just having a bit of a cash flow problem at the moment," said Lucy apologetically.

"We're all having trouble, Love, but I'm not a charity. I've got bills to pay too, you know," said the man.

Lucy was surprised by his lack of compassion. Perhaps the hair transplant clinic was chasing for its money? She realised that she'd have to change tactics. She took a handkerchief from her pocket and wiped her eye. It worked.

"Look, Love, I'll give you until next month, but that's it."

"Thank you so much," gasped Lucy. "I will have it, I promise."

The landlord almost felt sorry for her as he turned away. He pulled on the lead in his hand, and the dog followed.

As Lucy walked up the stairs back to her flat, the telephone began to ring. This time she was right. It was Dave ringing to arrange their trip the following day.

* * *

Anthony leant back as he crouched in front of the bike and admired his work. The gleaming metal was a just reward for the effort that he had put into his preparation of the machine.

"So, how are you getting on with the racing?"

His friend Simon seemed genuinely interested as he walked into the workshop with two mugs of coffee.

"It's going okay," said Anthony, taking a sip of his drink. "Just hope I can keep the team place now."

"No reason why you shouldn't, Mate. You just need a bit more racing experience and you'll be a permanent fixture at Willsby. Fame eh? Won't be long now, and you'll have all the girls after you."

Anthony grinned. Simon realised that he had hit upon a nerve with his friend.

"Don't tell me they've started already?" smiled Simon.

"Well, funny you should say that," said Anthony. "There is this one girl who seems a bit keen on me."

* * *

Although Lucy had been to the Yorkshire stadium before, she certainly didn't recognise the man at the gate. He, however, had recognised her. It was quite worrying. It had been clear from his expression that he wasn't pleased to see her again, but she just couldn't place him. It was surprising, as he had a distinct face with a bulbous nose and blotchy cheeks. Surely, she wouldn't have forgotten such features? Whoever he was, he had obviously known something about her, so she decided to steer clear. She had watched the racing from beside the track, instead of going to the hospitality suite, for fear of bumping into him again.

It was bloody cold down there. She would much have preferred the warmth of the box: but needs must. She hated being sprayed with grit from the bikes' back wheels every time they passed. How the riders managed to race under that bombardment amazed her; it was bad enough in the crowd, let alone on the track.

It had indeed been a pretty dismal day in all. What with that long journey in the uncomfortable van and Dave going on and on about his music collection. She had to feign her enjoyment of course, but did they really have to listen to that same Thompson Twins album three times on the journey? Dave had really believed that she loved it as much as he did.

It had been a welcome relief when Travis announced after the meeting, that it was back to his for a party. By 'his', of course, he meant the hotel. They were now sitting in the smoke-filled lounge bar.

The evening was turning out to be good fun. Dave had been quite amusing as he tried, albeit unsuccessfully, to keep pace with his new American friend. Travis was a party connoisseur, and it was clear that Dave just didn't have the stamina to match him. He had now fallen asleep on Travis's hotel bed and Mick suggested that they should take him up to his own room.

Mick had taken most of Dave's weight as Lucy helped to manoeuvre him along the hotel corridor. Mick, too, had had a bit too much to drink and was staggering awkwardly with Dave slumped on his shoulder. They reached the door, and Lucy fumbled with the key. Mick seemed relieved as he lowered his friend onto the bed. Lucy shut the door and turned on the bedside lamp. She sat on the bed and removed Dave's boots. He flinched as she moved him but then coiled into the duvet contentedly.

Mick watched it all through his inebriated eyes. Lucy was looking a little ruffled but extremely attractive. He was a little bit older than Dave and much nearer to Lucy's age than his companion. She stood up and walked over to him.

"Thank you, Mick," she said, her red lips as perfect as when they'd first picked her up earlier in the day.

Her almond eyes were fixed on his, and she had a coy smile on her lips.

"What would I have done without you?" she said in a whisper.

She was standing directly in front of him. In a more sober state, he would have taken a step back. Tonight though, he just didn't have the energy, and to be honest, the closeness was rather nice. As she stood there, Mick could almost taste the brandy aroma on her breath. He knew that he should turn away and leave, but something was keeping him rooted to the spot. He felt an enormous surge of guilt as he reached out a hand and ran his fingertips across her bare shoulder.

"Anytime you need a hand," he said.

Lucy said nothing; she just closed her eyes. She lifted her mouth close to his and opened her red lips in an alluring gasp.

Two hours later and Mick was restless. The inebriation was wearing off and he was slipping in and out of a confused sleep. It was hot in his hotel room as he wriggled uncomfortably in the huge bed. His muddled thoughts plagued his mind. What had he done? He'd taken advantage of his best mate's girlfriend, and while Dave slept in the same room as well. That had been bad enough; but his guilt went even deeper. Lucy had been vulnerable, hadn't she? He had taken advantage of that fact and to make things worse, he'd actually enjoyed it. It was little short of barbaric. If Dave had any inclination of what had happened, he would be livid. He'd never forgive him, would he? And to be honest, Mick wasn't sure he'd even be able to forgive himself.

Mick wasn't feeling any better by the time that he'd arrived in the hotel foyer the next morning. He sat on one of the brown velour chairs, arranged regimentally around a glass-top coffee table, and waited. He pictured Dave, storming into the reception, lunging towards him in an uncontrollable frenzy, hands outstretched ready to throttle him. He pictured Lucy, probably crying, as her new boyfriend laid into his once best friend as the realisation dawned on her that she'd been dramatically let down by both of them. Mick looked across to the receptionist. She sat relaxed, jadedly looking over her spectacles into the room, completely unaware of the events which could unfold shortly.

A bell sounded as the lift touched down on the ground floor. Mick's heart was pounding as the elevator doors opened. Mick's relief at seeing Travis was short-lived, as he realised his dilemma had merely been temporarily postponed.

Travis looked none the worse for his partying the night before. In fact, he had gained, at some point between midnight and dawn, a rather tasty-looking blonde who was hanging onto his arm like an oversized novelty shoulder bag. His smile was as wide as ever as he passed Mick.

"No Davy boy yet then?" beamed Travis.

"Not yet," replied Mick as he watched the American flashing his plastic payment card at the reception desk.

There appeared to be a problem. The receptionist tried to put the card through the reader. It didn't appear to be working. Travis took the card, rubbed it against his sleeve, and handed it back to the flustered woman. The problem persisted.

"Hey, Mick," shouted Travis, across the room. "Have you got any cash I could borrow? You Brits are stuck in the dark ages. This machine won't take my card."

"Why can't you just pay by cash like everyone else?" asked Mick as he looked in his wallet and walked over to the desk.

"I'm terribly sorry, Sir," apologised the receptionist. "We don't normally have a problem with these cards."

"You want to get that machine looked at, this is embarrassing you know Ma'am, having to beg from my friends," scorned Travis.

"How much is his bill?" sighed Mick.

He swallowed hard as the young lady reeled off the lengthy figure.

"That's just about cleaned me out, Travis," laughed Mick nervously as he handed the money across. "I don't earn that much in a month!"

"Cheers, Mick Buddy, I'll make sure you get it back," laughed Travis as the receptionist counted out the notes.

Mick wasn't joking. It really was more than he earned in a month. He slipped his empty wallet back into his pocket as he watched the American expressly exit through the automatic doors.

The bell of the lift sounded again. Mick had been distracted by the incident with Travis. Surely his day couldn't get any worse, could it? He really wasn't looking forward to seeing Dave and Lucy. What had she told him? Was he going to be throttled as well as having his wallet cleaned out? And all before breakfast too. He looked in the direction of the sound and instantly saw Dave and Lucy. Dave looked rough. His hair hung ruggedly over his forehead, looking rather like the yellow wool of a rag doll's hair. He seemed rather unsettled by the daylight that was pouring into the reception. Thankfully, he seemed far from capable of throttling anyone.

Lucy was dressed in the same black dress that she'd been wearing the night before. This morning, however, it extended to her knees and was hiding those long, tanned thighs. Lucy had an impish smile on her lips.

"Morning, Mick," she said.

Mick could just manage a smile. He looked desperately into her almond eyes for reassurance, but none was forthcoming.

"Dave's a little worse for wear," she said impassively.

Dave looked up pathetically from under his peroxide fringe.

"I know how he feels," said Mick, with a slight panic to his tone.

Lucy smiled knowingly but still not giving him the reassurance he so desperately wanted.

The journey home was quiet and awkward. Dave had fallen asleep and there was an unsettling déjà vu as Mick glanced across his sleeping friend to Lucy. He felt uncomfortable and wanted some sort of reassurance from her. Just how let down by him did she feel? Would she tell Dave what had happened between them the night before? Lucy's silence was unsettling.

"Thanks for keeping quiet," he said eventually, once his anxiety had reached breaking point.

She remained silent, staring doggedly ahead. There was a long pause before she spoke.

"Did you sleep well?" she asked nonchalantly.

It did nothing to ease Micks unease.

"No!" he exclaimed.

Mick's outburst had been instinctive and regretfully quite loud. He glanced into the back of the van. Thank goodness, Dave was still asleep, his head bobbing in time with the uneven road.

"No, I didn't sleep well," said Mick, this time in a whisper. "I kept thinking, you know, about what happened last night."

He glanced across to Dave again before continuing.

"Look, I'm sorry. I was out of order. I think I had one too many drinks last night. I didn't mean to…

"Me too," came a voice from the back of the van.

The vehicle swerved as Mick momentarily lost concentration.

"I think I must have had one too many last night as well," said Dave as his head appeared between the two front seats.

Lucy looked away, staring out of the window, and silence engulfed the vehicle once again.

"You two are quiet," commented Dave. "I guess we're all a bit worse for wear after the party, aren't we?"

Lucy and Mick said nothing.

"How about a bit of Thompson Twins to wake us up?" suggested Dave enthusiastically. "The tape's still in the deck. Pop it on will you Mick."

Lucy sighed as the familiar tunes filled the van and Dave crooned along with the lyrics.

"I feel awful, Mick," said Dave once they had dropped Lucy off at her flat. "I feel that I've let her down."

Mick laughed to himself at the irony of the comment.

"You see," continued Dave. "I'm sure she's angry with me for drinking too much."

Mick shook his head.

"If only I could remember what happened. Did I make a fool of myself?" asked Dave.

"You just fell asleep that's all," reassured Mick.

"But was Lucy angry? Did I upset her? She must have said something to you last night? What happened after I fell asleep? I must have done something stupid? You are obviously hiding something from me. I can tell you're not telling me everything."

"We just put you to bed, Mate, that's all."

"So, Lucy was left on her own with me snoring away? That couldn't have been much fun for her? You could have taken her back down to the party, Mick."

"She didn't want to go, Dave. Just leave it, she was fine."

"But she was obviously upset. She's hardly said a word all morning and you must have noticed she wasn't her normal self on the journey home?"

"She seemed all right to me," said Mick sternly.

"You wouldn't notice. You don't know her as well as me," Dave droned on.

"You're imagining it," said Mick harshly, the irritation in his voice obvious.

Dave was surprised by his friend's lack of compassion; perhaps he really was jealous after all?

* * *

Terry had not arrived and Anthony was growing impatient. He

was racing that evening and could have done without his brother's unreliability.

Anthony hadn't been keen to have Terry as his mechanic. It had been his brother who had wanted to do it, and Anthony hadn't had much choice other than to accept. If he wanted to ensure a team place, he had to have a good mechanic. Terry was that; unfortunately, he just wasn't very reliable.

Anthony glanced at the clock again. He knew this would happen. He knew Terry would let him down eventually. He felt no satisfaction though at having been proved right. He picked up his car keys, went out to his car, and loaded the trailer. He'd just have to drive to the stadium without his brother and hope that he turned up there later.

Terry was not at the stadium when he arrived. He unloaded the bikes from the trailer, leaving them at the rear of the pits before heading off to the changing rooms.

By the time he'd changed into his racing leathers and was walking towards the pits, he was relieved to see that Terry had finally arrived. He was unsurprised to see that his bikes hadn't been touched since he'd left them. Terry seemed more intent on socialising.

As he reached the pits, Anthony noticed that his brother was talking to the blonde girl who'd smiled at him the week before. Anthony felt humiliated. He had foolishly thought that the girl may have been interested in him, and here was his brother muscling in again, as usual. He felt embarrassed. As he approached, Terry tried to introduce the girl. Anthony walked on indifferently.

"Suppose I should make a start on the bike then?" said Terry as he made his way over towards it. Anthony glared at him but said nothing.

Anthony wasn't happy with the bike. Terry just hadn't been able to get it ready in time for his first race. The referee was fretful that the fourth rider in the line-up wasn't yet at the starting gate. A siren sounded, giving Anthony just two minutes to get to the start or face disqualification.

Terry made a last-minute adjustment and pushed the bike onto the track. Anthony didn't feel comfortable with it as he made his way around to the start. His thoughts weren't focussed. He felt tense as he took his place in the starting line-up. His bike was slow as the tapes shot up and he tried to pull away. The flying shale from the bike in front stung as it hit his body and impaired his line of vision to the first bend. He trailed in last place. He was now desperate to make up some ground.

The opponent in front should have been no competition for him. He tried to take a line around the outside of the track to overtake. It was a mistake. He hit an uneven patch on the dirt track and careered forward, clipping his opponent's back wheel. Both riders lost control of their machines. Anthony couldn't get away from his bike. The moment seemed to last forever as he plunged towards the fence.

He couldn't remember hitting the fence. The next thing he recalled was his head aching and his thoughts trying to make sense of the people milling around him. He could smell the gentle aroma of perfume and his thoughts were trying to make sense of where it was coming from. His vision was swimming in a bright light as the woman's voice was talking to him. She was urging him not to move and asking him where he hurt. He wasn't sure. He felt somebody remove his goggles. He was desperate to sit up, but the sweet-smelling woman was urging him to stay still. He lay there for a while as the woman was talking to him.

He gradually became more aware of his surroundings and what the woman was saying.

"You were unconscious. You'll need a trip to hospital," she said reassuringly.

He tried to sit up. It was at that point that the pain hit him. He felt the nausea suddenly and then the sharp pain in his lower arm. He knew instantly that his wrist was broken. His vision had stabilised and the floodlights above came into view. He certainly wasn't going to be stretchered off and instead stumbled to his feet. He was led off the track to a ripple of applause from the crowd.

* * *

Jane had noticed Lucy arrive in the clubhouse and watched as she bought a drink at the bar. As Lucy turned, Jane caught her eye and waved. Lucy, however, looked straight through her and made her way to the opposite end of the balcony. Jane wasn't convinced that she hadn't seen her. She was sure Lucy was avoiding her. Jane was a little perturbed. Admittedly, she didn't like the woman, but she didn't like animosity with anyone. She decided to leave Lucy to her own devices.

It was therefore a surprise to Jane when Lucy walked over to her at the end of the racing. She joined her at the table.

"Hi, Jane, I didn't realise you were over here."

Jane could tell she was lying.

"Can I get you a drink, Janey?" asked Lucy.

"No thank you, I'm fine."

Jane was feeling a little uncomfortable. She took a sip of her drink to break the tension. Lucy leant across the table.

"I've got a surprise for you later, Janey. You will be delighted."

Lucy smiled triumphantly before standing up and walking over to the balcony edge without offering any further explanation.

The women did not speak again before Dave and Mick arrived. Jane smiled at Dave as he approached. Her smile rapidly dropped from her face as she watched him walk over to Lucy and kiss her. The simple action had shocked Jane. She'd had no idea anything had developed between the two. Was that the surprise that Lucy had referred to? She looked across to Mick expecting him to be equally surprised. He wasn't. Admittedly, he did look a little uncomfortable though.

Lucy was enjoying her role. She acted her part out with a devilish show of affection towards Dave, loving every expression on Jane's and Mick's pained faces visible in the background.

Mick was growing extremely uncomfortable. He felt uneasy being with Lucy and Dave after what had happened in the hotel room, and now he had his sister's obvious disapproval to contend with.

"I want to get back early tonight," he said.

Jane wasn't that keen on staying under the circumstances either.

"That's okay Mick. I don't particularly want to hang around much longer either," replied his sister.

Mick shouted across to Dave.

"We'll take the gear home, then come back for you."

Dave nodded but Lucy had other ideas.

"It's okay. I'll take him home later," she said coolly.

Lucy stared at Jane; a cold victorious smile spread across her face.

"I'll see you tomorrow then," said Mick to Dave as he turned and walked away.

Jane followed him.

"See you again then Jane," shouted Lucy after the departing pair.

Jane said nothing. Lucy turned to Dave and sighed.

"Jane doesn't seem too keen on me. Have I done something to upset her?" she asked, once they were alone.

"I'm sorry," apologised Dave. "I just don't know what's wrong with her. She isn't usually like this. I think she's probably just jealous. She's always had the hots for me, you see."

Lucy smiled. Bless him, he really seemed to believe what he said.

"Do you mind if we make a move?" suggested Lucy after a few minutes.

"For sure," replied Dave as he stood up and led her to the door.

As they passed him, Travis interrupted them.

"Hey, Davy Buddy," he beamed, grabbing his friend's arm.

Lucy made her way to the stairs, leaving Dave talking to Travis and nervously watching her leave the room. It was a shame, she liked the American, but she had to press ahead with her plan. She was sure he'd understand. Lucy paused at the top of the stairs. It was at that point that Peter remembered where he'd seen her before.

"Of course, Sam Orpin. You were here with Sam Orpin. That's how I know you," he shouted up the stairs.

Lucy hurried down towards him.

"You must be mistaken," she replied, firmly but gently and out of earshot of her companion who was hurrying to catch up with her. "I've never heard of him."

The doorman felt the reprimand. He was certain that she was the same woman that he'd seen on a couple of occasions with Sam Orpin, but her denial was hardly surprising. Sam Orpin had been a sponsor of the club. He'd been involved in a burglary where an old guy had been stabbed. He'd been on trial for murder and, as far as Peter was aware, Sam was now serving his sentence in prison. As it turned out, it had been lucky for the club that he'd been arrested when he was. During the investigation, it had been discovered that he'd been defrauding the club. He'd also been taking an interest in Dave Chapman's personal financial affairs. Dave wasn't the brightest button and would, no doubt, have been conned one way or another himself, if fate hadn't had intervened.

Peter watched Dave and the woman walk away. She looked over her shoulder at him. He understood. He would keep their secret. After all, her new boyfriend wouldn't be too happy to learn that she'd once known Sam Orpin. It was probably best to let sleeping dogs lie.

As Mick drove home, however, his passenger wasn't feeling quite so forgiving. Jane had been going on about Lucy since they'd left the stadium.

"There's just something about her," she said as she sat beside her brother.

Mick looked at her uneasily. Lucy was the last thing he wanted to talk about.

"She's all right," he insisted.

"She was deliberately ignoring me tonight, Mick, at least until you guys arrived."

Mick looked at his sister with a disparaging glare.

"Seems like the other way around to me."

The sarcasm in his voice annoyed Jane.

"She's up to something, Mick, believe me."

Mick was feeling embarrassed, as thoughts of their night away nagged in his head, and his sister's persistence wasn't helping.

"I wouldn't mind betting she's after his money."

There was an awkward silence. Jane was unrelenting.

"I worry about him. He's obviously taken in by that fake charm of hers. He can't see through it like we can. He's so easily led. I mean, look what happened when he was nearly conned by that Sam Orpin. He'll only make the same mistake again if…"

"Just drop it will you!"

Mick's outburst was harsh as he tried to dismiss the niggling guilty memories of the hotel room from his mind. Jane was obviously shocked by his reaction, but he hoped not overly suspicious. He composed himself before he spoke again.

"How could she know about his money? She's only started coming to Willsby this year. We only met her a couple of weeks ago."

Jane wasn't convinced, but she said nothing more. Mick, for some strange reason, seemed to be defensive of Lucy. Perhaps he'd fallen for her charms too? These men were so gullible.

* * *

Terry looked down at his brother lying in the hospital bed.

"That's kind of put a damper on things hasn't it, Bruv?"

Anthony wasn't amused. His plastered wrist lay on his lap in front of him. Broken in two places and held together by metal rods. It had meant so much to him to get that team place, and now here he was on the sidelines yet again. He would be out for at least a month, if not more. He feared his future with the club had been jeopardised. If only Terry had prepared the bike earlier, none of this would have happened.

* * *

Lucy was worried. She wasn't used to things going wrong. It had been difficult convincing the landlord that she would pay the back rent next month. It just wasn't going to happen though, was it? If only she could find somewhere else to live? Besides, there was now the doorman at the stadium to contend with. She was frightened by how much he seemed to remember and petrified that he would tell somebody about her knowing Sam Orpin. If Dave found out, it could ruin everything between them. And then there was Jane. Both Mick and Dave were fond of the woman, and Lucy wondered how long it would be before they started believing her suspicions. On top of all of that, now Dave was in a strange mood.

He had been quiet all morning. She had not really wanted to take him back to her flat the night before, but with all the pressure on her, she felt that she needed to move quickly. She feared it had been a mistake. He was obviously unimpressed by his night in the cramped flat. Apparently, he was allergic to cats too; she hadn't done her homework there, had she? He'd had a restless night, and he had seemed preoccupied as they'd walked along the Esplanade to The Druids.

Dave returned to the table with drinks in his hands. There was an uneasy silence as Lucy's thoughts flitted in her head. Then Dave spoke.

"Lucy," he said solemnly.

Lucy swallowed hard. Dave paused. He seemed uncomfortable as Lucy's thoughts wrestled in her head. She appeared calm, but inside she was panicking, dreading what he was about to say. Surely, he hadn't found out anything about her past? That would be disastrous. Her fears were torturing her as Dave grabbed her hand and looked into her eyes.

"Why don't you come and live with me for a while? I think you'd like my house, there's plenty of room for us both."

Lucy could not disguise her relief. She felt the elation seep through her body. She cleverly seized her opportunity.

"Are you proposing to me?"

She of course knew that he wasn't, but how could she miss this chance? She sat glowing delight as she looked at him expectantly.

"Dave, of course I'll marry you."

Dave, naturally, seemed taken aback.

"I didn't…" he began.

Lucy interrupted.

"Shh. It's okay, Dave, you don't need to say anything. I knew you were going to ask me to marry you. I had this feeling while we were walking here. Intuition, I guess. We have something magical between us, don't we?"

Dave was obviously disorientated by the whole thing.

"Well, yes, but I didn't mean…"

Lucy took advantage. She turned to face the bar.

"Dave's just proposed to me. We're getting married," she shouted.

"Congratulations," came a chorus from the bar area.

"Get the couple a drink," said a stranger.

Dave looked completely bewildered. Lucy smiled.

"I just want us to get married as quickly as possible. Just a quick wedding. Nothing flash. One that will fit in with your racing schedule. We won't have many people there. Just our close friends like Travis,

Jane and Mick. That is what you want too, Dave, isn't it?"

Lucy was surprising herself with her enthusiasm. She just couldn't believe her luck. Dave had certainly fallen into her trap and now she just had to keep him there until he lost the will to escape. She walked over to the bar to collect their free drinks and handed the barman some money with a whisper.

"Put a double in my fiancé's will you, please?"

If she could get a few more of them in him, Dave wouldn't be in a fit state to broach the subject of the unintentional proposal, would he? Lucy felt proud of herself.

Lucy slept well that night. Admittedly, she'd woken a couple of times and was aware of Dave lying awake next to her. He had obviously been fretting, but that was quite a comforting feeling to her. She finally awoke late the next morning and was surprised that Dave was rather eager to visit Jane. Lucy, now confident that Jane would be of little danger, mirrored his concern at his being late to his summons, and offered to drive her new fiancé to see his friend. Dave was grateful. He grabbed his keys and wallet from the kitchen table. Crikey, he had spent a lot of money in the pub yesterday, his wallet was almost empty. No wonder he felt rough.

They arrived at Jane's small, terraced house within the hour. Lucy watched him knock on the door. She watched Jane open it and waved mockingly at the pair before driving off.

Chapter Thirteen

The doorbell rang. Lucy knew that she couldn't ignore it any longer. She walked resolutely down the stairs to the front door. The bell sounded again. The ring was impatient. Her month's grace on the rent had long passed and, although she'd found some money in Dave's wallet, it was nowhere near enough to pay her arrears. She took a deep breath, aware of the importance of the task ahead, and opened the door.

"Hi", she said shyly.

The landlord stood there with his dog, his grubby little rent book, and even more scars on his bald patch.

"I make it three months that you owe now."

"That's right," said Lucy. "I've got one month's payment together, and I'll definitely have the rest by next month."

The man looked at her. His preprepared speech halted in its tracks. He hadn't expected her to have any money, but at least there was a pile of cash in her outstretched hand, which would cover some of the arrears.

"I've put my car up for sale too. I've got someone coming later today to look at it. I'll be able to pay you in full then, of course."

The landlord took the money.

"And there's something else I wanted to talk to you about," continued

Lucy. "I was wondering if you'd agree to transfer my tenancy to a dear friend of mine. She's got a good job. She's an accountant."

The man looked intrigued. An accountant? That would make a change from the profession that most of his female tenants had.

"An accountant, eh?" he said, unintentionally out loud.

"Yes, with that local company in the High Street. She could get references if required," explained Lucy.

"Yes, I would need a reference. Don't want to take on any old Tom, Dick or Harry, do I?" said the landlord thoughtfully. "You'd still need to pay your arrears though," he said, suddenly remembering why he'd come to the flat.

"Of course, just as soon as the car's sold," said Lucy, gesturing to the vehicle outside.

It did seem a fair enough proposal. He'd noticed the sign on the windscreen of the BMW on his way in. It was a nice car: should raise enough to pay the arrears easily.

"Get your accountant friend to give me a call then," he smiled. "Ah, but don't mention how much you're paying, will you? I'll be doing some, you know, improvements to the flat, so I'll need to increase the rent slightly."

Lucy tapped her nose in understanding. The landlord tugged on his dog's lead and walked off towards his car.

Lucy waited until he'd driven away before removing the 'for sale' sign from her BMW.

* * *

It was Anthony's first meeting since breaking his wrist, and he was keen to show that he was still worthy of the Willsby team place. However, the chance to prove that was looking increasingly unlikely tonight. It had been raining all day and more had been forecast for the evening. Anthony knew that it was improbable that the speedway meeting would go ahead, but as there had been no official announcement, he made his way to the track.

There was still an air of optimism in the stadium as the fans filed through the turnstiles. Anthony was one of the few people in the stadium who didn't share that confidence. He knew that whatever the Willsby management decided, the consortium of riders would never agree to race in these conditions. He looked up at the dark sky and then around the crowd where the spectators huddled in small groups. He noticed the blonde girl, cocooned against the weather in her hooded jacket, standing with Graham. Perhaps she had braved the weather knowing that it was his first meeting since the accident? He smiled to himself as he dismissed the ridiculous thought.

There was a small group of riders standing looking at the track together with the team manager. Anthony joined them. They'd made their decision.

It took another ten minutes for the announcement to come over the public address system: the race meeting had been postponed.

Anthony made his way back to the car park. He wasn't too upset. He hadn't been completely honest about how much pain his wrist was still causing him. The extra week's recovery time would do him good.

* * *

Dave had already broken the news of Jane's separation. The fact that Jane had left her husband came as a pleasant surprise to Lucy. She'd have other things on her mind now, wouldn't she, so hopefully wouldn't interfere with Lucy's plan too much? Mick and Dave, however, seemed quite solemn in the van on the way home after the rained off speedway meeting. Nobody was saying much as they turned into the service station.

Dave climbed out of the van into the rain as Mick sat watching him with a long face. Lucy watched him too. Dave had filled up the fuel tank and was now running across the forecourt to the shop. He passed a bucket of flowers. They looked distinctly weather-beaten and dejected. A cheeky thought came into Lucy's head.

"Hey, Mick, why don't I go and buy some of those flowers for Jane, it might cheer her up?"

She looked expectantly at Mick. He let out a short cynical laugh as if her comment had amused him. Lucy was intrigued. She waited for Mick to explain himself but was disappointed by the simple response.

"It's kind of you, Lucy, but Jane doesn't like flowers."

Lucy didn't understand. Why was Jane so adverse to flowers? Had she unwittingly stumbled across some useful information here? Lucy would have loved to have learnt more, but Mick was reluctant to elaborate. Lucy reverted to her original plan.

"I've been thinking about Jane's predicament," she said enthusiastically. "I think I may have an idea that she'd be interested in."

Mick looked at her, intrigued, as she explained.

"Naturally, I'll be giving up my flat when I marry Dave. I thought perhaps Jane could take it over. I've had a word with my landlord, and he says it would be okay."

Lucy had been worried about the rent arrears. She was scared that Dave might have found out what a severe financial state she was in. The landlord hadn't mentioned a deposit for Jane to take over the flat, but if Lucy told Mick that he had, she could use that money to pay off her own rent arrears.

"Lucy," said Mick in an appreciative voice. "That's really good of you, and it's a brilliant idea. I'll mention it to her later. I'm sure she'll be thrilled."

No doubt Mick would have been pleased. He could hardly be relishing the thought of having his sister living with him indefinitely.

"I like to keep the whole family happy, in one way or another," said Lucy under her breath as Dave returned to the van.

The comment had brought back memories for Mick; uncomfortable memories of that night in the hotel room. He'd been trying to forget about it, but here it was again niggling at his conscience. He looked to the floor embarrassed as Dave climbed inside.

As they pulled up outside of Mick's house, Lucy was keen to get inside. She was eager to see Jane. She rushed into the lounge ahead of her two companions. Jane had obviously not been expecting her visitor. She discretely pulled her robe over her bare thigh. Lucy looked at the dimples of cellulite and smiled at the woman sympathetically. Jane did look rough, even more so than normal. Lucy sat down beside her, smiling impudently. Jane was tired and reluctant to talk. Her red eyes looked down to her lap where her crossed hands rested. Lucy reached out and took hold of her hand.

"I was so sorry to hear about your husband. If there's anything I can do?"

Jane's suspicious glare stabbed at her. Her reply was cold.

"Thank you, I can manage myself."

Lucy's feigned concern had been much more convincing than Jane's attempt at gratitude. Mick had noticed. He sighed.

"Jane," he began. "Lucy's had an idea."

The look on Jane's face was one of suspicion.

"What?"

"Well. They're getting married soon, aren't they?" continued Mick.

Jane didn't need to be reminded. Her concern for her friend was still prominent in her thoughts despite what was happening in her own life. She knew that Dave was making a huge mistake and that he was completely oblivious to the fact. Lucy had really manipulated him. Mick too, uncharacteristically for him, also seemed taken in by the woman. Jane had tried to warn Dave, but she realised the effort was pointless. She consoled herself in the knowledge that she would be there for her friend and her brother, when they eventually found out the hard way, what Lucy was really like.

"Lucy will be leaving her flat on the seafront empty," continued Mick. "She thinks she could persuade the landlord to agree that you take the tenancy over. You could move in there. I mean, we are a bit cramped here, aren't we? It would be good for you to have your own place, wouldn't it?"

"What a brilliant idea," said Dave.

He had obviously been unaware of the plan until that point. He smiled at his fiancée in a lovelorn appreciation.

"It's a lovely flat," lied Lucy.

Her forehead creased for a moment as she put on her sympathetic expression, and then the impish grin returned as she continued.

214

"It's just right for someone on their own."

The comment had been obviously malicious, and Jane was surprised that Dave and Mick hadn't noticed the fact. Dave remained naively enthusiastic.

"And it's handy for town," he encouraged.

"You'd be doing Dave a favour too," interrupted Lucy.

Of course, I'd have to be, wouldn't I, thought Jane. She bit her lip, tactfully keeping her thoughts to herself as Lucy went ahead with some sob story about her cat, and how Jane could look after it. Jane was reluctant to agree to the move, but the pressure from her companions was unrelenting. She had to think about Mick, didn't she?

"Okay. But only temporarily, until I find somewhere myself."

Jane watched as Lucy sat back in her seat, a show of triumph across her face.

* * *

After Friday's downpour, Anthony had decided against his usual training session on Sunday afternoon. He probably needed the practice but didn't want to risk aggravating his injury before the next Willsby match. Simon, on the other hand, was still keen to go, and Anthony had agreed to drive him there. Simon's speedway career was taking off now and he'd become a regular member of his team. Anthony was pleased for him. The regular income that his friend was now receiving had helped a lot. The negative effects on concentration and enthusiasm through lack of money was something Anthony thankfully didn't have. His late father had left him some money in his will. Admittedly, not as much as was left to Terry, but enough to help him through. Terry had also given him a driving job in their late father's business and the money from that came in useful too.

The drive to the practice track took about forty-five minutes, the long country lanes adding considerably to the journey time. The track was situated on a farm, a short distance from the marshy coastline. The land belonged to a temperamental old man, who had once, no doubt, been a successful farmer. Now, his livelihood depended on a few shabby sheep, and the inconvenience of letting the land out for race practices. Having strangers on his land seemed to make him even more cantankerous than normal; but needs must. He always kept a watchful eye on the trespassers, watching from behind twitching net curtains. Many of the younger boys tested his patience, scaling buildings, chasing his sheep, and deliberately leaving the gates open so that his animals escaped. Anthony felt quite sorry for him.

The track itself was small and basic and sat among a scattering of disused farm buildings. It was the place to be seen if you were a young rider as speedway's talent scouts would always be there. It rarely, however, attracted spectators. Anthony had, therefore, been surprised to see the young girl from Willsby arrive. She had watched a couple of practices before retreating behind one of the farm buildings. The land was so barren and close to the river that it seemed permanently windy. The few buildings were a welcome shelter from the weather.

The girl was sat in the long grass, her fingers playing with the green blades beside her. Anthony walked over.

"What are you doing down here then?" he said as he approached.

The girl looked around at him with large, startled eyes. She stood up. Grass seeds deposited across her jacket as she brushed past the tall grasses. Her hair was windswept, and her cheeks flushed red by the bitter wind, yet she still looked remarkably pretty.

"Anthony!"

She sounded shocked but at the same time almost excited. Anthony tried to remember her name. Terry had told him, but as he stood there looking into her eyes, he couldn't for the life of him remember it. He tried to hide his ignorance.

"Got bored watching the racing, did you?" he said.

He hadn't meant to sound as condescending as he had, and hoped the girl hadn't taken the comment that way.

"You could say that," she replied.

"I thought I spotted you arrive earlier," continued Anthony. "Didn't think you'd be that interested in a practice session though."

"Well actually, I came because I hoped you'd be racing," she whispered.

Anthony was shocked, yet flattered. He hardly knew how to respond.

"Wanted a sneak preview before next Friday, did you? Well sorry to disappoint you."

Again, he feared he'd sounded patronising, he hadn't meant it. He reached out to her and wiped the grass seeds from her shoulder.

"I'm sorry. I didn't mean to sound rude. I'm giving my wrist another week," he said, in a much more agreeable tone.

A frustrated silence developed between them, and Anthony leant towards her. They were interrupted by Simon's shout.

"Anthony, can we get off now?"

"Sorry, but I've got to go now," said Anthony as he instinctively kissed her cheek.

"Will you be at Willsby on Friday?" she asked as he turned to leave.

"Of course I will, I'm in the team, aren't I?" he replied.

Jeez, that had sounded belittling again, hadn't it?

He walked away, giving her a quick wave and smile as he left.

As Anthony sat in his house that evening, he thought about the girl. He felt flattered that she obviously liked him. Perhaps he could ask her out on a date sometime? As he pondered the idea, the doorbell rang.

Terry stood on the doorstep, a suitcase in one hand and Mandy holding tightly to the other.

"Hi, Ant, I don't suppose you could do your Bruv a favour?" toadied Terry.

Mandy's parents had found out about their daughter's relationship with Terry, a married man ten years her senior. He was hardly the ideal man for their wayward daughter. She'd had their lecture, and true to her rebellious form, had packed her bag and come running to the man she loved. Unfortunately, it wasn't that easy. Terry couldn't take her back to his house. He wasn't so sure that his wife would be quite as sympathetic towards the new girlfriend.

"It's just for a few days, Ant," he snaked, taking Anthony out of earshot of the girl. "If you can put her up for a few nights, I'll talk her into going home."

Anthony was reluctant to agree.

"Look, just until Friday," pressed Terry. "I'll take her off your hands then."

Anthony looked at the young girl standing dejected in front of him.

"Just as long as it's only for the week," agreed Anthony with a sigh.

Chapter Fourteen

The day of the wedding had arrived; all too soon for Jane's liking. She had reluctantly agreed to be a witness at the fiasco, but only to keep the peace with her brother, Mick, and her friend, Dave. Admittedly she had thought that it would have been called off before now. She'd expected Mick and Dave to have seen through Lucy's fake front to the real woman inside. Unfortunately though, the day had arrived, and Dave was apparently going to marry a woman that he hardly knew. It seemed ludicrous.

Jane had been trying to work out what Lucy was up to, but it just didn't make sense. Dave's inheritance seemed to be the most obvious reason, but that didn't explain why the woman was being so nasty to her. Lucy was definitely a very shrewd woman. Her story writing background had stood her well for her scheming. In fact, Lucy's life seemed to be one long play-act, with Lucy cast as the clichéd femme fatale. She had taken an instant dislike to Jane since their first meeting in the Willsby clubhouse. Perhaps she could tell that Jane wasn't as gullible as the others? Perhaps she saw Jane as a threat? Lucy put on a charming front, full of smiles and excessive amity whenever the men were around. Once she was alone with Jane, however, she never missed the opportunity to say something derisory or spiteful. Of course, it was always out of the earshot of Dave and Mick, who remained sucked in by her vacuous nicety.

The wedding day was a prime example of Lucy's manipulative skills.

"Couldn't you find anything to wear that suited you?" Lucy had whispered as Jane arrived.

The three men of course hadn't heard, and how could they have ever guessed by looking at the beaming smile on Lucy's face as she whispered her insult? Jane had ignored the comment, just as she had ignored all the subsequent seemingly innocent references to her clothing throughout the afternoon.

"And isn't Jane's outfit, well, *befitting* of her?"

"Take a picture of Jane. She looks so different in that *pertinent* choice of outfit."

Lucy had certainly mastered an art there, and Jane couldn't understand just why the woman was being so nasty. Jane had, nonetheless, remained calm, until that was, they were just about to leave after the ceremony.

Lucy caught Jane alone, out of earshot of the others, as usual. She walked over to her, holding out her small wedding bouquet of flowers.

"I know how much you hate flowers, Janey, so why don't you take these as a souvenir of the day? The day that I became Mrs Chapman and got all that betrothed money of his."

Jane couldn't ignore the provocation any longer. She wanted to lunge at the woman, but controlled herself, limiting her response to merely knocking the bouquet from Lucy's hand and shouting at her as she walked away.

Lucy had found the whole thing rather amusing. Luckily though, Dave had assumed she was crying as she tried to stifle her giggles into his shoulder.

Mick was angry with his sister.

"She's just so audacious," seethed Jane as they pulled away in the car.

"It's their wedding day for goodness sake. Couldn't you at least have tried to be nice just for today?" said Mick sternly.

Mick wasn't happy. His sister's behaviour had been totally out of order, but that wasn't the only thing bothering him. He was upset too. He had sat through that ceremony watching as Lucy slowly slipped away from him. He had been thinking about their time together after Travis's party. If only he'd met her before Dave had, it could have been him getting married to her today. Strangely, she had paused, before making the final commitment to Dave, and had glanced across at him. Mick had secretly hoped that she was having second thoughts. She'd smiled at him before continuing with her vows. Dave certainly was a lucky man.

"You just can't see it, can you?" continued Jane unrelentingly.

"There's nothing to see. You're just imagining it, Jane."

Mick paused, knowing that his impending comment would hit a nerve with his sister.

"You're just jealous of her!"

It seemed the obvious explanation to Mick. He could understand it. He was, after all, jealous of Dave, wasn't he? The difference though was that he could control his feelings, unlike Jane.

"You just wait, Mick," fumed Jane. "You'll find out. I just hope that by then it won't be too late."

* * *

Charlotte had been acting a bit odd tonight and Graham was concerned. Just before the last race of the evening, she had been over to speak to that mechanic again. He'd noticed her talking to him before, and he was worried. He'd heard things about Terry Myers and didn't like the idea of Charlotte mixing with his sort. She seemed so naive and vulnerable. He felt an obligation to look after the young girl. He'd considered himself a good friend of her father, and now that he wasn't around, Graham felt somewhat responsible for her.

He'd planned to leave after the last race, but was worried that Charlotte appeared to be hanging around waiting for someone. Concerned that she may be meeting the mechanic, he hid around the back of the clubhouse watching the man. He was talking to his brother, the speedway rider. Graham watched from a distance. He couldn't hear what they were saying, but it was obvious that the rider wasn't happy. He wondered what they were talking about and hoped it wasn't anything to do with Charlotte.

Terry had stopped Anthony as he walked across to the changing rooms after the evening's racing.

"Ant, can you do me a favour?"

Anthony had been expecting the question. Terry had been in a rather jovial and helpful mood all evening; the type of behaviour that normally preceded a bout of grovelling when he wanted something.

"What?" he snapped.

Terry winced slightly from the ferocity of the response, before composing himself sufficiently to continue.

"You know that Charlie?" he said. "The blonde one?"

Anthony recognised the name as being that of the young girl he liked. He nodded, his anger ebbing slightly.

"She wanted to stay with me tonight. Made up some sob story about her landlord wanting her to move out of her flat for the night. It was obvious she was just after me though."

Anthony's heart sank. Surely, Terry was wrong? He shook his head.

"Look, I already said that you'd..." began Terry.

Terry paused, noticing the disgruntled expression on his brother's face.

"Great!" interrupted Anthony sarcastically. "So now I'm a home for Terry Myers's unwanted girlfriends, am I?"

Terry smiled slightly; the comment had amused him. Anthony's face, however, was stern. Terry muffled his amusement as Anthony strode off across the green to the changing rooms.

Anthony had mixed thoughts about the prospect of taking Charlotte home that evening. It would have been great if it had been him that she'd wanted to be with, but it was Terry, wasn't it? She'd asked Terry to take her home, after all. What all these women saw in his brother was a total mystery to Anthony.

Graham had watched as Terry Myers had gone up to the clubhouse after his argument with his brother. He followed him, worried that Charlotte might be meeting up with him. Graham need not have worried. There was no sign of Charlotte in the bar. Graham was relieved.

Anthony was late leaving the changing rooms that evening. He had stayed behind with Travis Fengar. There had been an altercation earlier that evening during the racing. A Swedish guy from the opposite team had accused Travis of dangerous riding. There had been a heated exchange of words. Travis had been quite coarse with a play on words based around the other rider's sponsors: a company whose name, when read with its English pronunciation, took on a rather unfortunate suggestive connotation. The insult was, however, wasted on a man for whom English wasn't his first language. Anthony was concerned that someone may have explained the joke to him by now, and that Travis's rendition of Abba's *Dancing Queen* in the shower may have been provoking.

"Calm down, Travis," urged Anthony.

"What's up, Dude? Not an Abba fan? I do other requests?"

Anthony had stayed with Travis in the changing rooms. He'd sensed the animosity towards his colleague and wanted to make sure he didn't do anything too stupid. He also didn't think there was much point in hurrying out to meet Charlotte, she would probably have left by now as her plan to go home with Terry had failed. Once Travis had calmed down, they eventually headed for the door.

"Got time for a curry?"

"Not tonight, Travis," replied Anthony, noticing Charlotte stood in the shadows. "I've got to get back."

"See what you mean. Have a good night. Enjoy!" sniggered Travis before heading off into the darkness, continuing his Abba rendition as he kicked a discarded can.

Anthony waited until Travis was out of view until he spoke.

"Terry says you need a place to stay tonight?"

Charlotte nodded.

"That's right. My landlord's doing some work on my flat. I was hoping to find a guesthouse, but they are all full up. I'm really grateful to you for helping me out. Are you sure you don't mind?"

"I guess not. The car's over here."

He led her across the car park to his awaiting car.

"You rode really well tonight," she said suddenly.

Anthony was rather taken aback by the compliment. He wasn't sure how to respond so ended up saying nothing. There was an awkward silence before she spoke again.

"Is your wrist okay now?"

"I suppose so," replied Anthony, still unsure what to say.

"It was a nasty fall you had. The way you hit the fence like that must have really hurt. You were knocked out as well, weren't you? It's so dangerous," said Charlotte.

Anthony smiled but said nothing.

"I don't know why they haven't thought about using inflatable fences," continued Charlotte. "You know, something like the bouncy castles you see at fairs."

She was sweet, wasn't she? Only a girl would think of that. Can you imagine the stick the riders would get having blow-up, kid's slides around the edge of the track? Anthony sniggered at the thought.

He opened the car door, and she tentatively climbed inside.

Anthony was confused. It was obvious that the girl was lying about the sudden need to vacate her flat. Surely, her landlord would have given her more notice, or couldn't she simply have told him that it wasn't convenient today? He started the car. So, she'd made up the story in an attempt to go home with Terry. What could she see in his brother?

He pulled out of the stadium onto the main road and headed towards the centre of town. Anthony liked her. He wouldn't have thought that she was Terry's type, but he never could tell. It had been pretty much the same with Terry's wife, Maria. What was it that Terry had that he didn't? Apart from all these women after him, and the larger part of his father's bequeathed fortune, of course?

He drove through the centre of Willsby and headed out onto the country road to his house. So, if Charlotte was lying to be with Terry, why had she stayed and waited for him instead? Why not just go home? It didn't make sense. Perhaps she did like him, after all? He glanced across at her, suddenly realising that he'd been so engrossed in his thoughts that they had said nothing since leaving the stadium. She perched nervously on the edge of her seat. He'd been quite insensitive, hadn't he?

"We're nearly there now," he reassured as he drove along the familiar lane to his house.

She said nothing but stared ahead into the distance. She seemed taken aback as Anthony suddenly swung the car into his driveway and pulled up outside the house.

Anthony climbed from the car and was surprised that Charlotte did not follow. She sat motionless in the car, staring out into the darkness ahead of her.

"Are you coming then?" he asked.

Charlotte followed him tentatively to the front door and into the hallway.

"Make yourself at home," he said, pointing through into the lounge. "I've got to put the bikes away."

Anthony took the bikes around to the workshop. He really should have stripped them down then and there, but he didn't want to leave his house guest alone for too long. He'd do them tomorrow instead.

"You can sit down," he said as he returned to the lounge.

His guest was standing awkwardly in the middle of the room. Anthony walked over to the windows and closed the long, heavy curtains. Charlotte sat down gingerly.

"Would you like a coffee?" he offered.

"Yes, that would be great," she replied nervously.

Anthony made his way to the kitchen where he made two mugs of coffee. Charlotte appeared to have relaxed a little when he returned. He handed her a drink and sat on the other settee. He clenched his hand. His wrist did still hurt. He'd noticed it carrying those mugs in.

"Your wrist is still hurting, isn't it?" asked Charlotte sympathetically.

"It's ok. It could have been worse," he replied.

"It's so dangerous what you do," continued Charlotte. "Aren't you scared when you are racing?"

Anthony smiled to himself. A serious injury was the elephant in the room for speedway riders. Most of the time, the elephant was just sat in the grandstand, quietly filling in his programme. Most of the time, they didn't even notice him. Once they were out there on the track, the adrenaline took over, and the elephant was silent. Of course, they all knew it was dangerous. They all knew riders who'd had life-changing injuries. They even all knew of riders who'd been killed. It was something they never dwelt on though. You just wouldn't do it if you thought you'd get seriously hurt, would you?

"Don't really think about it," he answered, dismissing the thought as the elephant sat back down quietly in the corner of the room. "I just enjoy racing. It's the speed and the excitement. It makes me feel alive. It's addictive."

"I can understand that," said Charlotte. "I get an adrenaline rush just watching when those tapes go up, so it must be an amazing buzz doing it."

"You'll have to have a go sometime," smiled Anthony.

Charlotte laughed. That would never happen, would it? Inside her head, the elephant wasn't as subdued: it was wearing a pink tutu and juggling tennis balls, as the thought of her lining up at the starting gate briefly crossed her mind.

"I'll leave that to you," she giggled.

Anthony smiled too.

"Have you got another job?" enquired Charlotte. "Or do you just do speedway?"

"I wish I could just do speedway," sighed Anthony." One day I'd like to. I'm a driver for my brother's delivery company for now though. It's good. It fits around my racing schedule. I don't really like working for Terry, but I have to pay the bills on this place somehow."

Anthony fell silent again as he thought about Terry and their late father's business. He'd always wondered why his dad had left it to Terry rather than to him, or at least to both of them. He also wondered how he'd ended up working for Terry in what was essentially the business that, since he was born, everyone assumed would one day be his.

"This is a beautiful house," said Charlotte, diverting his thoughts. "Do you own it?"

Anthony relaxed more as Charlotte enthused about his house. He was enjoying her company and had almost forgotten that it had been Terry that she'd originally wanted to go home with. He was bought back to reality, with a jolt, as she suddenly asked.

"Do you live here alone?"

Anthony felt unsettled as he recalled Mandy's stay there. She was, of course, someone else whom Terry had let down, and Anthony was picking up the pieces from that still, wasn't he? Was he just repeating the same mistake with Charlotte? He hoped not. The difference this time was that he actually liked Charlotte. They seemed to be getting on so well. He couldn't face the thought of Terry ruining it. His response reflected his unease.

"Yes, of course, why do you ask?"

"It just seems like a big house for one," replied Charlotte.

Anthony smiled to himself as he thought about how much better it was since Mandy had left.

"I prefer it like that."

Charlotte had seemed to sense Anthony's unease and rapidly changed the subject back to his racing. He relaxed instantly, and they chatted for what seemed like hours about the Willsby team. She'd been a big fan in the past and had a comprehensive knowledge of the sport. They'd been fans of the Willsby team during the same era and exchanged stories of their memories. Anthony was impressed. It was refreshing to talk to somebody who shared some of the same childhood memories. It was surprising how much they had in common. She'd lost her father suddenly too. She clearly missed him. As she spoke, it comforted Anthony. He felt consoled to know that someone else shared those feelings that he had for so long suppressed after losing his dad. Charlotte seemed to understand how he felt. She seemed to understand his grief even better than his own brother, Terry, did.

In fact, Anthony had grown so engrossed in their conversation that he hadn't realised what the time was. Charlotte yawned.

"Am I keeping you up?" he apologised.

"I didn't realise how late it is," she replied.

"Come on. I'll show you where your bedroom is."

Anthony led her out into the hallway. He stopped outside the spare room where Mandy had been staying earlier in the week. It didn't seem right that Charlotte should stay in there. He led her instead along to the master bedroom at the end of the corridor and returned to the spare room himself.

The bed in the spare room was unmade. A towel had been flung across it; the dampness had seeped into the mattress. There was a covering of brown makeup on the table and fingerprints on the mirror. The room smelt of cheap perfume. Anthony opened one of the high windows. The sound of the rain on the glass intensified. He pulled shut the curtains, picked up the damp towel, folded it neatly, and took it along to the linen basket in the bathroom. Anthony thought about Charlotte as he walked down the corridor. The door to the main bedroom was ajar. He stared at it for a moment, then walked towards it and pushed it gently.

He stood in the doorway looking into the dark room. The duvet rustled.

"Anthony?" murmured the voice.

"You didn't really have to leave your flat tonight, did you?" he asked quietly.

"No. I'm sorry I lied, but I just had to think of an excuse to be with you."

Anthony was surprised.

"With me? But didn't you ask my brother if you could stay with him? I thought it was him you were interested in?"

"Good Lord no! What made you think that?" said Charlotte as she sat up in the bed.

"That's Terry for you. He thought you'd made up some excuse to spend the night with him. You've had a lucky escape."

"You don't mind me coming here tonight do you, Anthony?" she asked.

"I'm really glad that you did," he reassured as he brushed a strand of hair from her forehead.

* * *

Dave was sat upright in bed when Lucy entered the room.

"What the hell are you doing?" yelled Lucy, lurching for the brown paper envelope in his hand.

She had meant to hide the envelope. It held several important documents that she'd had to show to the marriage registrar, including the one renouncing her previous surname. She'd changed her name by deed poll last year, and certainly didn't want Dave finding out what it had been before. Dave flinched at the outburst. Lucy realised he was suspicious. She had to think of something quickly. Her eyes glazed over as she slipped the envelope from Dave's hand.

"I haven't mentioned much about my family because I'm a little embarrassed," she said softly as tears formed on cue in her eyes.

Dave forgot all about the envelope as he put a comforting arm around her.

"I come from a very dysfunctional and poor background, Dave, I didn't want you to know."

Dave looked into her eyes. He reached out to her as she discretely slipped the envelope onto the floor beside the bed.

"That's all behind you now," he reassured as he gently ran his hand across her cheek. "You don't need to worry about money now."

Lucy feigned inquisitiveness.

"I've got enough money to keep us both for years. You'll never go without now," he explained.

Of course, Lucy knew that, didn't she? He'd given her access to his bank account so that she could pay his bills. Had he really forgotten that? Lucy's expression faked bewilderment as Dave continued proudly.

"I inherited quite a large amount a few years back."

The expression on his face took her back to her childhood. She remembered her parents' faces on Christmas day when she opened her presents. Their faces had been a picture of pride and achievement when they gave their little girl the gift that they had saved so hard to buy for her. The gift that she'd already seen in the back of their wardrobe a few weeks earlier, when Lucy and her brother had found all their presents. Lucy didn't like surprises. How could you stay in control with surprises? Neither Lucy, nor her brother, had let their parents down. They thanked them on Christmas day with the fresh enthusiasm they'd been expecting. Lucy wasn't going to let Dave down either.

"I never realised," she said, almost believing the lie herself. "Why didn't you tell me earlier?"

Dave smiled to himself as he thought about Sam Orpin. He'd told people about his money in the past and look where that had got him. He'd had a lucky escape with Sam Orpin. In fact, if Sam hadn't had been arrested when he had, he certainly wouldn't be sitting here now with Lucy. He said nothing as he looked at her and smiled. She seemed to understand.

Chapter Fifteen

A nthony had been so captivated by Charlotte, that he felt slightly embarrassed as he awoke next to her in the morning. Her young face nestled in the pillow; her hair splayed out around it. She stirred as he moved.

Anthony paused, waiting for her to settle again, before climbing from the bed. He dressed and made his way to the workshop.

The bike stood dejectedly in front of him. He would normally have cleaned it immediately after a race meeting, but he'd neglected the task the previous evening, due to his impromptu visitor. His negligence would make the job even harder today. He felt a touch of guilt as he looked at the pitiful machine and began his work.

Anthony glanced out of the workshop. The bedroom window was visible across the garden. He imagined Charlotte lying, contentedly asleep in the bed, as he continued with the task ahead. As he progressed, the encrusted mud relented, and his bike began to come to life again.

It had been almost an hour before he heard movement from within the house. He walked around to the side door and into the kitchen. Charlotte was sat at the table. She looked a little distant this morning as if she had something on her mind.

"Have you been up for long?" he asked.

"No. I've only just woken up."

There was definitely something wrong. Perhaps it was his disappearing act early that morning? Maybe that had been a bit inconsiderate; but the task of cleaning the bike had been playing on his mind, and the job had needed doing.

"Sorry to have left you. I had to get the bike cleaned up," he explained. "I should really have done it last night, before the mud dried on."

"I see," said Charlotte, uncharacteristically showing little interest and staring into space behind him.

"Do you want some breakfast?" asked Anthony.

"Just coffee," she replied coldly.

Anthony made the coffee, noticing Charlotte's reluctance to look at him. He felt uncomfortable as he placed the mug in front of her and sat down. She stared into the steaming drink. Was she regretting having come here last night, perhaps? He was about to ask her if she was okay when she suddenly spoke.

"I ought to get back soon."

Anthony would have liked her to stay. He'd enjoyed her company the night before, and he wanted to find out what was bothering her. He had been hoping they could perhaps have spent a bit of time together today.

"Do you have to go so soon?" he asked.

"Yes, I do," she replied rather abruptly, standing up as she spoke.

Anthony sensed her urgency to get home. Maybe she had something pressing that she had to do today?

"Okay. I'll run you home, when you're ready then," offered Anthony.

Perhaps it was best not to push her for an explanation?

Charlotte left the room without looking back at him. He sat for a while watching the steam rise from her untouched mug of coffee.

As he sat pensively, Anthony noticed Mandy's makeup bag; she must have forgotten it when she'd left the previous day. It made the kitchen look untidy, and his having had Mandy stay wasn't something that he particularly wanted to be reminded of. He walked over and picked it up, placing it out of sight in one of the cupboards.

Charlotte returned quickly, her urgency to leave was obvious in her body language.

"Have you got everything?" he asked, not wanting her to leave anything behind like Mandy obviously had done.

She nodded.

"Are you sure you can't stay a bit longer?" he asked, sounding slightly desperate.

"No, I said I want to go home."

He felt the reprimand but didn't understand why. She clearly had something on her mind and needed to get home to sort it out.

The journey back to Willsby was long and silent. The country roads, that Anthony knew so well, today seemed uninviting and never-ending. Charlotte said nothing apart from some blunt directions when prompted. They pulled up outside her flat.

"I'll bring your bag in, if you like?" offered Anthony.

"No, I can manage on my own."

Anthony was disappointed but thought it best just to let her go.

"I guess I'll see you around then," said Anthony as she climbed from the car.

Once outside, she paused to look into the open window. She seemed to relax, free from the constraints of the vehicle.

"Thanks for letting me stay," she murmured.

She was sweet, wasn't she? Anthony watched her open the front door to the building, and disappear inside, before he drove off.

As Anthony made his way home, he thought about Charlotte. They'd got on so well the night before, and he couldn't imagine why she'd seemed so different this morning. Something was bothering her. Perhaps she felt embarrassed? He made up his mind to wait for a few days, and then maybe he could call around to see her again.

Anthony's welcome home was far from what he'd been expecting. He noticed Terry's car in the driveway. Terry was about to climb back inside it as Anthony pulled up alongside him.

"Hi, Bruv," said Terry enthusiastically.

Anthony wasn't quite as pleased to see his brother.

"What are you doing here?" he asked, fearing that he already knew the answer.

"Knew you wouldn't mind, Ant. Putting Mandy up again for me."

"No, Terry, I can't."

Terry gestured to the house.

"Well, she's in there, you can tell her for me, can't you? I've got to get off," said Terry as he got in his car.

Terry started the engine and drove off, ignoring his brother's pleas. Anthony kicked the gravel ferociously. He was angry, although angrier if the truth were known with himself, than with Terry. Why did he always let his brother walk all over him? He returned resolutely to the house.

"All right, Ant?" said Mandy, her red lips disfigured by her chewing.

"Sorry, lost me key. I was sure I left it here on the sofa, but I've looked all around and can't find it. Terry showed me where you keep the spare in the workshop."

Mandy lay slovenly across the sofa, her chubby white legs hung over the arm. Her red-painted nails tipped the wriggling toes of her crossed feet, and her discarded shoes lay on the floor.

"You can't really stay here anymore, Mandy," said Anthony firmly.

"It's okay, Ant, I won't need to," she said calmly.

Anthony was surprised by her certainty. She smiled at him and sat up. A trickle of chimes rang out as her bangles slipped down her arm to her wrist. She flicked her unruly hair away from her eyes, and a huge bubble exploded back onto her red lips. Her tongue darted out to collect the gum and retrieve it back inside her mouth.

"It will only be for the night," she said, between chews. "Terry's coming back for me tomorrow. We're going away together. He's going to leave his wife, and we are going to get a flat somewhere. Somewhere we can be together. Somewhere away from here."

Anthony looked at the girl. He felt ashamed, ashamed of being Terry's brother. He knew that Terry had no intention of going anywhere. Mandy's naivety and trust touched him. He could have told her the truth, but she wouldn't believe him, would she? At least not today. Tomorrow would be a different matter.

* * *

Lucy was looking forward to the dinner party. She realised that Jane must be feeling extremely lonely in that flat, over the other side of town to her brother. That morning, Dave had confided in his wife and had told her the story of Jane and Mick's sister's death, twenty years ago to the day. He realised that Jane had asked them around that evening to take her mind off the anniversary, and he certainly didn't want Lucy unintentionally saying the wrong thing. Jane disliked the woman enough already, so Dave felt it was probably best that Lucy was prepared.

Jane wouldn't have liked him telling his new wife the story. The story of how Jane had been the one to find the baby's body. She had taken it all very badly, and the memories had grown with her through the years. To a trained psychologist, it probably explained why she'd never had any children of her own; and even to the untrained, it explained why Jane hated flowers so much. The funeral had been a traumatic time for the young Jane. Flowers were a phobia that she had held onto into adulthood. They reminded her of the events of that day. No, Jane didn't like people knowing, but what harm was there in telling Lucy?

Lucy was enthralled by the revelations. Dave was right, she wouldn't now put her foot in it by saying the wrong thing, *unintentionally*.

Mick picked them up in his car later that evening. Lucy could tell that he was upset himself by his own memories.

"How's Jane settling into my flat?" she asked, breaking the sombre silence.

Mick met her eyes in the rear-view mirror.

"Really well. It was so good of you to arrange for her to move in."

"I wish Jane could see it that way. I do so want us to get along," said Lucy pessimistically.

Lucy's emphasis on the statement showed her sympathy. Mick was consoled by her efforts to befriend his sister.

They pulled up outside of the flat and parked. The windows of the tall building were ablaze with electric light. It was not long before Jane answered the summons of the doorbell.

As they climbed the stairs, Lucy looked at the floor. Two flats shared the staircase, and Lucy recalled how neither herself, nor the couple upstairs, had ever thought it their responsibility to vacuum the carpet. There had been a steadfast standoff. Jane had evidently relented.

"You've got the place lovely, Jane," she said as they entered the bedsitting room.

Jane glanced at her suspiciously, recognising the sarcasm.

Lucy followed her hostess into the kitchen, leaving the two men talking in the main room.

"So, Janey, this evening we're celebrating your sister's death, aren't we?" commented Lucy as she watched Jane dish up the meals.

Jane's eagerness to join the others was obvious, but she wasn't going to rise to the bait.

"It's hardly a celebration, but I do like to remember her," she said, trying to capture a little enthusiasm.

"How do you remember her, Janey?" laughed Lucy.

She paused before continuing.

"All grey and dead, wasn't it? All suffocated and blue?"

Lucy watched as the poison of her comment seeped into Jane, before increasing the dose.

"You could do with some flowers in here to brighten it up."

Jane flinched, but she remained calm.

"You know I don't like flowers, Lucy"

"Why ever not, Janey? They'd really look good in here. Remind me to buy you a bouquet one day."

Jane was eager to join the others.

"It's really hot in that kitchen," said Lucy as they entered the other room. "Isn't it, Jane? Really suffocating in there?"

They all sat down to eat in an awkward silence, which Mick tried to fill with the occasional topical news story.

Lucy leant back in her seat as she finished her food.

"Well, that's just about done me in. I think I'll die if I eat anymore."

Jane's glance across at Lucy was venomous, a fact that hadn't gone unnoticed by Mick. He glared angrily at his sister. Perhaps that hadn't been the best thing to say, but Lucy didn't know that, did she? Lucy couldn't have known about the anniversary that made the comment so painful for the siblings, could she? Jane was taking everything that Lucy said as a personal attack on her, and it was so unjustified. Lucy was only trying to be friendly.

Mick sipped his wine and glanced across at Lucy. She smiled coyly and Mick, having interpreted her undertones, looked away nervously. He didn't want Jane and Dave to notice the chemistry between them. He was certain, however, that Lucy knew what he was thinking. Ever since that night in the hotel room, Mick had felt jealous of Dave. He wanted to stand up there and then and declare his feelings, giving everyone the sordid details of what really happened that night after Travis Fengar's party. Of course though, he couldn't say a thing, could he? His sister would disown him, his best friend would floor him, and Lucy would probably never want to see him again. Or would she? Was she aware of how he felt? Did she feel the same? Even if she did though, what could she do? She was now married to Dave, wasn't she? And having his lights punched out by Dave wasn't high on his agenda, so of course, he kept quiet and instead looked sheepishly to the floor.

Mick's frustration was broken as Lucy took a sip of her wine and spoke.

"That wine's got a lovely bouquet, Janey?" she commented.

She sounded genuinely appreciative as she spoke. Jane's response, therefore, was totally unjustified.

"Why are you such an evil bitch?" she yelled, standing up suddenly. "Is it because I can see what you're up to, is it? Is that why you're picking on me?"

The outburst had been unexpected. Dave and Mick buffered the initial shock and tried to take control of the situation. Dave led his distraught wife to the door as Mick tried desperately to calm his sister. His efforts were in vain, and Jane relentlessly continued her verbal attack.

"What's come over you?" said Mick angrily as Dave and Lucy left the flat. "Why are you acting like this?"

"Can't you see what she's up to?" pleaded Jane.

"It's all in your head, Jane. How can Lucy know what today is? How can she know the memories we both have? I haven't told her. You're just reading things into her that aren't there."

Mick didn't know what else to say. His sister had gone too far this time. He left the flat, saying nothing, and ignoring his sister's tearful pleas.

Chapter Sixteen

"Why are you so insistent with lying, Terry?" asked Maria as her husband stood in front of her, his head hung in a mock shame. "I'm fully aware that you've been seeing that student girl."

"Of course, I haven't, Babe. You know I wouldn't do that," defended Terry, sounding remarkably convincing as he held out a reassuring hand.

"Don't patronise me," she snapped, dismissing his gesture. "I do know what's been going on."

Terry recoiled sheepishly. His wife's persistence both surprised and unnerved him. She had always seemed to believe him before, and her new strength of character made him feel uneasy. He panicked inwardly, unused to the feeling of vulnerability that was engulfing him. How could she know? He hadn't done anything differently, so how come, all of a sudden, she suspected him? His confused thoughts spun in his mind. He sought desperately to find an escape route from the captors of his wife's new-found determination. Perhaps it was Anthony? Perhaps he had said something about Mandy to her? How else would she know? But no, that didn't make sense. Anthony was too placid. He wouldn't have said anything for fear of upsetting Maria and getting drawn into the sticky tangle of the matrimonial web. It couldn't have been Anthony, but it did give Terry an idea. He looked to the floor pensively as he spoke.

"Ant told you about her, didn't he?" he said.

His ploy seemed to work. He noticed his wife flinch. He knew that Maria trusted Anthony, and that the revelation that he was aiding and abetting Terry's infidelity would shock her. She fell silent as Terry spotted his escape route, and his verbal attack ran for it.

"I knew I shouldn't have trusted him," he said. "I should have known he'd tell you that I've been seeing her 'round at his place."

Terry's onslaught seemed to be working. Maria had clearly been unaware that Anthony had even known about the affair. Terry knew that his admission of unfaithfulness would be disseminated by Maria's shock at Anthony's disloyalty.

"He's not so perfect after all, is he?" Terry continued, seizing his opportunity.

She fell silent and stared into his eyes.

"It must run in the family," she said with a renewed vigour.

She paused reflectively.

"But then that can't be right, can it? It can't run in the family if you aren't actually related to one another, can it?"

Terry flinched at the rhetorical comment. It had caught him unaware. How could he respond to that? He said nothing. He simply turned sedately and left the room.

Maria sat down, her body trembling as she heard her husband leave the house. Terry had been right. Of course, she'd suspected the other woman, and yes, it had been a shock that Anthony was mixed up in it all. She understood though. Anthony didn't want to get involved, did he? She felt exactly the same. She'd been harbouring her own secret from him, hadn't she? She too didn't want to have to face the consequences that her revelations would cause if they were to leak out.

It had been about six months earlier, when Terry had made the uncharacteristic slip-up. It was after one of his many drinking bouts at The Druids, when a few too many beers had lubricated the inhibitions of his vocal cords. Maria had been surprised by her husband's confession to the extent that, at first, she thought it was merely a joke. It was only when he tried to brush the admission off, that she realised there must be some truth to it. The fact that he wasn't actually related to Anthony was, let's face it, quite a revelation. Even in his drunken state, Terry had realised the gravity of his error. He'd laughed off his ramblings, digging himself deeper into the hole. There was a glint of panic in his eyes that day. Maria knew that he had slipped up. She knew she'd unwittingly become a party to Terry's biggest secret. He hadn't made the same mistake since, but Maria had kept her trump card close to her chest, and today had been the time to play it.

Maria longed to know all the details. How exactly had he passed as Anthony's half-brother? How had he tricked the old man into leaving him his money and business to the deprivation of his real son? She knew that without the full facts, her information would be of little use to Anthony, and anyway, she was a beneficiary of the fraud herself, wasn't she? The money and successful business were doing her very well, thank you. She wasn't about to play her trump card in public, just yet.

Maria wasn't the only person that Terry had let down today. It was early afternoon, and Mandy was still waiting for him to arrive. They were running away together today, and Terry had told her to meet him at Anthony's. Terry had promised. He was leaving his wife, and they were going to get a place together.

Of course, it was no surprise to Anthony that Terry hadn't turned up. It did, however, disturb him to see the hope ebbing away from Mandy. He had watched the inevitable progression of her emotions, from elation in the morning, to her now disappointment. Mandy's hopes had slipped away with each rotation of the clock hands. Anthony couldn't help but feel sorry for her. She had shut herself away in the spare bedroom. The silence and sombre atmosphere in the house gave Anthony the urge to go out. He walked through to the hall and knocked on the bedroom door.

"Mandy, are you awake?"

There was no answer, merely the sound of footsteps. The door opened, and Mandy looked at him through red, puffy, makeup-smudged eyes.

"I'm going down to the practice track," he said, trying to ignore the pained expression on her face.

"Can I come with you?" whispered Mandy.

Anthony was reluctant to agree. He just wanted to get away from all of this; just wanted a bit of time, with the lads down at the track, to take his mind off it all. But Mandy did look desperate.

"Go clean yourself up then," he relented.

Mandy smiled gratefully as she walked to the bathroom.

* * *

The previous evening had been awful. Lucy's snide comments, coupled with the memories of her sister's death, had picked at Jane's patience throughout the evening. Lucy had been trying to provoke her. Dave had obviously told Lucy about Jane's sister's death. Lucy had said those horrible things, and even when they were with the two men, she had been making references to the death: 'the heat's suffocating', 'I'll die if I eat more'. Jane was surprised that Dave and Mick hadn't noticed. Jane's eventual outburst was a culmination of anger towards Lucy, grief, and a frustration with her brother and Dave. Jane now regretted her actions. It had done little else but alienate her from Mick and Dave.

Jane hadn't slept well. Her head ached, and she was tired as she sat in the small kitchen sipping her coffee. The cat scampering around her feet wasn't helping either. He seemed possessed as he played with his catnip mouse, hurtling it into the air and then knocking it out of reach under the refrigerator. The cat sat staring into the dark gap, his tail thrashing back and forth. His black paw stretched into the dusty void; the mouse was just out of reach.

Jane cursed the animal. She wrenched the refrigerator forward and reached her arm into the gap. She felt the toy mouse and pulled at its tail. It was wedged in the space between the fridge and the wall, inside some papers. Jane gave it a short, sharp tug and it was free. She picked up the crumpled papers. They had obviously fallen behind the fridge some time ago.

The ink on the gas bill was faded, and the Indian takeaway menu was well out of date. The third document, however, was the one that caught her eye. The prison stamp on the top of the paper was as clear as the day that Sam Orpin had written his letter.

'Dearest Sister Lucy,' it read.

Jane couldn't believe her eyes. So, Lucy was Sam Orpin's sister! The same Sam Orpin who had tried to defraud Dave out of his money. The same Sam Orpin who was now serving a prison sentence for murder. Now everything was making sense.

Of course. That's where she'd seen Lucy before. She'd been with Sam Orpin at the sponsors' events at the track. No wonder Lucy was trying to turn Mick and Dave against her. She was a threat to her plans. Well, now she'd been found out, and Jane finally had the evidence that she needed to show to her brother and friend. Now they would realise that she had been right about Lucy all along.

* * *

Anthony and Mandy sat in the car at the practice track. Anthony was trying to keep his eyes fixed on the racing. Mandy was beside him, sniffling, obviously anxious for a sympathetic ear. He didn't really want to oblige.

"Look, I'm sorry this has happened," he finally conceded.

Mandy was looking at him, but Anthony avoided returning the gaze. This was difficult enough as it was. He sat staring at the steering wheel.

"So, what will you do now?"

Anthony's question was asked, not out of sympathy for the girl, but for fear of his own predicament. He didn't want to be lumbered with her.

She didn't respond.

"You'll be going home, I suppose?" he pressed.

There was still no answer. He looked across at her. Her eyes were puffy, and black mascara smudged panda-like around them.

"I can't go back, Anthony," she whispered.

"Why not?" asked Anthony, an impatient tone to his voice.

Mandy seemed upset by his insensitive and uncharitable question. "My dad will kill me."

Anthony felt guilty. Perhaps he should have been more sympathetic?

"Of course, he won't," he said, trying to reassure her.

"You don't know him," sobbed Mandy.

"Look, if it helps, I'll come home with you. Perhaps your dad will listen to you if I'm there."

"Would you really, Anthony?" said Mandy, leaning across and kissing his cheek. "You are so kind. I can't believe you and Terry are related."

* * *

When Mick arrived, Dave was still in the bathroom, so Lucy led him into the lounge. Dave had a race meeting that evening, and as usual, he was running late. Mick sat down beside Lucy. He didn't know what to say. His sister's outburst of the previous evening had embarrassed him, and he felt bad that he was unable to explain her actions.

"I'm sorry about Jane's behaviour last night," he finally said.

Lucy seemed grateful for his concern. She smiled at him, placed her hand on his knee, and leant over to kiss his cheek.

"It's not your fault, Mick," she said reassuringly. "But it is very sweet of you to apologise on her behalf."

She hadn't moved her head away from his. Her warm breath

whispered across his face. He turned his head to look at her. Her lips were now close to his. He raised his hand, running his fingertips across the smooth skin of her cheek, and kissed her.

The sudden noise from the bathroom startled Mick. He jolted forward in his seat. Lucy seemed calm as she very slowly moved her hand from his leg.

"Have you spoken to Jane since last night?" she asked as if nothing had just happened.

"No, I haven't," exclaimed Mick, in his embarrassment as he heard Dave approaching.

"Hi, Mick. Nice and early as usual, I see," said Dave. "I hope Lucy's been looking after you?"

"Of course, I've been looking after him," said Lucy, with a teasing smile.

Mick felt rather embarrassed.

"We'd better get off," he urged, feeling rather uncomfortable still sat there next to Lucy. "We're a bit late already, Dave."

"Crikey Mick. What's the rush?" asked Dave casually.

"Well, the traffic could be busy. You don't want to get there late, do you?" stuttered Mick.

"I don't know, Mick," laughed Lucy. "You are a worrier."

Dave kissed his wife.

"Now are you sure you don't want to come with us?" he asked.

Lucy paused.

"You should come," continued Dave. "It will be a good meeting. Me and Travis are on top form. I can't see anyone in the league beating us at the moment."

"If she doesn't want to come, don't force her," interrupted Mick.

The last thing he wanted was to have to be alone with Lucy, knowing that there was still a spark between them.

"I haven't said I don't want to yet," laughed Lucy.

"It will be a late one," blabbed Mick in his desperation. "I'm sure you've got other things to do."

Lucy paused pensively.

"Come on, Lucy," urged Dave.

Mick was now looking panic-stricken. Lucy raised her hand to her face and stroked her chin pensively. She was enjoying this.

"Please, Lucy." Dave encouraged.

"No. I think I'll give it a miss," said Lucy.

She couldn't help but smile as she watched the relieved expression on Mick's face as he hurriedly led Dave from the house.

* * *

Graham had been having a quiet drink in The Druids. He was sat at the window seat, looking out across the rain-soaked Willsby High Street, when he noticed Charlotte walk past. She was drenched from the downpour and looked uneasy as she scurried by. Her face was ashen and her eyes red. She looked like she'd been crying. What was she doing out on her own? Had something happened to her? Willsby wasn't the nicest of places after dark, and it was hardly the sort of place a young lady like Charlotte should be wandering alone. He hurried outside and ran after her.

"Are you all right, Charlie?" he asked as he grabbed her arm. "You look really upset. Has something happened?"

Charlotte said nothing as she shrugged him off.

"Let me walk you home. You look like you could do with a friend."

Charlotte quickened her pace.

"Leave me alone, Graham! I don't need any help from you or anyone," she sobbed.

Graham was concerned. She did seem upset, and her outburst was so out of character. He was worried about her. He was aware that she'd been talking to that mechanic at the Willsby stadium rather a lot lately. Graham had heard things about Terry Myers, and he was quite concerned about the influence he might be having on Charlotte. He was hardly the sort of character that she should be getting involved with. Graham wanted to make sure she was all right. He followed her down the road and along the Esplanade. He wanted to make sure that she made it home safely. She'd reached the cul-de-sac and he watched from a distance as she entered her flat. He returned to The Druids, content in the knowledge that she was safe.

* * *

Lucy had been alone at home for about an hour when the telephone rang.

"It's Jane," said the rather harsh voice on the end of the line. "Is Dave there?"

Lucy was surprised.

"Hi, Janey," she enthused falsely. "No, he's not back yet. How are you feeling now, Janey?"

"I'm much better now," answered Jane.

Lucy felt uneasy. Jane sounded uncharacteristically determined.

"Made up with your brother yet, have you?" asked Lucy, referring sarcastically to Jane's argument with Mick the night before.

"No. I haven't spoken to Mick yet, but I will soon. We are awfully close you know, me and my brother. It's funny that you should mention brothers though, Lucy. I've just found out who your brother is."

Lucy was panic-stricken. There was a long nervous pause as thoughts swam in her head. Jane couldn't know about Sam, could she? It was impossible.

"I haven't got a brother," she laughed nervously.

Jane couldn't believe what she was hearing.

"Lucy Orpin!" she said, "Sam won't like you disowning him like that!"

Lucy was speechless. How had Jane found out? She had been so careful. She felt disorientated and tried desperately to think of a way out. What exactly did Jane know? How could she get out of this? She didn't know how to respond, so she hung up the phone in her panic. Not wanting to risk Jane calling back, she left the telephone receiver hanging from the wall.

Lucy realised that she had made a mistake. She should have bluffed her way out of it. She had been caught out in that split second. One simple little mistake, just like Sam had made.

Lucy sat at the breakfast bar with the hum of the dialling tone buzzing beside her. The memories of the night that Sam had made his slip-up flooded back to her. She remembered how she'd been woken by him ringing her doorbell.

"What is it?" she had asked as Sam burst into the kitchen like a frightened, wild animal.

He was in a panic. Blood stained his hands. He frantically ripped off his shirt and rammed it into the sink, turning the taps on fully. His speech had been hysterical. Tears rolled down his face.

"Sam, Sam," Lucy had stammered.

"He came from nowhere, Luce. He had a knife. I had to respond. It was instinctual."

"Who?" Lucy had screamed.

Sam was frantically waving his arms around. Water gushed from the taps. Blood diluted in the sink. Sam crumbled to the floor, sobbing.

"I did a house up Cromwell Street," Sam had explained. "I thought it was empty."

"But it wasn't?" Lucy had clarified.

"No, he took me by surprise. Old boy waving a knife around. "

Lucy had looked at her brother.

"I panicked, Luce, it was self-defence."

"Is he?" she had paused, horror in her voice. "Dead?"

Sam nodded. Lucy placed her hand on her brother's shoulder.

"Look, don't worry. I'll cover for you; I'll say you were here all night with me. It's okay Sam."

Sam had lifted his head.

"No, Luce, I've messed up. I went to the stadium; thought I could lie low there and get cleaned up. Thought I could get some work done there and make that my alibi."

He paused to wipe his eyes with his sleeve.

"But Chapman saw me."

"Dave Chapman, the speedway rider with the money you were investing?" Lucy had asked. "What was he doing there?"

"He'd left something in the changing rooms. Had gone to collect it. Can you believe that? He saw me. He saw all this."

Sam gestured to the bloodstained shirt in the sink.

Lucy leant back in her seat as she recalled the events of that atrocious night. Sam may have been a bounder, but he wasn't a murderer. It was self-defence. That silly old sod coming at him with a knife. What was he expecting? Sam just needed a bit of money. He just did a couple of burglaries. He wasn't a murderer. He didn't deserve to be labelled as one because of Dave Chapman's misplaced morals. Dave had stood up in court and told the jury exactly what he had seen. He'd got it all wrong. He didn't know Sam. Sam wouldn't hurt a fly. It had been an accident. Without Dave's evidence, Sam wouldn't have been convicted. It was all Dave's fault, and she wanted to make sure that he paid for it. She couldn't let her brother down, could she? She certainly wasn't going to let Jane get in the way of her plans.

Chapter Seventeen

Anthony was feeling proud of himself. He hadn't realised that he had such good counselling skills. Mandy had calmed down a lot since earlier that day. Their long talk at the practice track had seemingly reassured her. She had finally agreed to forget about Terry, and to return home to her parents. She just needed a few more days to compose herself. Her father wouldn't be too impressed, and she just didn't feel up to confronting him at the moment. Would Anthony let her stay just another day or so, until she was ready to leave? Anthony had agreed.

Mandy had now gone to bed, and Anthony sat in his lounge alone. He straightened the cushions, left in that unruly state by his house guest. The grandfather clock in the corner ticked deeply as Anthony thought about his predicament.

Anthony wasn't especially keen on Mandy, but he couldn't help but feel sorry for her. They did have one thing in common, after all: they had both been let down by Terry Myers. It had been difficult for both of them, but things now seemed to be working out for the best.

Anthony's thoughts now turned to Charlotte as he sat on his green-checked sofa. He had been wondering why she had left so quickly before. Had he said something to upset her? He had been planning to visit her, but all this going on with Mandy had taken the priority. He would go tomorrow. He could call around at her flat, perhaps take some flowers as a peace offering in case he had upset her? Perhaps they could start over again, and he could make amends? He could, maybe, ask her out on a proper date? He sat back in his seat. There were a lot of things he'd been wanting to say to Charlotte. Tomorrow, he would make a start.

In the other room, Mandy lay on the bed in the darkness as tears trickled down her cheeks. She wiped her eyes again on the back of her hand and rolled over. Anthony had been kind, but she realised she couldn't stay with him much longer. She knew that he didn't really like her being there, and that she had little choice but to go home to her parents. She still hung onto the thought though, that Terry would change his mind. Perhaps he would ring? Perhaps he really would leave his wife as he'd promised, and they could run away together?

* * *

Dave was sitting in the bar at the speedway stadium with Travis. He was feeling uncomfortable about leaving Lucy on her own. He thought about how he could cheer her up and diffuse his guilt. He could stop off at the motorway services on his way home and buy her some flowers, couldn't he? That would do the job, wouldn't it? Confident in his plan, he ordered another beer for himself and Travis.

Lucy meanwhile was alone that evening. She sat staring into the flickering images of the television set. She wasn't really paying attention though. She was deep in thought. She was worried. Jane had somehow found out about Sam. It could only be a matter of time before she shared her newfound knowledge with Dave and Mick. What evidence did she have? How could Lucy get out of this one? Lucy's thoughts flitted through her mind, looking for that glimmer of light in the darkness that could herald her escape. Dave would be home soon. He'd been racing, and he and Mick would be on their way back. He'd already rung her to say he'd be late. He'd been delayed, which usually meant that Travis had insisted they stay behind for a drink and a curry. Lucy hoped so. The American was playing a vital role in giving her this reprieve. Lucy needed to stop Jane from speaking. It was the only way.

* * *

Mandy had seemed cheerful enough the next day. She had even offered to cook Anthony a meal that evening. It was her way of thanking him for his help. Anthony was touched. He mulled over the thought as he drove along the Esplanade on his way to see Charlotte.

Anthony passed the turning to Charlotte's flat; the little cul-de-sac was so well hidden, behind a cluster of old trees, that it had been easy to miss. He pulled up at the kerbside, allowing the car behind to pass, before turning around. He parked on the seafront and stepped out of the car. He picked up the flowers from the passenger seat.

Anthony crossed the road and walked up to the flats. The building was quiet as he stood in front of that huge wooden door. He pressed the doorbell and took a step back, clutching the flowers, as he waited for Charlotte. There was silence. Charlotte must be out. Maybe she was at work in the guesthouse? That was a shame. He returned to his car, replacing the flowers on the passenger seat. He'd try again tomorrow. Hopefully, the flowers would still look okay. He started the engine and waited as the old woman crossed the road, before he drove away.

Before she began her shift at the guesthouse that day, Mrs Shield had dropped around to see Charlotte. She was worried about the girl. She had sounded upset on the telephone earlier. Mrs Shield stood outside of the large Victorian house, her finger on the middle bell push. Perhaps she did have the 'flu, but Mrs Shield was concerned that Charlotte had sounded more upset than poorly. Perhaps she needed someone to talk to? She knew that Charlotte could be overemotional at times. Living in this place all alone couldn't help, could it? She had no family or friends in Willsby, did she? Mrs Shield was worried, and she wanted to help. She pressed the doorbell again. There was no reply. She stood back, looking up at the window. It was the first time that she'd been to the flat, and she wasn't completely sure that she had the right place. The flat appeared to be empty. She pressed the doorbell below. There was a clamouring behind the door, accompanied by a baby crying. A young woman opened the door, a small baby draped over her shoulder. She bounced the child in an irritated reassurance, as it bawled loudly.

"Sorry to bother you. I was looking for the girl upstairs, Charlotte?"

"Ain't seen or heard her all day," came the abrupt reply.

The woman stared at her from beneath her bleached fringe.

"Sorry to have bothered you," said Mrs Shield.

The door slammed shut as Mrs Shield turned away, relieved in her knowledge that at least her young friend wasn't at home. She walked back to the main road and glanced up once more at the window. A smile crept over her face as the thought entered her mind: perhaps she wasn't ill, after all, and had taken an impromptu day off work to go out with that Anthony? Yes, that would explain everything. Thank goodness for that. At least the young girl wasn't sat in that dreary flat on her own, was she?

That evening, the kitchen table had been set for dinner. Anthony's crystal wine glasses stood indignantly next to the bottle of cheap wine. The smell of simmering spaghetti Bolognese filled the room, while virtually every cooking pot in the house sat stacked dirty in the sink. At least Mandy was trying. Anthony went into the lounge and sat waiting for Mandy's summons to dinner. She appeared a few minutes later with a glass of wine. Even the Dartington couldn't mask the awful taste, but Anthony appreciated that Mandy was making the effort. She sat down beside him.

There was a short silence before the telephone rang. Mandy bolted from her seat, rushing to the kitchen after the first ring. Anthony sighed, sensing that she was hoping it would be Terry. He knew that was highly unlikely. She was clearly upset when she returned.

"He's ringing me up now, trying to freak me out. Hasn't he done enough already?" she sobbed.

Anthony was confused.

"What?" he asked in bewilderment.

"Terry. He's ringing me up. I picked up the 'phone and there was just silence," explained Mandy. "Just silence. So, I hung up."

Anthony didn't understand. As far as Terry was concerned, Mandy was just a bit of fun, a young girl flattering an older man. He certainly didn't care about her and certainly wouldn't be bothered to play mind games with her.

"Are you sure?" he asked.

"Grow up, Anthony! Who else could it be? Anyway, I know it's him. I can hear the sea in the background. He's probably ringing from outside The Druids."

Mandy started to cry again. She stood up and flounced off to the bedroom.

The meal was forgotten, and the cheap, red wine was poured down the plughole.

* * *

Lucy still hadn't heard from Jane; she had been disturbingly quiet. Was she waiting for the right moment to break her deadly news to Dave and Mick? If this was Jane's strategy, it was working: Lucy was scared.

Dave was none the wiser about the turmoil inside his wife's head. He sat staring into the television screen at the sitcom. Mesmerised, he laughed, prompted by the canned laughter of the show.

As the telephone rang, Lucy froze. Was this the moment she had been dreading? Was this the moment that Jane would impart her new-found knowledge to Dave? In her mind, Lucy could picture Jane, holding the receiver on the other end of the line. She stared blankly into the cold fireplace, awaiting her fate as the ringing continued.

Dave glanced across to his wife expectantly.

"I'll get it, shall I?" he said, with what appeared to be a touch of sarcasm.

He sprung to his feet. Lucy watched him leave the room. She felt condemned as the ringing stopped. She could hear the muffled tones of his voice, but the noise of the television drowned his words. Was he talking to Jane? The canned laughter chuckled callously as Lucy stood up and walked across to the doorway. Dave was quiet, listening attentively to the caller.

"Who is it?" asked Lucy, awaiting the gallows of his reply.

Dave placed his hand across the mouthpiece.

"It's Travis," he said enthusiastically. "He wants me to go over tomorrow. He's having a party."

The relief shot through Lucy's body.

"Travis is one long party!" she laughed, as the fix of her reprieve seeped through her veins.

Chapter Eighteen

M andy walked into the kitchen, throwing her luggage in a heap
beside Anthony.

Anthony looked at the bulging bags. It saddened him to think of
all her lost hopes crammed inside.

"Will you take me home now, Anthony?"

"Of course," he nodded. "There's just somewhere I need to go first."

Mandy looked at him inquisitively as he picked up his car keys
from the table.

"I'll only be a couple of hours."

He stepped over the discarded bags.

"Where are you going?" asked Mandy.

"Just got someone I need to see."

Mandy sighed as she watched him leave and heard the car pull
away. It had taken a lot of courage to decide to go home. She had
hoped Anthony would have taken her straight away. It would be
difficult maintaining this composure for another few hours. She
walked over to the kettle, filled it with water, and plugged it into the
wall socket. She reached into the cupboard above for the teabags. She
paused, noticing the full whiskey bottle on the top shelf. She didn't

particularly like whiskey, but it did seem more appealing than tea. It would help kill the time that Anthony would be away.

Mandy ignored the click as the electric kettle turned off, and instead twisted the top from the whiskey bottle, and poured herself a glass. She sniffed it. It smelt warm. She raised the glass to her lips.

The first mouthful burnt her tongue and throat; the second seemed to numb the sensation. She carried the bottle and glass into the bedroom. As she sat on the bed, she noticed the remains of the sleeping pills that she'd been taking the night before. Perhaps another couple now would help her sleep away the next few hours, while Anthony was away? She opened the bottle, placed the pills on her tongue, and swallowed a mouthful of whiskey to wash them down.

It didn't matter how hard she tried; she couldn't get Terry out of her thoughts. Perhaps there was still time for him to come back? Even Mandy didn't believe that now. She took another swig of whiskey, another couple of pills, and lay on the bed, waiting for Anthony's return.

She'd managed to sleep for a while, but her dreams had been maliciously intent on reminding her of Terry. She looked at the clock. Anthony wouldn't be long now, would he? Mandy drank some more whiskey and took some more tablets. She felt drowsy, her head ached, and her thoughts were foggy.

Anthony wasn't on his way home yet though. He was on his way to see Terry. There were no prizes for guessing where he'd be, and true to form, his car was parked outside of The Druids. Normally, Anthony would have avoided Terry when he'd been drinking, but today was different.

Terry sat slouched across the bar. He didn't notice Anthony arrive until he pulled up the stool beside him.

"Hi Bruv," said Terry, seemingly unperturbed by his visitor's humourless expression.

Terry knew how placid Anthony was. He enjoyed the feeling of power that his brother's docility gave him. Strangely though, he seemed different today.

"I'm taking Mandy home later," announced Anthony.

"She still with you then?" said Terry nonchalantly.

He looked into his pint of beer and laughed to himself.

"It's not funny, Terry. That girl is really upset because of you, and I'm fed up with having to pick up the pieces all the time."

"Relax Bruv. I'm sure you'll have an enjoyable time consoling her," replied Terry, resting his hand on Anthony's shoulder.

Anthony shrugged him off. Terry wasn't sure what to make of the uncharacteristic change in Anthony. It aggravated him. He looked at him, waiting for Anthony's submissiveness to return. It didn't come. Terry felt unusually threatened and instantly became defensive.

"What's your problem?" he shouted.

The public house fell silent as the other patrons looked on. Terry stood up, kicking the stool to the ground. The crash was amplified by the silence that had consumed the room. The bar steward looked up, anticipating the worse.

"I don't want any trouble in here, lads," he pleaded.

"It's all right, I'm going," snapped Terry, kicking the stool one more time as he left.

Anthony watched him go, and whispers returned to the room. The screech of car tyres on the tarmac outside confirmed Terry's departure. The bar steward appeared beside Anthony, picking up the stool.

"I'm sorry about that," said Anthony.

"It's okay. There's no damage done," reassured the barman. "I know what Terry's like when he's had a few. You know, he really shouldn't be driving. He'd downed several before you arrived."

Anthony sighed as he left.

As he reached his car, he looked up the road towards the turning to Charlotte's flat. Perhaps he should try her again? She may be in now? He could do with someone to talk to right now.

He drove around to the Esplanade and pulled up outside of her flat. He grabbed the flowers, which he'd left on the passenger's seat the day before, and walked to the door. There was no reply again. He was disappointed. He looked at the flowers and laid them on the path next to the door. There wasn't much point in his keeping them, was there? He pulled out the card that he'd written and read over his message, before slipping it back behind the stems. Hopefully, she'd see them when she got home and give him a call?

He turned to leave, not noticing as the breeze caught the card and blew it into the bushes. He returned to his car. He'd better get back to Mandy. She would be waiting for him, wouldn't she? As he started the engine, a frightening thought crossed his mind; surely Terry wouldn't dare have gone there, would he?

As Anthony pulled into his driveway, he was beginning to regret having aggravated the time bomb of Terry Myers. His fears seemed well-founded: Terry's car had been abandoned outside his house. Anthony's earlier bravery had gone. He was nervous as he pulled up behind the haphazardly parked car. He climbed out of his own and walked to the house. He noticed a deep scratch on the side of his brother's Mercedes. That was fresh; had Terry been in an accident on his way back from The Druids, maybe?

The house was quiet. The gentle ticking of the car's engine cooling was the only sound as Anthony approached the slightly ajar front door. As he pushed the door, a sudden noise from the spare bedroom caught his attention. He turned to his left and entered the room.

The curtains were pulled shut, and the darkness momentarily blinded Anthony. Then he noticed Terry, sat on the floor, slumped against the wall, an almost empty bottle of whiskey in his hand. Terry looked up and blinked in a short confusion.

"No more bother now," he belched, laughing to himself.

The whiskey bottle sat uncomfortably in his hand. The last few trickles of alcohol escaped onto the wooden floor as Terry chuckled.

Anthony's eyes turned to the bed. Mandy lay there perfectly still. The initial delusion of her peaceful sleep was, however, suddenly shattered as his eyes became accustomed to the darkness. Something wasn't right. Her face was almost black. Her eyes were open and terrified. Anthony rushed to her, lifted her heavy head, held her clenched hand, and desperately willed life into the still body.

"What the hell have you done?" he screamed.

Terry remained silently slumped against the wall.

"Terry, she's dead. What have you done? Don't you realise what you've done?"

Terry looked up, his mouth gaping open, his eyes trying to focus on the voice.

"Didn't do it," he slurred.

Anthony scowled.

"She's dead, Terry. You've killed her," he screamed.

"Didn't do it," repeated Terry, a fatigued impatience detectable in his voice.

Anthony was silent. He stared at his brother in shocked bewilderment.

"I said, I didn't do it!" shouted Terry, apparently trying to justify his nonsensical ramblings.

Anthony couldn't believe the horror that was unfolding around him.

"What?" he yelled.

"That bird of yours, you know, that Charlie. She did it."

Terry looked up through blurred, languid eyes.

"She came in here. I was sat here."

"How could Charlotte kill anyone, Terry? You aren't going to get her involved in this."

"She came in," said Terry. "She saw Mandy asleep on the bed and started calling her things. I stood up, agreeing with everything she said. Then I gave her the pillow."

Terry paused. For such a ridiculous story, he sounded very convincing. He continued:

"I gave her the pillow, and I told her to hold it over Mandy's face. She did. But she wasn't that strong, so I helped a bit. Mandy was struggling, but me and that Charlie, we held her down. Charlie just needed a bit of help."

Anthony dropped the body. It fell heavily onto the mattress. He rushed over to his brother, grabbing his arms, and shaking him frantically. Terry rocked limply back and forth. He was still smiling to himself and put up no resistance as the bottle fell from his hand, rolling noisily across the floor.

"What do you mean?" demanded Anthony. "Where's Charlotte? What have you done to Charlotte?"

Terry looked at him through glazed, apathetic eyes.

"I don't know. She ran off," he sniggered.

Anthony let go, and Terry fell back against the wall.

"We won't tell anyone I was here," said Terry with calculated confidence. "We'll just say we found the body, and I'll say I saw Charlie running away."

Anthony couldn't believe his ears. The horror was evident on his face. Terry seemed to sober slightly.

"Ant? Bruv? We are going to cover for each other, aren't we? We are brothers, after all. Bruv?"

Terry staggered to his feet.

"Bruv. You can't let me down."

Anthony said nothing. Terry started to grow angry.

"You can't let me down," he repeated. "You promised your dad you'd look after me. You can't betray your dad."

Anthony stared at his brother defiantly for a moment and then rushed out of the house. He had to find Charlotte.

* * *

Dave was visiting Travis and would be out for the rest of the day. Lucy was alone in the house. The music was deafening as she turned up the volume on the radio.

She waited. As expected, it was only a matter of minutes before the banging started. The old man next door always made his irritation known in the same way. Lucy pictured him now, behind the partitioning wall, banging with all his puny might. The silly old bugger!

The knocking continued.

Using a paper handkerchief, Lucy carefully picked up the flowers that Dave had bought for her a couple of days earlier. They were still in their cellophane packaging, and she didn't want to leave her fingerprints, as well as Dave's, on the wrapper.

She left the house through the back door. The old man would be so engrossed in his remonstration, that he wouldn't notice her driving away, nor even realise that he had just become her alibi.

The country roads were empty as Lucy headed for Willsby. The town centre was quiet as she snaked through the streets. The old buildings looked down impassively as if waking up ready for the day's inevitable invasion of tourists. It didn't take long to reach the Esplanade.

Lucy parked on the wide seafront road, opposite the turning to the cul-de-sac. The tall trees obscured the house as she climbed from the car. She shivered. It was deceptively cold today. Staring out at the grey sea as it whipped at the pebbles, she breathed in deeply, feeling the resolute determination fill her body. She pulled the gloves from her pocket and wiggled her fingers inside. Reaching to the passenger seat, she pulled out the flowers from the car. She slammed the door shut and turned the key before heading across the road to the flats. She looked at her watch. Her timing was perfect: the people upstairs would have left for work by now, and the single mother downstairs would be out on the school run. Jane was alone in the building, for sure.

Lucy felt a strange sensation of déjà vu as she unlocked the heavy door. The familiar hallway welcomed her into the dark arms of its imposing staircase. She climbed the stairs and carefully unlocked the door to her old flat. There was a noise from the bedsitting room at the end of the short corridor. Jane was in. Lucy quietly shut the door and turned into the kitchen. She placed the flowers in the sink. Barnaby had been asleep, in a cardboard box under the kitchen table, and stirred as Lucy approached. She ignored him as she slipped her hand into the draw, pulling out the knife. She hid the weapon behind her back as she returned to the hallway. The floorboards squeaked. She heard Jane's voice from the other room.

"Who is it?"

There was silence as Jane approached the doorway.

"Lucy," she gasped, relief seemingly ebbing through her body. "I thought you were a burglar for a minute."

Lucy said nothing as she walked slowly towards Jane. Jane began to look a little uneasy as her visitor approached.

"What do you want?"

There was silence.

"Why are you here?"

The lack of a response to her questions was intimidating. Jane stepped slowly backwards into the bedsitting room. Lucy continued her calculated approach, a smile creeping across her lips. Jane stepped back again, this time she felt the corner of the bed jab into her thigh. She stopped and grabbed the bedpost with her hand to steady herself. Lucy stopped too; her brown eyes fixed on Jane.

"What do you want, Lucy?"

Jane tried to compose herself, but her voice trembled as she spoke. The foreboding gaze and menacing silence of her visitor frightened her.

"Lucy, what do you want?" she pleaded.

The corners of Lucy's mouth curled; her lips parted as she began to laugh.

"I've got something for you, Janey," she said.

For a brief second, Jane felt relieved. The woman's voice, although hardly friendly, had at least broken that ominous silence. The relief, however, was short-lived as Lucy brought the knife into view. Jane's horror contorted her face as Lucy spoke again.

"I've thought it through, you know," she said as she swiped the long blade across Jane's bare wrist.

Jane pulled her arm into her body with a sharp intake of breath. She eyed the cut nervously as beads of blood appeared along the pink line. Lucy chuckled again in her intense thought.

"I was wondering what the best way to stop you talking would be," she whispered.

Jane's eyes glanced down nervously at the shining blade. Lucy seemed amused by her fear and once again lurched towards her, catching her arm again with the edge of the blade.

"I'd planned to suffocate you at first. Had it all worked out in my head. I've gone over and over the scenario. I was going to use a pillow to suffocate you in your bed."

She smiled demonically as her eyes too turned to the knife. She rotated it in her hand.

"That's how your little sister died, wasn't it? Suffocated in her little cot?"

Lucy's voice was cruel in its tone.

"And poor little Janey found her, all grey, and stiff, and dead."

The comment was wicked, but Jane hardly cared. She was more

concerned by that huge blade waving around in front of her. She said nothing as her mind raced.

"No, this way is best," continued Lucy. "Sam would have done it this way. I wanted to make it look like suicide to start with, but then I had a wonderful idea."

Lucy seemed engrossed by her thoughts as the knife waved erratically through the air.

"I've got it all planned you know. Dave will get the blame for murdering you and trying to cover it up. I'll get to keep his money; it won't be much use to him in prison, will it? I've got an alibi you know. Just check with my neighbour; I've been at home all day playing my music. But Dave? Where's Dave? I don't know. I'll tell the jury that the last I saw of him was when he stormed out of the house on his way to see you. When I told him how horrible you've been to me, he was in such a rage, he could have been capable of anything."

"What do you want, Lucy?" pleaded Jane in desperation. "I'll do anything you want. I won't tell anyone about Sam. I promise. Whatever you want, Lucy? Whatever."

Jane reached out in her plea. The sudden movement disturbed Lucy from her musings, and she instinctively thrust the blade forward into her victim's chest. Jane's legs hit the bed behind her. She jolted, coiling around the embedded weapon. Her chubby hands grasped for the knife, her face distorting in pain and panic. She fell sideways onto the bed as her life seeped from within. Lucy watched her fall, intrigued by each contraction on her face, contemplating the thoughts behind those terrified, wide eyes. Finally, the victim was still on the bed. Lucy wrapped the dead woman's hands firmly around the protruding knife's handle and rolled her onto her front. The knife penetrated deeper as the heavy weight pressed upon it.

Lucy returned to the kitchen. Now, she had to cover her tracks and make it look as if Dave had been there. She remembered a glass vase that she'd left in one of the wall cupboards. She tried a door. It was stiff, so she pulled harder. The door relented, catching her cheek as it opened suddenly.

"Damn. That will leave a bruise," she cursed as she retrieved the vase.

She wiped the dust from the vase and filled it with water. She ripped off the cellophane wrapper from the flowers, taking care to leave the shop's name visible to link them with Dave's purchase a few days earlier. She arranged the flowers in the vase and placed the cellophane into the peddle bin. She bit her lip in thought, as she partially retrieved the wrapper. That was better, any self-respecting police officer would notice that now, wouldn't they? She carried the vase into the bedroom and placed it on the mantel beside the picture of Mick and Dave. She stepped back and admired the arrangement.

"Don't they look beautiful, Janey?" she mused. "And to think there are witnesses who can confirm that it was Dave who bought them."

She dragged her old typewriter from under the bed and lifted it to the table. The paper was already in place. She typed the brief note, making sure it was full of grammatical errors. Dave wasn't that bright. His spelling was atrocious. It would look like he'd typed the note to cover his tracks, and to make it look like Jane had committed suicide.

She took one last look around the room. Everything was perfect. She left, leaving the door ajar: that way someone would surely discover the body.

Lucy made her way home, stopping at the payphone just down

the road from the house. She rang her neighbour's number, leaving the receiver hanging as she returned to her car. She imagined the old man staggering to the telephone. He'd be so fixated with answering the ringing 'phone, that he wouldn't have noticed her driving into the shared driveway. She pulled around the side of the house and parked in front of Dave's car. Dave was out in his van. He'd want to make a hasty retreat later, and this way her car would be the most obvious choice. She entered the house and turned down the music.

"All right, you've got your way!" she yelled through the adjoining wall.

Now all she had to do was wait for Dave's return.

Dave sat for a moment, his hands gripping the steering wheel. The blonde girl had run out in front of the car. He should have noticed her, but his mind had been wandering. He wondered if he should check up on her? She seemed okay though as she ran into the telephone box. Dave pulled away and headed down the driveway to his home. Travis had kept him out longer than he'd expected and now he was feeling guilty. Lucy was waiting for him as he walked into the lounge.

"Got caught up in traffic," he explained.

"It's okay," she replied unconvincingly.

Dave sensed that his wife wasn't happy. She was probably angry that he'd been out with Travis all morning.

"I'll make it up to you," he said as he placed his hands around her waist. "I know I shouldn't have stayed so long with Travis. You know what he's like though."

"It's not you, Dave," she said reassuringly, turning her sad eyes towards him. "I went to see Jane today."

Now it all made sense to Dave. That's why she looked so upset.

"I wanted to try to sort things out. I wanted so much for us all to be friends. She was so nasty though."

Lucy's voice was changing to uncharacteristic desperation.

"I'm frightened, Dave," she whispered.

Lucy pictured the body as she'd left it, lying on the bed, the knife penetrating the flesh, and the red blood staining the duvet.

"I'm really frightened that she might do something stupid."

Lucy managed to stop the smile creeping across her face.

"She was so horrible to me today, Dave. Look," she said, turning her face to show off the massive bruise that her encounter with the cupboard door had left earlier.

"She did this."

"Jane hit you?" asked Dave.

Lucy said nothing.

"She's gone too far now," asserted Dave.

He sounded resolute as he spoke.

"I'll go and see her now."

"No!" urged Lucy.

"I've got to sort this out, Lucy," he said protectively as he held his wife's shoulders. "I'm not having her treat you like this."

Lucy held him close to her, slipping the key to Jane's flat into his pocket without him even suspecting: that would surely incriminate him when that was found.

"I won't be long," he reassured.

Lucy watched as Dave left and climbed into her silver BMW. She was right, he had chosen her car rather than his own in his haste. She waited for the sounds of the car door closing, the engine starting, and the car pulling away, before running outside.

"No Dave. Don't! Please don't do it!" she yelled loudly after the departing car.

Dave had not seen her. Good. She fell, feigning her sobbing, onto the gravel driveway.

"No Dave. No! Not Jane!"

She sobbed for a while before clambering to her feet. The curtains twitched in the neighbouring window. Good. Her witness had her alibi.

Lucy returned to the house. She closed the door behind her, slumping up against the heavy door. Her sham tears dried instantly, and she began to smile.

She just had to wait now. Surely, Jane's body would have been discovered by now? The place would be swarming with police. It was only a matter of time until Dave stumbled into the middle of the crime scene, and the finger of suspicion pointed in his direction.

Chapter Nineteen

"I still can't believe that he would do such a thing," said Maria, as they walked together down the staircase from the courtroom. "It was so horrible, reliving the whole thing like that. How could he? Even lying under oath like that. Not even admitting it with all that evidence against him. I had him completely wrong, you know. I feel so foolish."

Tears were welling in Maria's eyes as she spoke. The trial had been difficult for her and the strain was showing on her drawn face. She recalled him sitting there beside that sombre prison officer. He had looked across at her, his eyes seemingly begging for her help. She had looked away. She had once thought they were soulmates, but he had let her down, hadn't he? She wasn't going to help him now.

"You were great," she said, as her red eyes looked across at the man beside her. "This must be so difficult for you too. The audacity of his trying to blame you for murdering that poor girl. I know you didn't get on that well, but you did care about him, didn't you? I mean you are his broth…"

He raised his hand to her mouth and stopped her as she spoke.

Maria smiled knowingly. Of course, they weren't really brothers, were they? She'd known that for ages, but that was all in the past now. All that earlier deception had paled into insignificance with what he had done now.

The bright sunlight outside blinded them for a moment as they left the confinement of the courthouse, and with it, the murderer that Maria had once been so fond of.

"I know it's difficult," he comforted. "It's so hard to believe he could have done that. I mean murder? I wouldn't have thought it possible. If only I hadn't found Mandy's body when I went 'round there, I wouldn't have had to testify against him, would I? It was hard, but I had to do it. Try to forget about it now Maria. We have each other now. We've both got to look to the future."

She smiled and looked into his reassuring brown eyes.

"I can't tell you how grateful I am to you, Terry."

"The worst is over now. Anthony is paying for his crimes," sighed Terry as he took hold of Maria's hand with a victorious smile.

* * *

Lucy looked up from her writing. She was glad that the story was finished. It had been fun. It was such a shame that it now had to be destroyed. It was getting dark, and her eyes were straining uncomfortably. She slipped the pen between her teeth and leant back in her chair, cradling her manuscript.

She knew what she had to do. She carried the papers over to the fireplace. The story she'd written was too damning on her to be kept. It had helped her plan out so many things, including Jane's murder and the framing of Dave. Trying out her options on those two girls in her book had really helped her focus her thoughts. It had helped her realise that suffocating Jane was too risky on her own, and that the stabbing was the best option. It had helped her ensure that she'd covered her tracks. She daren't let the story be seen. It had been for her eyes only. She had to destroy it before anyone else read it. She couldn't leave any clues. She owed it to her brother, Sam, not to slip up.

Lucy sat on the hearth, her knees curled up under her chin, her hands hugging the manuscript close to her chest. The heat warmed her as she tore off the first page. She fed it teasingly to the fire. The flames nibbled the corner before enthusiastically consuming the entire sheet. The orange flames reached into the darkness before dying back down to a contented consumption of the charred paper. Lucy ripped off another page. Another. Another. Sheet after sheet she fed them to the ravenous fire. The unbearable heat was making her feel faint, but she had to persevere. Page by page, she fed the story to the flames. The flames devoured their paper feast, eating through each word, each paragraph, each chapter. There was no dampening their hunger as they consumed their way through the transcribed characters, cremating their existence. She thought about her creations as they were consumed by the flames. Some of them had been based on the people she'd seen each day: that old woman in the guesthouse, Graham at the speedway stadium, Peter the doorman, Anthony the Willsby team's junior rider and of course, the ever flamboyant, Travis Fengar.

She would miss her made-up characters too. There was the student, Mandy, the downtrodden wife, Maria and there was Charlotte. Charlotte: what depth of her bizarre imagination had she originated from? The immature, innocent, and naïve Charlotte. The victim who had to be sacrificed to save the hero.

Ah yes, the hero of the story: Terry. What a clever and shrewd invention he was. He was the saddest to burn. He was the clever one, outwitting all those pathetic, paltry characters. The confidence trickster, who with his clever deceptions, had been welcomed into a wealthy family. He'd tricked his victim into writing out a will and saw to it that it was promptly executed. By his clever manipulation, he'd ended up with a large share of the family's wealth. How ingenious he was. He was a true vigilante. The world and all its unfair wealth distribution needs people like Terry to even things out. A modern-day Robin Hood, you could say. Lucy had especially liked Terry.

The raging flames were creating devilishly menacing shadows on the walls as she fed her reams to the fiery furnace. It was hellishly hot in the room but she continued resolutely with the task ahead. Finally, Lucy ferociously launched the final sheets to the fire, then lifted her glass from the floor, and toasted her flickering shadow. She walked over to the green-serge settee. She sat down, watching the flames devouring her tracks. All she had to do now, was wait.

An hour had passed when the doorbell finally rang. Instead of answering, she calmly walked over to the telephone and dialled the number. Everything was going to plan. The telephone rang twice before Mick answered.

"Hello."

"Mick? It's Lucy. Something terrible has happened with Dave. Can you come over straight away?"

The desperation in her voice was obvious. Mick was worried.

"What's happened? Are you okay?"

"Just come quickly, please Mick."

The telephone went dead.

Lucy's doorbell rang again.

Mick stood holding the receiver for a while before the urgency of the situation struck him. What was Lucy talking about? What had happened? Was she in trouble? He had to get over to Dave's place. He could be there in ten minutes. He grabbed his car keys and left the house.

Lucy finally opened the door.

"Mrs Chapman?" enquired the younger of the two police officers who stood at the door.

Lucy stepped back, giving them room to step inside.

"Yes," she answered. "What's wrong? What's happened?"

The older officer wiped his brow. Boy, it was exceptionally hot in this house.

"Mrs Chapman. I'm sorry to have to tell you, but we've arrested your husband."

Lucy raised her hand to her mouth.

"Oh, my Lord! Not Jane. Tell me he hasn't hurt Jane?"

Her concern was obvious to the two officers, who looked at one another in a silent understanding.

"He was so angry when he left here. I was scared of what he might do," continued Lucy. "Is my dear Jane okay?"

"I'm sorry, Mrs Chapman, I'm afraid your friend is dead."

Considering how hot it was in the house, the ashen look that crept across Lucy's face was quite an accomplishment.

"Would you mind coming down to the station, Mrs Chapman? It sounds as though you may be able to help?"

Lucy wiped the tears from her cheeks.

"Of course," she murmured. "What's going to happen to my husband?"

The two officers said nothing as they led her out to the waiting police car. The youngest helped her into the back seat, while his colleague went across to the neighbour's house. Lucy watched the two characters at the neighbour's doorway. The old man gestured to the officer, no doubt telling him how he'd seen Dave drive away in a temper, and confirming that Lucy had been at home all day, playing annoyingly-loud music.

Suddenly, a car approached down the driveway. It came to an abrupt stop, and Mick jumped out. He ran over to Lucy, climbing into the backseat of the police car beside her. Lucy silently congratulated herself on the perfect timing.

"Lucy, what's happened?"

Lucy's eyes glazed over.

"It's too late Mick. I thought you may be able to stop him, but it's too late now. Dave has *murdered* our dear Jane.

In the end

"I still can't believe that he could do such a thing," said Mick, as they walked together down the staircase from the courtroom. "It was so horrible, reliving the whole thing like that. How could he? Lying under oath like that, not even admitting it with all that evidence against him. Even trying to drag poor Travis into it, by saying he'd been with him when Jane was murdered. I had him completely wrong, you know. I feel so foolish."

Mick was obviously distressed as he spoke. The trial had been difficult for him, and the strain was now showing on his drawn face. In his mind, he could still picture Dave, sitting callously beside that sombre prison officer in the courtroom. Dave had looked across at him, his eyes seemingly begging for help. Mick certainly wasn't going to help Dave now. He had looked away.

"You were great," he said, the distress obvious in his eyes. "This must have been so difficult for you too, after all, he is your husband."

Lucy raised her fingers to his lips and stopped him as he spoke. He smiled and slipped his hand into hers, reassured by her presence, as they left the courthouse.

The bright sunlight outside blinded them for a moment, as they left the confinement of the dark building.

"I know it's difficult," she comforted. "It's so hard to believe he'd do such a thing. I mean murder? I wouldn't have thought it possible, if I hadn't had heard all that evidence with my own ears. But Dave's being punished now, and we must look to the future."

Mick smiled and looked into her almond eyes as she spoke.

"I can't tell you how grateful I am to you, Lucy."

"The worst is over now," she sighed, as she held his hand tightly. They had reached his car.

"Will you be all right driving home on your own?" she asked.

"Yeah. I'll be okay. Thanks for everything, Lucy. I'll be in touch soon."

Mick climbed into the car. Lucy waited until he'd driven away. She wiped the fake tears from her eyes and made her way across the car park to the awaiting van.

She opened the passenger door.

"Guilty! The jury found Dave guilty of Jane's murder," she announced triumphantly as she climbed inside.

"Well, who'd have thought that?" said the man at the wheel. "Can we get something to eat now?"

"Yeah, how about a curry?" suggested Lucy.

"Right on, Babe," smiled Travis. "I could do with a hot, chicken curry."

THE END

BV - #0099 - 040521 - C0 - 198/129/16 - PB - 9781914195402 - Matt Lamination